The author was born in 1941 in Bidford-on-Avon. He has lived in Coventry all his life. He was educated at John Gulson Grammar School and then at Lanchester Polytechnic, where he studied Building Management. He went into business at the age of 24, successfully taking one company to the stock market. He is married to his second wife and has a son and a daughter from his first marriage. Mike Price is now retired.

Fran

Enjoy

Mike Price

To all my family, especially my wife, Marie, for their support.

Mike Price

A COLD MOON

AUSTIN MACAULEY PUBLISHERS™

LONDON • CAMBRIDGE • NEW YORK • SHARJAH

A CIP catalogue record for this title is available from the British Library.

ISBN 9781528931502 (Paperback)
ISBN 9781528966696 (ePub e-book)

www.austinmacauley.com

First Published (2019)
Austin Macauley Publishers Ltd
25 Canada Square
Canary Wharf
London
E14 5LQ

Chapter One

The thrill of excitement sent a shiver through him, it was always the same. No matter how many times he heard the sound and no matter how many times he had been disappointed, it was still the same. It grew louder in his ear, the *ping ping* of the detector now shouting in its own alien language.

He lay the detector down, slid the knapsack off his shoulders and set it down on the grass. Inside were his notebook, pencil and hand trowel for scrapping back the earth. Strapped to the outside of the bag was a short shovel, about a meter long, which he used for deeper digging if the 'treasure' was well buried.

The turf peeled back easily, the recent rain having loosened the earth, and he scrapped eagerly at the exposed soil with the trowel. He was pleasantly surprised when, having dug down only a few inches, the trowel clanged as it hit the metal object. His pulse quickened as little by little the box was exposed.

It looked like a rusty old tobacco tin and he felt a flash of disappointment, but his curiosity forced him to carry on. Pulling the box loose from the last sod holding it down, he wiped off the mud and shook the box to check if there was anything in it. There was no sound. The lid was tight and would not budge. Holding the box in his left hand and with the trowel in his right, he used it as a hammer to knock the lid off. The lid spun away, falling to the ground, the open box revealing a piece of paper.

He slowly opened the folded sheet to reveal the writing.

"FOOLS GOLD, BAD LUCK WILL, TRY AGAIN"

He spun round to see if anyone was watching him, but the only people in the immediate area were a few mothers, their children playing on the swings and they were paying him no attention.

It was obviously one of his so-called friends who knew he came here regularly and must have thought it great fun to plant the box. He could see the funny side of the joke; he just hoped that they, whoever they were, had not seen the excitement on his face when he first located the 'find'.

He packed his trowel back into the knapsack, picked up the detector and headed home. He had lost interest, for that day anyway.

Chapter Two

David Shakespeare had been saddled with the nickname of 'Will' since his school days. When he was just thirteen, he had entered a short story competition for under sixteen-year-olds which the local paper ran and, much to his surprise, had won it. His mickey taking pals had called him Will which stuck. Even the teachers often referred to him by the sobriquet. Now only his bank manager and the tax man addressed him as David.

He had met his wife, Julie, at University when they were both studying to be teachers, graduating in the same year. He had obtained a post in a junior school in Kenilworth and Julie, who was a Catholic, had been lucky to get a position at Bishop Ullathorne Senior School, which was situated on the south side of Coventry. They moved in together just before the start of term, renting a two bed flat in Kenilworth. It was ideal for both as it only took her fifteen minutes to drive to Coventry and he could walk to his school.

Will had never been proficient at sports, but like most of his contemporises, he was happy to watch others sweating and straining on the pitch. Having lived in Leicester for most of his childhood, he had, with his father, supported Leicester City, staying loyal even through the dark times when they had been relegated to the First Division, effectively the third tier of English football. Now they were in the Championship and currently in the top six, so a play-off for promotion was on the cards. When he and Julie had moved to Kenilworth, she was originally from Bradford, he had continued to support 'The Foxes', even though he did not always manage to attend every away game. At least, it meant there were lively discussions with his pals in the local on Friday nights, as most of them supported Coventry City.

But now, he had a new passion which had caused a few raised eyebrows amongst his friends. He had read in the papers about the 'Staffordshire Hoard' and how an amateur with a metal detector had found gold on a farm near Litchfield in July 2009. The gold was worth three point three million pounds, which was shared with the farmer who owned the land. He had researched all he could on the subject. It was believed that the Hoard was a war bounty because there were no feminine objects in the collection. It dated back to the Seventh Century when Anglo Saxon Britain was ruled by warring kingdoms, Mercia was the biggest, stretching down from the Humber almost to London and west to the Welsh boarder. King Offa had built Offa's Dyke to separate the Welsh from Anglo Saxons and in Warwickshire was the village of Off-church, or 'the church of Offa'.

Will had reasoned that as there was an old Castle in Kenilworth, then maybe that had been built on the site of one of King Offa's headquarters. It had not taken much for him to think maybe Abbey Fields, with its ruined Abbey of St Mary built by Henry 1st's Chamberlin Geffry de Clinton in 1124, who had also built the Castle, was part of an original settlement and therefore, might hide riches of its own.

Fired by the thoughts of becoming the next Terry Herbert, the finder of the Staffordshire Hoard, he had gone onto the internet and found a site that sold metal detectors, but was confused by the wide variety on offer. Not really knowing which was best, he had settled for a basic model complete with earphones, which he purchased for a hundred and sixty-nine pounds.

He knew it was a mistake the minute he showed his new toy to the guys in the pub. The general consensus was that he had just wasted his money, but undeterred, he ignored their banter. He would show them.

Even Julie, who was normally very supportive of him, thought that he would be better off spending his money on lottery tickets but Will was convinced that there was a chance of finding something, and anyway, it was interesting and it was certainly cheaper than golf!

Every Friday, he had to suffer the weekly questioning from his pals at the Local.

"What treasure had he uncovered?"

Once they had gone through this ritual humiliation, or at least that is how they viewed it, then the evening could get down to some really important issues like football. Tonight was different. The five Friday regulars, John, Dave, Robin, Geoff and Will had arrived almost at the same time and after ordering their pints, seated themselves in the corner by the open fire, their 'reserved spot', the landlord shifting anyone who presumed to sit in their sanctum.

There was an atmosphere apparent from the outset and the normal banter was muted. It was Will who broke the silence.

"I had a find this week," he said.

"Any good?" Robin smirked.

"Yes. A box full of gold, some fool must have lost it."

"No, no you've got it wrong, its fool's gold not a fool." John was not the brightest of people and the others looked daggers at him.

"How would you know that, John?" Will tried, desperately, to keep a straight face.

"I … er… oh bloody hell! You know, don't you?"

"Of course, I just didn't know which one of you it was."

They all laughed; at least, Will had taken it in good part.

"You'll all laugh on the other side of your faces when I hit the jackpot."

The friends had had their sport and now it was time for some serious drinking.

Will never stayed late at the pub, saying goodnight after a couple more pints. It was only a ten-minute walk to the flat and he was home by nine. He appreciated the fact that Julie never complained about him having a drink with his friends and not being a big drinker, did not want to abuse her feelings, and there was another reason for not drinking too much.

For the last eighteen months, they had been trying for a baby. After more than eight years together, they had decided the time was right for a family, but it had proved to be more difficult than they thought. At first, Will was quite pleased that they did not conceive immediately, for it meant that the increased sexual activity would continue, but after a year, Julie had begun to worry. In spite of her doctor telling her that sometimes, when a couple set their minds on starting a family, the 'pressure' they put on themselves actually works against them and nothing happens. The doctor had told her to relax and let nature take its course, but another six months had elapsed and still nothing.

Saturday morning, they had an appointment with the gynaecologist to test them both and Will certainly did not want to go there with a high alcohol content in his blood stream.

He did not sleep well that night, the thought of the morning's appointment playing on his mind.

They hardly spoke as they dressed and showered. The appointment was for ten o'clock and they both felt nervous, but neither could broach the subject. The journey to the consulting rooms took less than fifteen minutes but still nothing was said.

As they entered the building, Will squeezed her hand and she squeezed his in response. They gave their names to the receptionist who asked them to take a seat whilst she informed the consultant that they were here. Still nothing was said between them.

After a wait of ten minutes, which seemed like an hour, they were ushered into the consultant's room.

"Good morning, I understand that you have been trying for a baby for eighteen months and so far nothing has happened."

Jason Graham was a big man in every sense of the word; he had a booming voice which seemed natural for a man who must have been seventeen stone. He had a large head with a red nose that looked as though he enjoyed more than one glass of wine. He wore thick glasses and had a mass of curly hair, which was in urgent need of a visit to the barbers, and yet, for all this mass he gave off a calm reassuring persona.

"I have read the notes your GP sent me and as far as I can see, there is no reason why you, Mrs Shakespeare, should not be able to conceive. We must, therefore, assume that it is you Mr Shakespeare that might be the cause of this road block."

Will was taken aback, there was nothing wrong with him, he was perfectly healthy, in fact, he never went to the doctors, didn't even know his doctors name.

Mr Graham continued, "I would like you to provide me with a sample so that we can test it and check we are on the right lines."

"A sample, what sample?" Will was at a loss to what he was talking about.

"A sperm sample. If you would go with my nurse, she will take you to another room and provide you with a few magazines which should help." The smile was not as reassuring as it was surely meant to be.

Mr Graham pressed a button on his desk and the receptionist reappeared in his office.

"Nurse, would you take Mr Shakespeare to room three please?"

The nurse needed no further instruction; she knew what room three was for. Will followed her out, still in a daze. He was not sure he would be able to provide a sample that easily.

The magazines worked their magic but not until he got to the pages depicting the girl on girl action and then it was plain sailing!

They left the consulting rooms and walked back to the car.

"Was it very embarrassing?" she asked.

"Well, if you've got a girlfriend who wants to come round for the evening, I'll tell you all about it." He laughed and she hit him, a gentle poke in the ribs.

"You dirty old man, you were supposed to think of me."

"Oh but I did."

She hit him again, but this time with a little more venom. The tension had been broken and they both felt more relaxed, they just hoped there was no serious impediment to them conceiving.

A week later, they received a letter from Mr Graham telling them that the results of the test had been received and could they attend at his rooms the following Wednesday at 4.30 pm.

On arrival at Mr Graham's, they settled down for the customary wait and scanned the out-of-date magazines, not really giving them more than a cursory glance.

After about fifteen minutes, the nurse showed them into Mr Graham's room.

"Good afternoon, I trust you are both well." His booming voice seemed to reverberate around the room.

"Fine thank you, but naturally, keen to know the results of the test," Will replied.

"Yes, of course. Well, it's as I suspected. Nothing to get worried about," he had seen the look of apprehension appear on Will's face. "You have a low sperm count, you'd be surprised how many men have the same symptoms."

Julie squeezed Will's hand. She wanted to reassure him that it was all right.

"So what happens now?" Will's voice seemed to be detached from his body, as if this was all a dream. Surely, there must have been a mistake, he felt as fit as a fiddle.

"I can see this has come as a surprise, but let me reassure you this has no effect on your health and is nothing to worry about. It means that conceiving a child naturally is just a little more difficult. It is still possible, and if you want to keep trying then there is a chance you will be successful, but the chances are much less."

"What are the alternatives?" It was Julie who asked, seeing that poor Will was not his usual effusive self.

"I would recommend IVF. You can get it done on the National Health and the waiting list is not that long, I'd say between three and six months. Of course, you can go private, but it is expensive and it would still be me that you would see."

"I think we need to talk things over and get back to you." Will had regained his composure and wanted to get back home as soon as possible, away from doctors and nurses, and have time to think. They left the consulting rooms and drove home, neither wanting to be the first to break the silence to discuss the situation. Once home and with a large whiskey in his hand, Will pulled Julie to him and hugged her.

"Darling, it's up to you, whatever you decide then I'm happy to go along."

"That's a bit unfair putting it all on me. This should be a joint decision."

"No… no… I'm sorry, that came out all wrong. What I mean is that you are the one that will have to go through the procedures, so if you don't feel comfortable with that then we just carry on and hope we conceive naturally. However, if you want to try IVF, then I'm with you one hundred percent."

They were still holding each other, as if drawing strength from the other person. He gently cupped her face in his hand and pressed his lips to hers. The kiss soft at first became more intense the longer it continued. Julie reached her hands behind his neck and pressed tighter to him, so that he could feel her firm breasts with their hardened nipples against his shirt.

"We could start trying right now if you like?" his voice was husky and his body was trembling with excitement. She could feel him hard against her groin and let out a little moan.

"I just hope nobody comes calling in the next hour."

She was already undoing his belt, and quickly slid his trousers and pants down to his ankles. Whilst she undressed him, Will had unzipped her skirt and unbuttoned her blouse. In seconds they were standing in the kitchen, both stark naked.

Had anybody rung the doorbell, it would have gone unnoticed, such was the intensity of their lovemaking.

Chapter Three

After talking things over at some length, they decided to forget about trying for a baby, letting nature takes its course and, if after three months nothing had happened, then they would go on the list for IVF treatment. Their life went back to normal and 'the baby thing' was not discussed. As Will so quaintly put it, 'it was on the back burner'.

The lads at the pub had been warned that the subject of babies was strictly off the agenda, a request happily agreed to. After all, there were far more important subjects like football, and now there was a general election looming. Although they did not all agree on their party loyalties, one thing they had agreed on was they would never fall out about the subject.

When Tony Blair came to power in '97, Will had been an enthusiastic supporter, even reaching the point of joining the Labour party, but having obtained all the forms never actually completed them. As time went by, he got more and more disillusioned, the final straw being the invasion of Iraq, on the false premise, there being 'weapons of mass destruction' which could be used against Britain. He had decided that maybe it was time for a change, even before Gordon Brown called the election, but who to vote for was the question? The expenses scandal exposed by the Daily Telegraph had shown that MPs from all parties were more interested in lining their own pockets than representing their constituents.

Will had decided he would go to the meetings of all the candidates standing in the new constituency of Kenilworth and Southam, listen to their arguments, then make his mind up. His friends in the pub were scornful when he explained what he had decided. Although they were split in their support for the two main party candidates, they were all agreed that you had to be loyal to your party. Despite their reaction, he had made up his mind and nothing would change it.

Dave and Robin were especially strong in their condemnation. They were both staunch Labour supporters and they felt that Will was 'letting the side down'.

"You can't just abandon your class, you're a working man." Dave could not understand Will at all.

"I'm not abandoning my class, I'm just fed up with all the bullshit that comes out of their mouths, and anyway, Tony Blair was not exactly a Socialist, was he?"

"But the Tories are only out for big business and don't care about the little people," Rob trotted out the party line that his father had fed him since he was a boy.

"Listen you two, the old divisions are gone, nowadays, there's not a lot to choose between them, so I'm going to listen to the candidates and see if any of them want to do something for Kenilworth, or are they just cannon fodder for the party machines."

John and Geoff said nothing, although they were staunch Tories, they could see that Will had a point, they just weren't going to give him the pleasure of agreeing with him.

Will called time on politics, for that night at least. He wanted to talk about football. Leicester was still in with a chance of finishing in the play-off positions, whilst Coventry, who only a few weeks ago was a couple of points behind them, was in free fall, sliding down the table at an alarming rate.

"You really know how to put the boot in, don't you?" Dave gave a thin smile.

"Well, that's more than Cov's forwards do," Will could not resist the riposte.

"You've still got to win the play-offs, so there's a long way to go," John said, although in truth, he was not that bothered being more interested in Rugby Union.

"I bet you all a tenner that Leicester go up. Anyone brave enough to take me on?"

The odds were against Will, but he had a feeling that this was Leicester's year and £40 was not the end of the world if he lost. As a man, they all agreed to take the bet.

"You don't want to bet on the outcome of the election, do you?" Geoff asked mischievously.

Will ignored his remark; he was not getting drawn back into a political debate. He looked at his watch, nine o'clock. The evening had flown by. He got up, said goodnight to the group and left for home, there were other more pleasurable duties to perform that night.

Chapter Four

The following Wednesday after school, Will had decided, as the weather had turned warmer, he would walk to Abbey Fields and try his luck with the metal detector. The nights were lighter now and he could spend a good two hours before Julie would have their dinner ready. He left the house equipped with knapsack and detector, and set out along the lane towards the fields. He had a map of the area, which he had divided into squares, each time, he religiously scanning each 'square'. Having completed a full pass over the area, he shaded it in on his map. He had so far worked the whole area from the main road past the boundary wall of the church yard and up to the old Abbey ruins. The next 'blocks' on his map would take him up to the hedgerow that divided the park area from the field containing the pond.

Part of this next area had been tarmaced to provide a play area for children, and the council had erected swings and slides there. He realised that he could not search over this area and just hoped that there was nothing of any value underneath, for if there was, it would stay undiscovered. There were a few mothers watching their children playing on the apparatus, which were now used to seeing Will, and took no notice of him. Some of the children had been curious when he first started searching the area, but soon lost interest when he found nothing.

Will had methodically worked his way up and down the grid as drawn on his map, and after an hour and half, had not even had a peep out of the machine. He was now working down the side of the hedge that separated the two fields. What looked like an old lamp standard, but without the top that would normally hold the lamp light, stood next to the hedge about twenty feet from the Abbey ruins. Will was getting tired and thought he would just finish this last grid then call it a day, as the detector swept around the base of the lamp, the bleep…bleep burst into his earphones. For the last ten minutes, he had been on autopilot thinking what Julie might be preparing for dinner, so the noise startled him. He passed the detector over the spot again and the noise returned. He stopped, turned round to see if anyone had heard the sound, or noticed what he was doing, but there was no change in the scenery, the children were totally oblivious to him. He bent down, and taking the small trowel, scrapped away at the grass at the base of the pole. It was early April and had not rained for a few days, so the ground was hard, the trowel making little impression. He realised he would need the shovel to dig into the ground. He looked at his watch, Julie would be expecting him back within the next fifteen minutes, there was not enough time to thoroughly dig down to investigate properly. The location was easy to remember as it was at the bottom of the old lamp standard. Will made up his mind to leave it for now, go home, have his dinner and come back much later that evening, when, hopefully, there would be no one around to poke their noses in.

Will packed his note book away and clipped the detector onto his knapsack. It had occurred to him that this might be another wind up by his friends and by walking away now, if they were watching, would not give them the pleasure of him digging away for another disappointment!

Julie was in the kitchen when he arrived home and shouted to him as he entered.

"Will? Glad you're back, I was just about to ring you on the mobile. Dinner is ready, roast chicken, okay? Can you set the table?"

"Yes boss," he said it without rancour. They both cooked, and whoever made the dinner the other set the table and opened the wine.

Will poured them each a glass of wine and they settled down to the meal.

"Well, tell me, did you find anything?"

"I'm not sure. I got a full strength signal but it was getting late so I didn't stop to dig down, anyway, the ground was fairly hard so I will need the shovel. It's probably a false alarm, but I'm going back later when it's quiet and hopefully, no one's watching."

She smiled at the memory of the joke his friends had played on him. She knew how disappointed he had been and desperately hoped that he would find something, even if it wasn't a treasure trove.

After dinner, Julie settled down to mark some homework she had set and Will caught up with the day's papers including the election manifestoes which had been published over the previous two days. He had to admit that neither of the major parties was very inspiring, and more and more he was leaning towards the Lib/Dems. Throughout the credit crisis, he had been impressed with Vince Cable, their Treasury spokesman, and whilst not agreeing with everything he said, he liked his honesty and straightforwardness, which seemed in sharp contrast with the constant sniping and failure to answer any questions from Labour and Tory spokesmen. If only they were not so keen on Europe then he would be inclined to vote for them, he might even do so in spite of his antipathy to the EU.

He looked up from the paper, it was already ten o'clock. He had not realised how quickly the time had passed and he wanted to go back to his 'find'.

"I'm just popping out for about half an hour to see if it was a genuine find or just another rusty old nail."

Julie looked up from her marking.

"Do you want me to come with you?" She was pleased when he shook his head. She had at least another thirty to forty minutes marking and needed to get it completed that night.

He pulled his Parka on, picked up the knapsack and shovel, before setting out to the fields. Although the days had warmed, the evenings were still cold and the difference in temperature was at least ten degrees. The night was dark and, as it was a new moon, there was no illumination, save for the street lamps. As he walked towards the park, he remembered when he was a boy his father taking him into the garden to show him the stars in the sky, teaching him the names of the constellations, showing him the pole star and explaining the Latin names together with their more common names. On nights like tonight with no moon visible, it being either the start of a new moon, or the waxing of the old moon, his dad always called it a 'cold moon', explaining that with no light emitting, there was no warmth. As he grew older and knew that the moon did not give any heat, he challenged his dad on the term, but his father would not budge.

"It's a cold moon and always will be," his father had insisted.

Will did not argue, the term seemed appropriate, even if it was not logical. From that point onwards, he also referred to a new moon as a cold moon.

Tonight was a cold moon.

Will reached the spot under the old lamppost and set the knapsack down on the grass. He had not bothered to bring the metal detector; it was just a case of how far down before he struck pay dirt.

Although the top layer of the grass and soil was firm, underneath it still held the moisture from the winter rains and the digging became easier. He had dug down about one and half times the depth of the shovel's blade when he heard the sound of metal on metal. He knelt down, carefully scrapping away at the soil, as he did so another clang, then another encouraged him to continue. Taking out the pencil torch from his knapsack and shining into the hole, he could see a glint as it played on the metal object. Holding the torch in his teeth, he crouched down and scrapped away the earth around the object to reveal a silver case. Gently digging under the case, he loosened it free. It was a silver cigarette case.

He wiped the case with a cloth, the silver shining in the light of the torch. It had a hallmark on the back with a monogram on the front bearing the letters M D G.

This was defiantly the most valuable item he had ever found and although not ancient treasure, must still have a value. He wondered if there was any clue to its owner inside as he clicked the clip that held it shut. The case opened to reveal a piece of folded card. He opened the card, which had been folded into four and spread it out on the grass.

Will's mouth fell open with surprise. He blinked and looked again, but there was no doubt. The card was in fact a photograph, but not one that he would have ever imagined.

The image was of a room with a bed in it and a naked young man bent over it with his hands outstretched on the bed cover. Behind him was another man who seemed older, also naked… buggering the young lad.

Will felt sick. He was not a prude and certainly not homophobic, but to see the act so graphically represented had shocked him.

Will quickly filled in the hole that he had recently excavated and packed away his tools. He needed to get home and have a drink, preferably a double.

Julie heard the front door shut and called out from the living room.

"That didn't take long. I suppose it was another false dawn." There was a hint of irony in her voice for she secretly hoped that one day he would come home with a knapsack full of gold. When there was no response, she got up from her chair slightly put out by Will not acknowledging her. He was in the hall hanging up his Parka.

"What's up? You look as though you've seen a ghost? Do you want a cup of tea?"

"No... but I could do with a large whisky."

She was surprised. Will was not a big drinker and it was unusual for him to drink spirits during the week as he liked to have a clear head in the mornings. Even young children could be very demanding and certainly very noisy. She poured him the whisky and he slumped into the chair.

"Now will you tell me what's going on?"

"I found a silver cigarette case..."

"But that's good, isn't it?" she interrupted.

"Just let me finish. As I said, I found this case and opened it to see if there was any way of identifying the owner and..." His voice faltered, his mouth dry, not able to get his words out.

"Come on, what was in it?" She was getting irritated now; it was not like Will to be so reticent.

"Look for yourself." He took the photograph from the case and handed it to her. She stared in disbelief at the image.

"Good God! Why on earth would anyone take a picture of that?"

"That's exactly what I thought. As you can see, the picture was taken from the side and you can't see either of their faces. The older man has turned away from the camera and the young man's arm is blocking his face. The only thing I have noticed, looking at it again, is the older man is wearing a gold Rolex and there seems to be a tattoo of some description on the back of his wrist partly covered by the watch."

"What are you going to do, report it to the Police?"

"I don't know. It's not exactly illegal, is it?"

"Yes, but the case is lost property, you should really hand it in."

"I can't see anyone rushing into the police station wanting to claim it, can you?"

She laughed and it seemed to lift the tension that had been present since he came in. Even Will had to smile, though the whole thing still seemed unreal. What should have been a little celebration at finally finding something, had turned into a dilemma of what to do next. He decided he would sleep on it; there was no urgency. No one had seen him digging, so no one needed to know anything about it, he could throw the case in the bin and forget the whole incident. None of his friends thought he would ever unearth anything, so there would be no questions from them; they had stopped asking how the hunting was going long ago.

He finished his whisky and made his way up to bed. Julie was in the kitchen making a cup of tea to bring up with her. By the time he had undressed and got into bed, he had convinced himself that he should forget the whole incident.

Chapter Five

Will had put the incident of the cigarette case out his mind, but had not thrown it in the bin, which had been his first thought. Instead, it was sitting at the bottom of the drawer in his bedside cabinet.

A week had gone by and the newspapers were full of election fever. All the parties had announced their candidates and published their manifestoes. The divide between the two main parties was closing and the smart money was on a hung parliament, with the Liberal Democrats in the position of 'Kingmaker'. Will had made up his mind; he would attend the public meeting of each of the candidates. Initially, four candidates had been announced, Nicholas Milton (Lab); Nigel Rock (Lib/Dem); Jeremy Wright (Con) and James Harrison (Green) but a fifth had thrown his hat in the ring a few days after the others. Martin De Glanville (Independent) was standing as an anti-sleaze candidate. Will was intrigued and was interested to know just exactly what De Glanville hoped to achieve. He had read a piece De Glanville had written in the local paper. It appeared the main thrust of his policy was to reduce the expenses MPs could claim and cut out the blatant corruption the majority of the last parliament had managed to get away with. On the face of it, Will had to admit he had a lot of sympathies with the guy's sentiments, but failed to see how one man could make a difference. Will, nevertheless, decided to attend his meeting, which was to be held that Friday. To get a bit of background on the man, he went on the internet to find out where he had come from. It appeared he was an ex-Tory who had tried unsuccessfully to get his name on the short list for the new Kenilworth constituency, but had not even made the last four. He lived in London, was a hedge fund manager who had made a lot of money in the boom years, and had been wise enough to foresee the credit crunch, moving out just in time. He was married to the daughter of a Baronet, who had been a model, but was now running a fashion boutique in Kensington. All in all, he did not, on the face of it, appear to be a man of the people and certainly, in Will's eyes anyway, not a champion of the little man, so the anti-sleaze label did not appear to fit well.

If nothing else, Will was a fair-minded person and resolved not to go to the meeting with a preconceived opinion, even though it was hard not to!

"I wonder why he has chosen Kenilworth to try and get elected," Julie said as they got themselves ready to go to the meeting.

"From what I've found out, he thought he would be a shoe in for the Conservative nomination, even bought an apartment in the High Street so he could play the 'local' card. I think he wants to try and split the vote. Call it an act of revenge."

"I thought you were keeping an open mind," she teased.

The early evening was dry and warm, and as the days were lengthening, the sun still shone behind the rooftops. They arrived to find the room only half full. Clearly, this was not the normal well-oiled party machine the other candidates could rely on. Looking around, Will recognised some of the people in the audience, men he had known from the time that he had flirted with the labour party, clearly, they were here on a 'fishing trip' and not to support the candidate. A few more people drifted in and the low drone of chattering permeated the room as they waited for the candidate to arrive.

An earnest young man of about twenty-five walked onto the platform and coughed, to try and gain the audiences' attention but it had little effect. He looked nervous and unused to appearing in public.

"Ladies and Gentlemen, if I could have your attention please," he shouted the words and the room fell silent, like naughty schoolboys being admonished by the headmaster. The result even surprised the speaker and, for a second, he was lost for words. Having recovered his composure, he continued, "I am the agent for your, Independent Anti-Sleaze Candidate, who I will now ask to speak to you. May I present Martin De Glanville."

There was some polite applause as De Glanville came to the microphone. He was a tall man; about six foot three, with dark hair flecked with silver, handsome, with a smile that played around his mouth and bright piercing blue eyes. He reminded Will of Sean Connery in the old Bond movies.

Julie squeezed Will's arm. "He's got my vote," she whispered.

"Behave," he replied out of the corner of his mouth.

"Ladies and Gentlemen, firstly, I would like to thank Tony, my agent, for that rousing introduction." A ripple of laughter went round the room and de Glanville paused to emphasise the joke. "You will have to forgive him, he's a little nervous. His last job was a traffic warden so he's not used to being amongst friends." The room duly responded again whilst poor Tony sat on the platform turning a deep shade of red.

Having got his audience on his side, De Glanville moved to outline his policy.

"I realise as one man I cannot influence the big decisions on health, police, defence or tax, but what I will promise is that I will represent Kenilworth and Southam to fight for your interests. Whoever wins this election, we all know that we are going to have to batten down the hatches for the next few years to get out of this economic mess and we will only succeed if all the country work together. Too often in the past, politicians have gone to Westminster and forgotten who put them there… Well, I can tell you… It was decent folk like you in this room tonight! Westminster has become a gravy train, with MPs thinking that they could take, take, and take. I will expose anyone who abuses the system. In the last parliament, whilst ordinary people in this country suffered under the credit crunch, hundreds of MPs were fiddling their expenses and lining their pockets at your expense. My platform is a simple one, reform of the pay and expenses of Members, and be a voice for the minority."

He took a drink of water whilst his words sank in.

"I sometimes think that once people get elected to Westminster they forget why, they forget that they are there to represent their constituents. In this country, poll after poll indicates that a majority of the population wants to bring back the death sentence for certain categories of murder. Yet, every time there is a vote to bring back hanging, it is defeated. How often have you seen MPs being interviewed on TV after such a vote and being asked the question why did they vote against capital punishment when the vast majority want its return, and do you know what they answer?

They think they know better!

Unbelievable!

They have the audacity to say that they know better and such matters cannot be decided by the people. How arrogant is that? They forget who put them there in the first place.

I believe in Referenda and think on important issues like this the people should have the final say.

The other big issue that seems to have been quietly brushed aside in this election is Europe. All the major parties, including the Conservatives, see our future as part of Europe. Perhaps it is too late to change that now, but we are constantly being flattened by new European laws that are slowly strangling the legitimacy of the British Government, with the worst law being that on Human Rights. This seems to me, is a charter for the rights of the perpetrator, not the victim. We need to curb the gradual ceding of our powers to Brussels before it is too late."

A ripple of applause showed that he had struck a chord with his audience.

"The list goes on and on with Red Tape, and Health and Safety legislation stifling our ability to trade out of our economic difficulties. We are a nation of inventors and designers, but are being held back at every turn by petty laws and regulations that hamper true entrepreneurship. Bureaucracy must not be allowed to prevent recovery."

A larger round of applause greeted this last statement and Will found himself warming to this man. Some of his views were perhaps a bit further right than Will felt comfortable with; but nevertheless, he had to acknowledge it was basically common sense.

"Ladies and Gentlemen, this is a small island, and one that has developed a wonderful multicultural pattern that enriches the lives of everybody. I, for one, endorse that feeling and am happy living in this society, but and there is a but, we cannot continually take in more and more immigrants where ever they are from or whatever colour they are, without some sort of control. People who want to come to this country must prove that they have a worth… they must put in as well as take out. I believe that a basic knowledge of the English language is a necessary prerequisite for anyone wanting to take up residence in the UK, along with the prospect of a job to go to. If we adopt this course of action, then any new immigrants will be welcome to these shores."

Many in the audience rose as one to applaud. For the first time in his life, Will felt that a politician was saying what he was thinking and never once had De Glanville derided or criticised any of the other parties.

"Ladies and Gentlemen, I have kept my speech as short as possible as I know we politicians can be boring and I did not want you all to doze off too early." Again, polite laughter and he waited, like a good actor, milking the moment. "I would now like to open the evening to a question and answer session, so you can ask me what really concerns you, and hopefully, I will have the right answers."

There was no doubt that he was charismatic and had the ability to make each person in the room feel as though he was addressing them solely.

"I hope you don't mind, but it is such a warm evening, with your permission, I would like to remove my jacket before we start the next part." Without waiting for a reply, though it would not have been negative, he took of his jacket and rolled his sleeves up. "That's better. Now does anyone have a question?"

Will and Julie were sitting near the front to the right hand side of the hall, and had a clear view of the platform and the speaker. Will's mouth dropped open as his gaze fell on the candidate's bare left arm. He was wearing a gold Rolex watch and had a tattoo of a dagger partly covered by the watch! His eyes moved up to De Glanville's head and now he noticed the flecked grey around the temples… it was the same as the picture of the naked man with the young boy. He felt Julie squeezing his hand. She had noticed the watch at the same time!

Will could not believe what he had just seen. He stared ahead not hearing anything, the questions and answers seemed to be in a different time zone. He felt numb.

Julie was trying to whisper something in his ear, but it did not register. She shook his arm and eventually, he turned towards her. She pointed to the door and mouthed the words, 'Let's go'.

They made their way outside and stood for a moment, neither speaking at first.

"It's just unbelievable. Now what do I do?" He looked at Julie almost pleadingly, but she was just as confused as he.

Chapter Six

Martin grabbed another glass of champagne as the waitress pressed her way through the crush of people. He had been invited to the opening of a new gallery in Jermain Street which his friend Toby was opening with an exhibition of Australian aboriginal art. Toby had been a contemporary of his at Westminster and the two, although not close friends, had stayed in touch. More importantly for Toby, he wanted as many wealthy people as possible at the launch and he was hoping that some might even buy from the exhibits on show.

Martin certainly fell into that category. Since coming down from Oxford, his rise in the city had been rapid and he had earned, the not too flattering, nickname of 'Golden Balls', for it seemed he had the Midas touch. Martin was proud of what he had achieved, but it had not been easy, in fact, it had almost cost him a nervous breakdown with the punishing schedule he set himself. For the last ten years, he had not taken a single holiday and worked at least a sixteen-hour day often only having Sunday afternoon away from the phone or computer. In that time, his reputation as one of the leading fund managers had grown and made him a small fortune and more importantly, he had seen the credit crisis coming, making sure all his investments were well protected.

He had set himself a ten-year plan and now that stage in his life was complete. He now wanted to enjoy the fruits of his labour, but had no intention of letting go, just easing off a little. His next goal was to move into politics and he had a plan for that as well. He would need to cultivate old friends with political connections getting adopted for a constituency ahead of the next election, which was only eighteen months away.

David Cameron was riding high in the polls and, with the economy in turmoil; Gordon Brown's star had fallen to an all-time low. It was obvious that no election would be called until the very last minute, but when that date arrived, probably spring 2010, the Tories would sweep to power and he wanted to be on the bandwagon.

Although Toby thought Martin was doing him a favour being at this soirée, it was just the sort of function that Martin wanted to be seen at.

He spotted Giles Latcham and made his way across the room to speak to him. Giles was one of Cameron's speechwriters, but his official title was communications officer at Central Office, he was definitely someone to court.

"Giles, hi." Martin held out his hand. "I hope you remember me, we met at Westminster, though I was in the year below you."

Giles turned round and shook Martin's hand.

"I'm sorry old man, but I can't say I do."

Martin was not easily put off.

"No matter. Look, I wondered if we might have a drink sometime, I would like your advice on something." Martin passed him a business card. "Or perhaps dinner if you're free?"

Giles read the card.

"Are you the guy they call 'Golden Balls'?

Martin blushed slightly.

"I have been referred to by certain members of the press by that soubriquet."

"Yes, okay then, dinner. I'm free this Friday, would that suit?"

"Fine by me. I'll book a table at the Ivy, say seven thirty."

Giles nodded his agreement, then turned back to the couple he had been talking to before Martin had interrupted.

Martin moved around the room looking to see if there were any other people that might be useful to him that he could cultivate but although he recognised a number of the guests, they were of no relevance to his latest plans.

He stopped and admired one of the paintings hanging on the white painted wall at the rear of the gallery. It was vibrant with strong colours and although he was not exactly sure what it represented, he felt strangely drawn to the picture. Toby came up behind him.

"It's beautiful, don't you think?"

Martin turned to face Toby.

"What is it?"

"It depicts an aboriginal villager stalking a Kangaroo and he is just about to kill the animal. I think it is really powerful. Primitive Australian art is getting really popular. It's a good investment."

The words 'good investment' resonated with Martin, but more importantly, he really liked the picture.

"How much is it?" he asked.

"Ten thousand, but you can have it for nine if you buy it now."

Martin pulled his chequebook from his pocket, and wrote out a cheque there and then.

"You don't waste any time do you?" a woman's voice said

A number of the guests had gathered round whilst the transaction had taken place and Martin turned to see who the speaker was. A woman in her early thirties smiled back at him. She was about five foot eight with long dark hair and a sun-tanned complexion, large brown eyes and high cheekbones, which gave her an aristocrat look. Her figure could only be described as stunning and to Martin, she appeared to have stepped straight off the catwalk. She was by far the most attractive woman he had ever come across.

"I'm sorry I don't think we've met before. I'm…" He did not finish his sentence.

"Martin De Glanville aka Golden Balls. I know, I've been watching you." The smile still played around her lips, which she licked every so often as if polishing them. She was toying with him, almost goading him to ask her who she was. They stood there for a few moments, sparring in silence waiting to see who would speak first.

Graciously, he broke the silence. "And you are?" he asked.

"Madeleine Verity, but my friends call me Maddy."

"May I call you Maddy then?" He returned her smile.

"If you invite me to see your new picture when it's hung, then yes you certainly may."

Martin was used to forceful women. In his line of work, some of his women competitors were far more aggressive than their male counterparts, but socially, all the women he had known had been far more reserved, Maddy was certainly different.

"Good then, next Tuesday at my flat, say seven thirty. Do you like Chinese food?" He did not wait for an answer, "I'm a dab hand at stir fry. I'll look forward to seeing you." He passed her his business card with his private address scribbled on the back.

"I can't wait," she said as she put the card into her handbag, turned and was swallowed up in the crowd.

Toby had been witness to the whole episode and had stood there, his mouth gaping open, his hand still grasping Martins cheque.

"You be careful, old son. Maddy usually gets whatever she wants and I have a feeling she wants you."

"Well, that's not so bad, is it Toby? She is stunning."

"You just mind you don't bite off more than you can chew, that's all. Anyway, I'd better get this picture wrapped and sent round to your place for the unveiling next Tuesday." He grinned as he said the words unveiling, as though there was some hidden meaning in them.

Martin left the gallery pleased at the turn of events. He had secured a meeting with Giles Latcham who was right at the heart of the Conservative machine and if anyone could help, it would be Giles, then there was the bonus of meeting Maddy. There was something about the woman that intrigued him and he looked forward to getting to know her better. His mind explored the possibilities of a friendship with Maddy and what advantages that might give him in his pursuit of a political career. With a spring in his step, he crossed the road and hailed a cab to take him to his favourite wine bar, which was situated only a short walk, or stagger, from his flat.

Chapter Seven

Martin sat at the bar sipping a gin and tonic whilst constantly looking at his watch to check the time. He had arrived early, at seven fifteen, as he wanted to make sure he was there to greet his guest. By a quarter to eight, he began to get anxious, was Giles coming? He had not rung to cancel the appointment, so there was no reason to believe he was anything other than late. Martin was used to promptness and made it a point never to be late for a meeting he was attending, as it immediately put you at a disadvantage, and most of his meetings involved negotiations dealing in millions of pounds. Having the advantage was of prime importance, but this was different, this time he wanted something from Giles.

Another glance at his watch, it was now five to eight. He called the waiter and ordered a glass of water. He didn't want to be drunk before the evening had even started!

As the glass was set down in front of him, Giles appeared by his side.

"My sincere apologies, I hope you haven't been waiting long."

"No, no just arrived myself as matter of fact. Would you like a drink?"

Giles nodded and asked for a gin and tonic.

"What's that you're drinking? It's not water, is it? Good God, are you teetotal?"

Martin gave a hollow laugh. "No, I just thought I'd start with water, I like a clean pallet before drinking wine."

"Bit of a connoisseur, hey."

"No, not really, just like what I like." Martin, in fact, knew quite a bit about wine, but did not want to appear to be superior, on the contrary, he wanted Giles to feel top dog.

"Shall we go through to our table?"

The maître d' showed them to their table giving them each a menu, the wine list he gave to Martin.

"Do you dine here often? They seem to know you." Giles was obviously impressed.

"I do come quite a lot. It always impresses the clients and a good meal often loosens them up." He gave Giles a knowing wink.

They ordered their meals and Martin asked the Sommelier to recommend the wines.

"I always think that if you have an expert on hand, why not use him," Martin said by way of explanation.

They passed a few pleasantries, the usual small talk, whilst eating the starters.

Martin was wondering how to broach the real reason for the meeting when Giles brought the conversation around to the present state of the economy.

"You know, Martin, Brown has got to call an election by June 2010, and with the way things are, I can see him hanging on until the very last minute, that's why we have started gearing up for the fight now. We're riding high in the opinion polls, but a lot can happen in eighteen months. If the economy starts to pull out of this recession, and I think it will, then Brown is going to claim he has all the answers."

"But, surely, the electorate knows that he got us into this mess. He was the one who said 'no more boom and bust' and here we are, bust!"

"Yes I know, and you know too, but he is putting all the blame on the global downturn and profligate bankers. Christ, you're in the system, you should know better than anybody."

"Giles, I can't deny we have all been on the gravy train and I have done very well, but I saw the way things were heading and moved out of properties months ago. If I could see the way the wind was blowing, surely, the treasury should have been aware."

"I think they were, but the politicians didn't want bad news so ignored them. Anyway, here we are and it's going to get worse before it gets better, you mark my words. Look, I'm sorry, been going off a bit, you wanted to talk to me?"

"Yes, as I said I've been very lucky and made myself financially independent. I'm looking for other interests now; I'd like to put something back into the system."

"Well, Martin, I can tell you the party is always looking for donors, after all it's our lifeblood. If you want to help swell the coffers, I'm sure we could get you a gong for your support, I'm afraid a 'K' will cost you big time." He gave a chortle.

"No, no I don't want to donate, I want to be active… I want to become an MP."

Giles was taken aback, he had totally misread the situation, he had done some checking on Martin, and knew that he was seriously wealthy and had assumed he was looking to buy his way into the honours system. Not once had it crossed his mind that Martin wanted to become a candidate.

"Sorry, old boy, got the wrong end of the stick. Well, if you're serious, the first thing you need to do is join the party, then I can set up a few meetings with some influential people and if they like you, then we can try and fast track you to a suitable seat. I warn you though, it's not easy and as a newcomer, you'll be way down the list. The party is not in favour of parachuting Central Office's chosen 'Wonder Kids' into the home counties. That's frowned on these days. I can help by putting you in front of the right people though. By the way, you're single, aren't you? The old ladies in the Shires like their young men to be married with two point four kids. Have you got a girlfriend?"

The questions were coming thick and fast and Martin was reeling from the onslaught.

"I'm seeing someone and it's pretty serious." He was sure that finding a suitable escort would not be a problem, though in truth he had not bothered with girls since university, he had not had the time! He had been too busy making money.

"Good. Then the first thing is for me to send some forms for you to fill in and get you on the 'books' so to speak. I'll put them in the post tomorrow and if you can get them back to me, I'll press the start button, but don't expect things to happen straight away. This is the Conservative party remember, not the stock exchange." He laughed. He laughed a lot at his own jokes.

Martin steered the conversation away from politics back to money, which seemed to fascinate Giles. Martin had achieved what he wanted and the meeting had been a success even though the bill was a whopping four hundred pounds, but then you had to speculate to accumulate. That had been his watchword in life and it had always proved to be right.

Chapter Eight

Martin felt pleased with himself, the meeting with Giles had gone well and he had been as good as his word, the enrolment papers to join the party had arrived first class on Saturday. Hardly bothering to read the small print, he had filled in the forms and put them in the prepaid envelope. He included a cheque for a thousand pounds. His short time with Giles had taught him that, as far as party loyalty goes, it was always better if sweetened with a little financial sugar. He spent the rest of the weekend working on some papers. Saturdays and Sundays were much the same as any other day to him; the only difference being the computer was in the spare room and not the office.

His secretary was surprised when on Tuesday he informed her that he would be leaving at five o'clock sharp so not to book any evening appointments or conference calls. She was not at all unhappy by the request as it meant, for once, she would get an early night. She was, however, a little taken aback by his next request. He passed a list of items that he wanted her to get for him from a delicatessen in Chinatown.

"You should find everything on the list easy enough, most of the supermarkets stock the majority of ingredients, but they never seem to have authentic rice wine." He saw her puzzled look and smiled. "I'm entertaining tonight and want to impress."

"Well, I hope she appreciates it." She smiled back. It was the first time he had ever mentioned entertaining anybody; she had him down as a confirmed workaholic bachelor.

"I'll let you know how I get on," he promised.

At five o'clock sharp, he collected the dinner ingredients and made his way to the car park. His pride and joy was his Ferrari, bright red, it shone like a beacon amongst the plethora of standard silver BMW's and Mercedes. Clicking the remote as he walked amongst the rows of cars, he could not help thinking that his car was probably worth two to three times as much as any of the others standing to attention in their military like rows. He even had a special place, which was originally a space for two cars, but he had rented the extra space by saying that he needed two cars at any one time, one being for clients. Somehow, his totally illogical explanation had been accepted and now he was the envy of all the other owners.

The engine gave that throaty roar that sent a thrill down his spine no matter how many times he heard it, and the car moved smoothly away like a panther preparing to sprint after its prey. His apartment overlooked the Thames and in truth, he could have walked the short distance from the office, but even with the burden of the Congestion charge, the pleasure of nestling into the leather and feeling the raw power under his control was worth every penny.

He glanced at his watch, five twenty, plenty of time to prepare the meal, and leave the chicken and beef to marinade whilst he showered and changed. The beauty of cooking Chinese food was that it could be prepared in advance and the actual stir-frying only took minutes.

He went to the fridge and collected the chicken breasts, then slicing them into strips, placed them into a bowl of mixed egg white and corn flour, making sure they were completely coated, then returned the bowl to the fridge. Next up, he sliced the small fillet of beef into bite size pieces and added them to a bowl of corn flour, rice wine and soy sauce, which went into the fridge to marinate. There was nothing else to prepare, it was that easy.

He left the kitchen and headed for the dining room. It only took minutes to lay the table putting chopsticks at the side of the chargers, and in Maddy's place, adding a spoon and fork just in case she was not proficient in the art of oriental eating. He had bought six red roses which he placed in a vase in the centre of the table. Standing back, he surveyed his handiwork, the lights reflecting around the room from the cut glass wine glasses. He gave a smile of self-satisfaction… *yes, that looked just right,* he thought. As he left the room, he turned the dimmer switch down low. There was just enough time for a shower and a change of clothing before she was due. A shiver of nervous tension ran through his body, he was not quite sure how the evening would evolve, but of one thing he was sure, it would be interesting.

The intercom buzzer startled him. Although he had been expecting it, it still made him jump, he had not been this apprehensive since his first interview at Cambridge. He picked up the receiver.

"Hello."

"Martin, it's Maddy."

He pressed the release button. "Come on up."

He walked to the door and opened it ready for when she stepped out of the lift. Hearing the whoosh of the lift and the clunk as it stopped for the doors to open, he stepped forward so that she would see him as soon as she got out. She smiled as she saw him and walked the few paces to where he stood.

"Hi, nice to see you again, I've been looking forward to this. I hope I won't be disappointed."

Martin lent forward and kissed her lightly on each cheek.

"I told you Chinese food is my specialty."

"I'm sure you have other hidden talents," she smiled again as she said this.

He had the distinct feeling that she was playing with him, teasing him and he had to admit he was quite enjoying it.

"Drink? What would you like?"

"You choose."

"Dom Perignon?"

"Fantastic, it's my favourite."

He took two champagne flutes from the cabinet and poured them each a glass. The bubbles exploded to the surface as they clinked the glasses together.

"To the future," she said.

"To the future," he returned the toast. "Right, I'm going to start cooking, so if you want to go into the living room, make yourself at home."

"I'd rather stay and watch the master at work, that is if you don't mind being watched."

There was something in her voice as if there was another meaning to what she was saying, like a naughty schoolgirl who was hiding something from her teacher, yet, the innocent look on her face made him wonder if he was just imagining it.

He had a large range style cooker and more than one wok. He quickly stir fried the chicken then set it to one side. He had a mixture of lemon juice, chili, garlic, soy sauce and chicken stock which he heated in the wok, then added the chicken pieces and a little corn flour to thicken. The whole process was completed in less than five minutes. He similarly cooked the beef, but this time, added stock and oyster sauce. Both dishes he poured out into the heated serving dishes. Finally, he took some boiled rice which he had made previously and stir-fried it, adding frozen peas and two beaten eggs. The fried rice turned a light golden colour as the eggs cooked in the mix. He tipped the mixture into a third serving dish. The meal was complete, total time, fourteen minutes.

"You're a genius, I'm impressed," she said.

They took the dishes and the heated plates into the dining room.

"I've cheated slightly; I have to confess. I bought the prawn crackers from the deli."

She laughed. *Not exactly what I would call cheating,* she thought.

"Chablis okay?" he asked.

"Umm, lovely."

She helped herself to rice and chicken, saying she would try the beef in a minute. He was pleasantly surprised when she eschewed the fork and spoon, and expertly ate with her chopsticks.

The room was quiet, save for the click of bamboo on china. They were both busily eating and conversation was taking a poor second place.

"Where have you hung your new picture? I can't see it," she said, her eyes searching the room.

"It's in my bedroom facing the bed so that it's the first thing I see in the mornings."

"I can't wait to see it, especially from that angle." She smiled as she spoke and licked her lips. He was not sure if it was in appreciation of the food or something else.

"Plenty of time to show you the picture. You still have the beef in oyster sauce to try."

"Well, if it's half as good as the chicken, then I know it will be sensational."

"I've got a bottle of Gevry Chamberten, which I think will go well with the beef, do you drink red?"

"I drink anything, especially expensive wines and I can see you only have expensive wines, so please pour." Again, she licked her lips and this time, he knew it was not the food she was thinking of!

They finished their meal and she helped him clear away the dishes. Having switched the dishwasher on, he walked back into the lounge and poured two large brandies, not even bothering to ask if she wanted one or not.

"Any particular music you fancy?" he asked.

"No, you choose."

"Rhapsody in Blue then, it's my favourite."

The wine of the clarinet could be heard above the piano as he sat on the settee next to her.

"Excellent choice of music, and brandy," she said as she moved closer to him.

For a moment, there was an awkward silence whilst neither spoke then, together, they both started to say something.

"Sorry, you go first," he said.

"No, no please what were you going to say?" She looked directly into his eyes as though she was reading his soul.

"Well, I… er… thought you might like to hear about my future plans."

"I certainly would, especially if it means you will be seeing more of me."

"You may find it a bit dull," his words seemed to catch as if he was finding it hard to breathe. "I am hoping to go into politics. In fact, I've already applied to join the Party and am looking for a prospective seat for the next election."

"I take it you mean the Conservative Party?"

He laughed "Of course, who else?"

"Well, you might have been a left wing trendy. What do they call them, champagne Socialists?"

"Heavens, no!"

"That's alright then. You have my full permission." She was giggling now, the effects of the wine and brandy showing in her cheeks, which had got redder as the evening wore on. "You know, you're a very handsome man Martin. I think the electorate will fall for you big time." She drew close to him and kissed him gently on the lips, not lingering but long enough to be meaningful.

"And you, Maddy, are well-named because you are madly attractive."

"Who gave you permission to call me Maddy," she teased. "I said you could call me Maddy if I saw your new picture hanging on the wall."

"In that case, you must see the picture, follow me." He stood up, and rather unsteadily she got to her feet and followed him to the bedroom. The curtains were open, revealing a large panoramic view of the Thames, with the lights of the buildings reflecting on the water. The room was high up, so not overlooked from outside. The ceiling lights were turned low but the picture was illuminated by a single light above it. Maddy crossed the room and sat on the bed, with the pillows behind her, facing the picture. There was no doubt about it, the picture had a raw power that drew the viewer into it almost as if you were there at the kill.

"Come and sit beside me, I won't bite, you know," she said.

Martin sat on the bed next to her, kicking off his shoes so that he could stretch out on the cover.

"You have certainly got taste in pictures. Do you have the same taste in women, I wonder?" she let the question hang in the air for a few seconds. "Would you like to taste one?" She turned to him and placing her hand at the back of his neck pulled him to her. This time, the kiss was not gentle and her tongue searched his mouth, darting backwards and forwards. He felt a warm pleasure. He was being taken on a ride into the unknown, and was happy to sit back and enjoy it.

For a second, she pulled away from the embrace, but only long enough to breathlessly say, "Unzip me please."

He felt for the zip at the back of her neck and slid it downwards. As it fell from her shoulders, her tanned skin shone in the glow of the lights. She wore nothing underneath, no bra, no knickers just hold up stockings! He looked down and saw the bulge in his trousers, there was no turning back now… even if he wanted to.

Chapter Nine

Martin woke and looked at his watch, seven am, just like any normal day, but this was not any normal day. He turned to look at Maddy but the bed was empty.

"Are you in the bathroom?" he shouted. There was no answer. He rose and padded across the room. On the table, he noticed a card and picked it up and read it.

"Thank you for a wonderful evening... Had to dash to the Boutique... Will ring you later... Top marks for food, wine and sex!!! Love, Maddy."

He stood for a moment trying to take in the events of last evening. It had all happened so quickly and he realised now that he had not been in control of things. Maddy had made all the running and now in the cold light of day, he was not sure if he liked that or not. There was no doubt that she was beautiful and intelligent, though, in truth, they had not had chance for any meaningful conversation! She was definitely more experienced in the bedroom department than he was and had taken full control, bringing him to a peak twice, the second time orally, which he found the more enjoyable.

He was intrigued by Maddy and wanted to see her again, only this time to find out a bit more about her, after all, he only knew her name!

He arrived at his office promptly at eight am, his secretary already there. She smiled as he passed her.

"How did the meal go?" she queried.

"She was duly impressed," was all he offered in return.

His secretary knew better than to press the point, he would tell her more in his own good time.

As the day went on, he found himself wondering if she would call him and by six that evening, he thought that maybe he had dreamt the previous evening. His mind was not really focused on work, so he decided to call it a day and go home. His secretary could not believe her luck, two early nights! She hoped he would see more of this woman if this was the effect she had on him.

He arrived home, showered and changed, and was deciding whether to go to his club for a few drinks before eating, or go straight to his favourite Italian restaurant just round the corner, when the phone rang.

"Hello," he said rather breathlessly.

"Martin? This is Toby. Just rang to ask how things went with the unveiling?"

There was a half-concealed laugh in his voice.

"Oh, it's you." There was disappointment in his voice, he hoped it was Maddy. "Yes, everything went well. As you said, she is a bit of a handful."

"In more ways than one," he teased. "Are you seeing her again?"

"Definitely, I think I will be seeing a lot more of her." Quite why he said what he did, he was not sure.

"I bet you have already seen quite a lot of her." Toby did not even bother to suppress the school boy giggling this time.

"Go away," Martin said, but good-naturedly.

The line went dead.

He went back into the bedroom and finished getting dressed. The phone rang again and this time, it was her.

"Hi, sorry I had to dash off early this morning, but I had to open up shop, you can't rely on the staff. Thanks again for a wonderful evening. I meant what I said in the note."

"When can I see you again?" The words were blurted out. He had not meant it to be like that but she had that effect on him.

"So I did make an impression."

Again, he felt that she was toying with him, playing him like an angler would a salmon. He could almost see the smile on her face and her tongue licking her lips.

"Can we meet for a drink or a bite to eat?" he said.

"I'm all yours! Do you like Italian? I know a little place that serves the most divine pasta, my treat."

"What now?"

"Of course, I live in Kensington, over the shop actually. Pick me up in half an hour."

She dictated her address and phone number just in case he got lost.

He put the phone down and sat for moment thinking. Was he doing the right thing? She was in control again as though she was manipulating his every move and yet, did it matter? What he needed for his move into politics was a wife, and she was definitely attractive and would fit the bill. *Christ,* he thought, *I've only met her once and I'm contemplating marriage. Perhaps I should slow down and see what happens.* But the more he thought, the more he knew she would be just what the old ladies in the shires would like!

He found the Boutique easily and a parking space in the side road next to the shop. He walked back around the corner and spent a minute looking into the shop window. It was definitely up market and although he knew very little about women's fashion, he could tell that the clothes were expensive.

A door next to the shop was the entrance to the flat and he rang the bell. He waited but nothing happened so he rang again. Suddenly, the door swung open and Maddy appeared. As always, she looked stunning. She wore a knee length dress and alarmingly high heels. It was cold and for warmth, she had 'round her shoulders a pashmina. She was not dressed for walking; this was strictly a 'car to bar' outfit.

He kissed her on either cheek and she smiled up at him.

"Hi," she said

"Hi," he replied, and for a few seconds, they just stood there as if frozen in time.

"Can we go to the car? It's not that warm," she said, stating the obvious.

"Sorry, of course. I was just admiring your beauty."

"Corny, but very flattering." She laughed, but not in a critical way.

He smiled back, as they walked the few steps to the car. The familiar roar of the engine drowned out the hustle and bustle of the London evening as the car pulled away. In no time, they had reached the restaurant, Maddy expertly directing him. He dropped her at the door and drove a few yards to a vacant bay to park the car. She was waiting just inside the entrance when he returned.

"Now, young lady, I want to know all about you," he said with every ounce of authority he could muster.

The waiter guided them to a table and took their order for drinks before handing them a menu each.

"You're the regular here so I'm in your hands, I'll let you choose and don't worry, I have no fads about food." He laid his menu down and sipped the Campari the waiter had brought them both. He suddenly realised that, without thinking, he had put her in charge again.

She ordered spaghetti carbonara and bottle of Frascati, and once the waiter had left them, looked straight into his eyes.

"Well, what do you want to know?" It was not a challenge, more like opening a picture book and asking what page should we read first.

He smiled at her.

"I would like a potted history of your life and what you do, at the moment, you're a complete enigma."

She laughed and her face seemed to light up. It was not a guffaw more a delicate chortle. She sat back in her chair and for the next half an hour, he sat hardly saying a word while she relayed her life thus far.

She was the daughter of a Baronet, who was the third generation to hold the title, had a younger brother who was an officer in the household cavalry and had fought in Iraq. Sadly, her mother had died from Leukaemia when she was only thirteen and the loss had affected her deeply. She became difficult to handle at school, and at the age of fifteen, was expelled for drinking and smoking in the dormitory. She had been expected to eventually go to university and her father was bitterly disappointed in her. However, she was his favourite and she managed to get back into his good books quite quickly.

Yes, I bet you did, Martin thought to himself, but said nothing.

Her father employed a private tutor for her, but although she was bright, she did not take to authority and after a difficult twelve months, when she reached sixteen, he admitted defeat. The tutor's services were dispensed with and as she put it, she was free. Although rebellious, she was not lazy and had a succession of jobs, ever searching for something she could take to. Her father indulged her and gave her a generous allowance, most of which she had the foresight to save in a deposit account. Her wages she lived on, or rather squandered on partying, smoking, flirting with social drugs like cannabis, but never getting into the drugs scene, she was too smart for that. Eventually, she took a job in a local dress shop and found that she actually enjoyed working there. The owner was a middle-aged lady who had run the shop for years and was happy to make a living out of it with no pretentions to expand or diversify. Maddy learnt all she could from this woman who was only too pleased to have a keen attractive assistant. The owner let herself be persuaded by Maddy to expand her range to include dresses for younger women and not just her normal 'thirty to forty somethings'. After a couple of years, Maddy was virtually running the shop, including buying the clothes. She found she had a gift for spotting the latest trends and soon, the shop was making a name for itself, as well as, good profits. Her father was pleased that she seemed to have settled down, though he still did not approve of her social life as she seemed to come home at all hours. However, no matter what time she rolled in, she was always on time for work.

Her life changed dramatically when the owner of the shop, after she had been there about four and half years, told her that her husband was seriously ill and she would have to sell the shop to nurse him full time. Maddy was at first devastated by the news but once it had sunk in, she quickly decided what she would do, buy it herself! It did not take much for her to persuade her father what a good investment it would be and, as it was coming up to her twenty-first birthday, the deal was done. Since then, she had sold that shop at a handsome profit, offered to pay her father back his investment, though she knew he would not accept and bought the lease on her present shop. The clientele was more up market and as she put it, 'paid through the nose for her garments'.

Martin had sat there listening to her story, fascinated. She was just like him. She set herself a goal, and went out and achieved it.

He had finished his pasta and noticed hers was only half eaten. *Very difficult to talk and eat at the same time*, he thought to himself, but it had not stopped her drinking! He caught the waiter's eye and asked for another bottle of Frascati. She had consumed most of the first bottle and he had made sure that he drank plenty of water with his couple of glasses of wine. The last thing he wanted was to get breathalysed; the Ferrari was certainly an attraction for young coppers out to make their mark.

"Fascinating, and what about your love life? After the other night, I can't believe you've been celibate up to now," he said it without rancour; it was more to confirm the obvious.

"No, I've not been a nun." She grinned at him. "But I'm not relating my past exploits to you, let's just leave it that I like sex and what I like I have."

He grinned back at her. Touché!

They finished their meal and as promised, despite his objections, she paid the bill. There was still half a bottle of Frascati on the table, and to his surprise, she called the waiter over and asked him to put a cork in it so that she could take it home. Once the bottle had been returned, they left. The cold night air hit them like a knife cutting through the flimsy dress. The restaurant had been warm and the difference outside was a shock. He quickly ushered her back into the entrance and told her to wait while he brought the car around. In only a couple of minutes, he was back, the Ferrari's engines throbbing, a warm invitation to escape the cold.

He pulled up at the door of the flat, waiting for her to get out.

"You're coming in."

It was not an invitation; it was an order.

"Of course."

He reversed the car around the corner, his parking spot still empty from earlier. He locked the door and walked quickly back to the flat. The door had been left open but there was no sign of her. He walked in and found the door to the living room. It was empty.

"I'm in here," she called out and he traced his way along the hall to where the voice had come from. He opened the door to what was her bedroom. She was lying half-propped up by the pillows on the bed, two champagne glasses in her hand and the bottle, unopened, on the table at the side. She was completely naked!

"I told you I like sex," she said.

He smiled at her, but inwardly gave a groan. *This is too much,* he thought, *she's insatiable.* His mind flashed back to the last time he had made love, that is, before he met Maddy, and realised that it was five years ago. He recalled that it had not been very successful neither he, nor the girl in question had been very experienced. He had not bothered since then, that is until Maddy came on the scene. On reflection, she had been the one who had taken charge on their first encounter, and he had basically followed her lead. Now he was expected to perform again. It was not that he found her unattractive, on the contrary she was gorgeous, but physical sex had never held that much of an attraction for him.

She looked up at him.

"What's the matter? Don't you fancy me?"

"Sorry. I was daydreaming. Of course, I do, I just hope I can perform after all that drink," he lied.

Fortunately, she had not noticed she was the one who had drunk most of the wine. He undressed and lay beside her.

"Open the champers then, you're the man."

He sat up, opened the bottle and pored them both a glass. She took a sip, and then poured some of the liquid onto her stomach and it ran down between her legs.

"Oops, I've spilt it, I'm afraid you're going to have to lick it all up." She grinned like a child who is playing a game and obviously winning!

He lowered his head to her belly and gently, softly began to lick following the path that the liquid had taken.

"That's it... oh yes... oh yes... oh I love it"

This is going to be a long night, he thought.

Chapter Ten

Over the next few weeks, he saw a lot of Maddy, but as he knew that she expected sex whenever he met her, he contrived numerous different reasons for either having to come home, or rise extremely early in the mornings. By these subterfuges, he escaped having to perform! Each time he excused himself, she sulked like a child who cannot get her own way but she soon came 'round with each expensive present that he bought her. He did not, however, extricate himself from her advances on every occasion and had more sex in six weeks than he had all his previous life! He realised his sex drive was well below hers, which would have blown the Richter scale through the roof, but other than her insatiable desires, he did like her company. She was well educated and knowledgeable about the arts, and shared his love of the opera and ballet. *All in all,* he thought, *as long as I can control her bedroom activities then we are a good team.*

It was with this thought in his mind that he rang up Giles.

"Giles, hi, it's Martin."

"Hello, old man, how are you?"

"Fine, thanks, just wondering how things are going with trying to find me a constituency." He had never been one for talking around a subject, far better to get straight to the point.

"Oh yes. Well, I have been sounding out one or two of the members of the selection panel and they have come up with only one possible seat."

"Go on, tell me then," Martin's voice betrayed his eagerness.

"It's a new seat, one of those where the boundary commission have redefined the area so we don't know if it will be a safe one or not. It's Kenilworth and Southam." He paused, waiting for Martin to take in the information.

"Excuse my ignorance, Giles, but where the bloody hell is that?"

There was a chuckle at the other end of the line.

"I thought that might be your reaction," Giles said, a trace of laughter still in his voice. "It's just outside Coventry on the way to Leamington Spa. You've surely heard of Coventry."

"Yes, yes." Martin was annoyed as much with his own ignorance as that of Giles condescending tone. "So what's the next step?"

"The next step, old man, is to get you in front of the local committee and onto a short list."

"Oh I see." There was disappointment in his voice, he had expected that it would be a straightforward case of being introduced to the locals as their new candidate, he had not expected a beauty parade!

"I'll fix things up and let you know when they want to see you. I should be able to get back to you within the next two weeks. By the way, how's the love-life going? I hear on the grape vine that you've been seeing quite a lot of Madeleine Verity. Are wedding bells on the horizon? Her old man is a party stalwart so she would definitely fit the bill."

Martin could imagine Giles winking at this comment if they had been face to face.

"Oh yes, we're announcing our engagement soon."

"Good show, Congratulations. Look, sorry, I've got to dash. My secretary's waving furiously at me from the next office. Bye."

The phone went dead before Martin had even had chance to say goodbye. *Bloody liar,* he thought, *I bet he doesn't even have his own secretary, just wanted to get rid of me.* He sat back in his chair to think over what the selection panel might want to ask him and realised that he was a little out of his depth. He would need some helpful advice from somewhere. He went over the conversation in his mind, Kenilworth and Southam, not very inspiring but it was a start anyway.

It was another five minutes before it hit him, what he had said at the end of the call, 'we're announcing our engagement soon'. Fuck! Why on earth had he said that? He would look a bloody fool if he asked her to marry him and she said no, he'd be sunk before he even set sail on the good ship Kenilworth!

Martin never deliberated over anything for too long. All his business life had been characterised by making firm decisions fast, not foolhardily but, nevertheless, swiftly. He picked up the phone and dialled her boutique's number.

"Maddy. It's Martin."

"Hello, darling, what's up? You don't normally ring the shop, is there something wrong?"

"No, not at all. I just wondered if you fancied going to the Ivy tonight. I've spoken to Giles and he thinks he has something for me. I thought we could celebrate over dinner."

"You know I love the Ivy, of course, that would be great."

"I'll pick you up at seven thirty, then we'll go back to my place for drinks, is that okay?"

"I'm looking forward to it… and darling, make sure you haven't got a headache!" She laughed, and he laughed with her.

He called his secretary into his office and told her to hold all calls for the next two hours, if anything really urgent came up to ring his mobile, but other than that, he would be unavailable. She was a little surprised as work usually came before everything, but she had noticed since the day of the Chinese meal, he had not been his old self, though the new Martin was a distinct improvement.

He left the office and hailed a passing Taxi.

"Where to, Guv'nor?" the cabbie asked.

"Asperys, the jewellers," he replied.

It was only a short trip and Martin doubled the fare by way of a tip.

"Thanks and good luck." The driver left him at the kerb and sped away. He crossed the road and entered the jewellers. The shop was not busy, and a smartly dressed young man approached him and asked if he could be of service. Martin suddenly panicked, he had decided to buy an engagement ring and propose to Maddy on the spur of the moment, now here he was, at the Queen's jewellers, not knowing what to get.

The shop assistant repeated the question.

"Can I help you, sir?"

"Yes, yes, sorry I was miles away for a second. I want to buy an engagement ring please."

"Have you anything in mind?"

"No not really, it's a surprise." *To me as well,* he thought to himself!

"Well, sir, a lot will depend on how much you want to pay. Shall I show you a range of rings and a range of prices?"

"Thank you, that would be most helpful."

The assistant left him but soon returned with a number of trays holding an assortment of rings, some solitaire's, some with a cluster of diamonds around a centre stone and some had three or five diamonds set together. As well as the various configurations, there was a choice of gold, white gold or platinum bands. He stared at the array of precious jewellery. If only he'd thought to ask Maddy first and then choose a ring, but it was too late, he had decided on the big romantic gesture and now he had to go through with it.

His eyes ran over the rings for the fourth time and alighted on a large solitaire on a platinum band.

"Can I see that one a little closer please?"

"An excellent choice, sir."

I haven't chosen it yet, Martin thought. "How much is it?"

"Fifteen thousand pounds, sir," the assistant replied in a matter of fact way, as if he was giving the price of a loaf of bread at the general store.

Martin panicked for the second time since entering the jewellers.

"What if it doesn't fit?" he asked.

"No problem, sir, just bring it back to us and we can size it to suit, but this is an 'N' and in my experience, that is an average size which fits most ladies."

Martin breathed a sigh of relief.

"Thank you, I'll take that one then."

He passed over his credit card, which had a limit of twenty-five thousand pounds, and the assistant went to the office to ring through to the card company to check that it was in order. He returned after only a couple of minutes.

"Thank you, sir, everything is correct, do you want it gift wrapped?"

"No thanks, just in its box will be fine."

Martin left, the ring safely tucked away in the inside of his jacket pocket, and once outside, started to walk back towards the city, keeping his eye open for a passing cab. He had only walked a few yards before one appeared coming in the opposite direction and, waving furiously, he hailed the taxi.

Within two hours, he was back at his desk, fifteen thousand pounds lighter in his bank account, but feeling very pleased with himself.

As always, she was ready to leave when he called to collect her that evening. One of the many qualities he liked about her was her punctuality; she never kept him waiting whenever they met. She was wearing a red off-the-shoulder dress, with matching shoes and bag. He wondered if she ever sold any dresses from the shop, or whether it was just a channel for her own cloths. He kissed her lightly on the lips by way of greeting.

"This is a nice surprise; I can't wait to hear your news."

He smiled to himself. *I hope it really is a nice surprise,* he thought, as the engine burst into life and they roared off down the Kensington Road.

The Ivy was packed but Martin was a regular and somehow they had always managed to find him a table. When he phoned to make the reservation, they had at first said they were full, but once he gave his name, they miraculously found there had been a late cancellation.

The maître d' showed them to their table and Martin ordered a bottle of Krug. He sat deep in thought, unable to decide whether to propose before the meal or after it.

"What's the matter? Is there a problem? I thought you were happy that things were moving with Giles." She looked at him quizzically, this was not like Martin, he was usually very buoyant; confidence was his middle name.

"Sorry, no, there's no problem." He had come to a decision

He filled her glass and then his own, and they chinked together as he said, "To us."

"To us," she repeated the toast.

He cleared his throat and then slid his hand into his jacket pocket. Withdrawing the ring, he held the box open in front of him. She looked at the ring, sparkling in the reflection of the room lights, her mouth wide open in surprise.

"Maddy, will you marry me?" The words, so carefully rehearsed only a few hours ago, rushed out so that they were concertinaed into one long word. She had not taken her eyes off the ring but had, nevertheless, deciphered the message.

"Martin, it's beautiful, may I take it out of the box?"

"Only if you say yes to the question?"

"Of course, it's yes. I've been wondering how long it would take you to ask."

The relief swept through him and taking the ring from the box gently slipped it onto her finger. It fitted as though designed especially for her. The waiter had seen the tableaux being played out and had discreetly left them alone, not wanting to disturb the proceedings for the mundane matter of taking their order. Eventually, Martin released her right hand, which he had been holding all the time she had been admiring the ring. He looked up and the waiter took it as his signal that he could proceed, and within seconds, had appeared at their table to take the order.

Later, during the course of the meal, he related the conversation he had with Giles and told her that he intended to visit Kenilworth to meet the local party chairman, to 'smooth the way', before they compiled their short list of candidates.

Of course, the evening did not end once they had finished their meal. He had picked her up by taxi which, considering the amount of wine they consumed, had been a wise decision. They were swaying gently as they left the restaurant to take the taxi the Ivy had called for them. She was giggling as she almost fell out of the cab once back at his flat, and it crossed his mind that maybe she would just go straight off to sleep once inside. As he turned the key in the lock and they entered, she seemed to get a second wind, and walking straight into the kitchen, found the wine fridge and pulled out a bottle of Dom Perignon.

"Night cap, darling?" she asked.

"Why not," he groaned inwardly, knowing he would have a long night's work in front of him! He had prepared himself for the prospect of her carnal desires and had got hold of some Viagra tablets to counter the negative effect the drink might have on his libido. She had already found the glasses and poured two drinks by the time he had reached the kitchen. He slipped the tablet into his mouth and washed it down with a gulp of champagne without her noticing. *I just hope the thing kicks in quickly,* he thought, knowing that the next room they would be entering would be his bedroom.

Chapter Eleven

Martin woke next morning, a stale taste in his mouth, the result of a combination of wine, brandy and champagne. Maddy was still fast asleep as he slipped out of bed to go to the bathroom. He was surprised to find that he still had an erection, perhaps he should not have taken a whole tablet, but it certainly worked for him last night. She must have had at least three orgasms and he even admitted to himself, as he padded across the bedroom floor, that he had enjoyed things more than usual!

He showered and dressed, leaving her still fast asleep, and went to the kitchen to make breakfast. She was still asleep when he carried the tray into the bedroom with her breakfast of scrambled eggs on toast and a mug of steaming hot coffee.

"Wake up," he called as he set the tray down on the table beside the bed

She stirred, rolled over and opened one eye.

"What time is it?" she asked.

"It's eight o'clock," he replied.

"Christ, Martin, it's Saturday, don't you ever have a lie in?"

He laughed at her good-naturedly.

"Don't you remember anything about last night?"

"Of course, I do, we got engaged, came back here and you made love to me for what seemed like forever, it was wonderful."

He laughed again, flattered by her description of the evening.

"No, I meant at the restaurant, I told you that I had spoken to Giles about the new Kenilworth and Southam constituency, and that I was going up to meet the chairman of the party."

"Yes, I vaguely remember you saying something, but I didn't realise it was today that you were going."

"You know me. I like to strike while the iron's hot. I rang him, a fellow called David Smythe, and asked if it would be convenient to call and he said it was not a problem and that Saturday would suit him better."

"Do you want me to come with you?" she asked.

"Don't you have a shop to run? I would have thought that Saturday would be your busiest day."

"Well, yes, but I have Jane and there's a young girl who works on Saturdays, and she's very good. I could easily ring through and tell them I won't be coming in."

"No, it's fine, and anyway, it's only the first meeting. I am sure once they have chosen me, they will want to meet the future Mrs De Glanville." He smiled and she returned his smile fingering her new ring, which glistened in the morning light, which was streaming in through the window.

He left her to finish her breakfast and went back to the living room where he had left his own coffee. It was cold now so he returned to the kitchen to pour a fresh mug.

He had decided not to wear one of his business suits, instead opting for grey flannels, white shirt and of course, a blue tie. A plain blue blazer with black brogues completed the outfit. He wanted the effect to be smart, but not smart Alec.

Maddy had just stepped out of the shower when he went into the bedroom to let her know he was off. She stood facing him drying off the remaining water and looked up.

"Can I tempt you with a quickie before you go?" she asked mischievously.

"You're incorrigible," he replied as he kissed her goodbye. "I'll ring when I get back."

He quickly made his escape; he had seen that look in her eye before and recognised the danger signals! He settled into the Ferrari and, exiting from the car park, made his way through the traffic heading to the Edgeware Road. The roads were not very busy and soon he was on the MI heading north. Conscious that the car was a magnet for traffic patrols, he sensibly kept to a sedate eighty plus miles an hour, which was difficult as the Ferrari, like a dog straining on the leash, wanted to roar away. The last thing he needed was a speeding fine on the way to an interview to become the next Conservative candidate for Kenilworth!

Before he knew it, he was heading along the A46 from Coventry. The satnav's monotone voice cut in telling him 'to take the next exit and turn right at the roundabout'. He was soon in Kenilworth High Street and two minutes later, parked on the forecourt outside the Conservative Party local office. The journey had taken under two hours. It was five past eleven and his appointment was for eleven fifteen. Feeling pleased with himself, he got out of the car, locked it and entered the building. To his surprise, the reception area was empty. He coughed, rather loudly, in the hope of attracting someone's attention, and as if on cue, a door opened and a man of about fifty-five came into the room.

He had sandy hair, which was receding, and being light gave the impression that he was balder than he was. The man was short, about five-six, rather overweight, the paunch trying to burst out his trousers, with rounded cheeks that reminded Martin of a hamster he had as a pet when he was a boy. Martin stifled back the urge to laugh as the memory crossed his mind. The man walked towards him.

"Mr De Glanville?" he asked. "I'm David Smythe, the party chairman, we spoke on the phone."

"Pleased to meet you, please call me Martin."

"Sorry about the empty office, but we don't usually have anyone working at the weekends, that is unless we're in the middle of an election campaign and then we're open almost twelve hours a day. Please come through. Would you like a cup of tea or coffee?"

"Coffee would be fine, thank you, white, no sugar."

He followed David through into a large room which had a long table and at least sixteen chairs set around it. He assumed this was the party meeting room. A coffee percolator was making a spitting noise in the corner of the room. David pointed to a chair and motioned Martin to sit down. David poured two coffees and set the cups on the table then sat himself down at the head of the table with Martin next to him.

"This is just an informal meeting, Martin, to get to know a bit about you and to answer any questions you might have about us."

He had a note pad in front of him and a piece of paper with itemised points on it. Martin assumed this was his aid memoir that held the questions he wanted to ask.

"I've got all the boring stuff like name and address, and occupation, what I would like to talk about is you and why you would like to represent us. I must tell you before we go any further, our little constituency seems to be very popular. We have applications from twelve prospective candidates and I am seeing each one to whittle them down to a short list of three, then, we will ask the three remaining to meet the full committee and give a little presentation. Is that okay with you?"

Martin realised that the last bit was not a question, it was a statement! He felt disappointed; he had expected that the interview would be just a formality and that the Chairman would automatically recommend him to the committee, the whole thing then being rubber-stamped. He nodded his head by way of agreement.

"Good, then if you could give me a resume of your opinions on current party policy and what, if anything, you would seek to change should you be successful at the next General Election, I would be grateful." Smythe pulled his chair closer to the table and picked up his ballpoint pen ready to make notes.

Martin had prepared a list of all the current policies and his own views on them, and had read them over and over again, so that now he could repeat them almost verbatim without resorting to any notes. He had learnt his lines like actor and felt that would impress his audience more, giving the impression what he said came straight from the heart. Giles had given him a few tips stressing whatever he believed himself; he should stick to endorsing Central Office policy. He could be a rebel, once elected!

Smythe sat quietly without interrupting whilst Martin explained his views on everything from Trident to Europe. The whole performance lasted about half an hour and Martin felt pleased with himself when he finished. He was sure he had covered everything and noticed that Smythe had made numerous notes whilst he had been speaking. He tried to see what was written on the note pad, but Smythe had turned over a blank sheet at the very instant he finished speaking.

"Thank you, Martin, that was very interesting."

Martin could not detect from the tone of Smythe's voice what he was thinking; it was neither approving nor critical.

"By the way, I forgot to ask if you are married."

"I've just got engaged as a matter of fact and intend to get married in a few months."

"Excellent!" It was the first time Smythe had shown any emotion during the whole interview. "Have you any questions that you would like to ask me?"

"A couple. When do you expect to have your short list and, if selected, I would like to buy an apartment in the area, so that I can spend more time with my constituents, so can you recommend a good estate agent?" Giles had told him the party liked their MPs to live in the locality if possible and if he said he intended to move into the area, it would go down well.

Smythe wrote an address down on his pad, and tore the sheet of and passed it to him.

"These are probably the best in the area, but I should wait until after you have been selected before you buy." For the first time, he actually smiled and Martin could have sworn that he winked at him. "The answer to the other question is that I have already seen six candidates and expect to see the other five over the next week. I will make my recommendations to the full committee and the short list will be drawn up at our next meeting, which is a week on Tuesday. Letters to all candidates will be sent out the next day so you should hear within two weeks. Well, if that is all…"

He pushed his chair back mid-sentence and stood up. The interview was obviously over. Martin took his cue and stood up and held out his hand. Smythe shook his hand, rather too vigorously, as though trying to shake him off.

"Thank you for coming all this way, Martin; it's been a pleasure to meet you."

"Thank you for seeing me, I look forward to our next meeting."

"Yes, yes, of course."

Smythe ushered him to the door and gave a cursory wave as Martin walked to his car. *Bit of a cold fish,* Martin thought to himself as he opened the car door, *didn't give much away as to what he was thinking.* Martin sat for a minute going over in his mind what he had said. He was sure he had covered all the major points and stuck rigidly to the party line, even though there were some aspects that he did not personally go along with. No, all in all, he was happy with the way the meeting had gone and now needed to talk to Giles for advice on how to present himself when he went to the full committee, once the short list was announced.

He took the piece of paper, with the address of the estate agent that Smythe had given him, out of his pocket and tapped in the postcode on his sat nav. It was only a couple of minutes away. Why waste another journey, he could get some details now.

He started the engine and reversed off the forecourt. The monotone voice immediately burst into life... 'In a hundred yards, turn right, turn right...'

There was nowhere to park outside the estate agent's but he noticed a large 'P' sign just ahead and followed the sign to a large car park. Having locked the car, he retraced his steps back to the agents.

"Can I help you, sir?" A young man who looked no older than twenty greeted him as he entered.

"Yes, I'm interested in an apartment; preferably centrally located, do you have anything?"

"To rent or buy?"

"Ideally to buy."

"Please take a seat and I'll get some details."

Martin sat on a chair next to a coffee table while the young man collected some printed details of various properties. He returned and placed the leaflets in front of Martin.

"Would you like to look through these and pick out what you might be interested in? Then I can give you some more information, or arrange a visit."

Martin worked his way through the particulars of flats and apartments, but nothing stood out as being acceptable. Most were one bedroomed, or of a poor standard and in need of repair. He knew he would not have anything like his London pad and didn't need that amount of luxury, but if he was going to use it for more than the odd night, then he certainly wanted something with a few mod cons.

He called out to the young man. "Have you anything more modern? These all seem to be very old or conversions of old houses."

"Certainly, sir. We have a development at the top of the High Street. They have just been built and there are two and three bed flats available." He walked over collecting the particulars from a stand at the side of the office.

The development was indeed modern and the artist's drawings showed that even one of the bedrooms had an en-suite bathroom. *That's more like it,* he thought.

"Can I view one of these?"

"Certainly, sir, we can go now if you like, it's literally five minutes' walk away."

Martin nodded his agreement, and the agent, stopping only to speak to a young lady in the rear office to tell her that he was popping out and would she hold the fort, picked up a bunch of keys and ushered Martin to the door. It was indeed only five minutes and Martin was impressed when he saw the new development sitting at the end of a parade of shops opposite the town's main hotel. From the outside, with its location to shops and restaurants, it seemed perfect.

The agent let them in to the main entrance and they took the lift to the second floor, then along a gallery. He opened the door and Martin followed him in.

"This is the show apartment the developer had furnished. It is a two bed, and there is only this and a three bed left. I have to say, they have all been sold very quickly, it's a most popular development."

Martin was not listening to the sales patter. He would make up his own mind. He followed the agent as he showed him the main bathroom, the double bedroom with en-suite shower/toilet, the single bedroom and the main living room, with a kitchen area in one corner completely fitted out with fridge, oven and hob, it even had a built in microwave. A dining table with four chairs was situated in the corner next to the kitchen area. The lounge part consisted of a sofa and easy chair, with a flat screen television on one end wall, and there was a full-length set of sliding doors, which opened up onto a small patio. Martin walked across the room and unlocked the patio doors. He stepped onto the balcony. The view took in all of the High Street. *This place is ideal,* he thought.

"How much is this one?" He asked.

"Two hundred and ninety-five thousand."

"Does that include the furniture and fittings?"

"I'd have to check, but I'm sure something could be agreed."

Martin had made up his mind.

"Tell the developer I'll give him a cheque for three hundred thousand if he throws in the furniture and fittings, or if he prefers, I will arrange a banker's draft, but I want to do the deal today. Can you contact him on a Saturday?"

The agent was taken aback; no one in his memory had ever offered cash for a property! If he had known just what Martin was worth, he would not have been at all surprised.

They closed the flat and walked back to the estate agent's office. Once there, he quickly contacted the developer and within an hour, the deal had been done, subject to all the legal documentation. Martin left particulars of his solicitor and shook the agent's hand before leaving. As he walked to the car, he had a smile of satisfaction playing on his lips. That had been a good day's work, he was sure the full committee would be impressed when he came for his second interview and told them that he had a dwelling in the town, so he could be close to his constituents.

As he pulled out of the car park to head back to London, still mentally congratulating himself on what he had accomplished, his mind moved to the next stage of his strategy. Having become engaged to Maddy, he wanted to get married as soon as possible. Giles had impressed on him the importance of having a suitable wife who would be acceptable to the local party. Maddy certainly filled the bill, not only was she attractive, but also intelligent, and her father was a baronet to boot, so the sooner they were married, the better.

On the way back down the MI, he put his foot down and felt the power of the Ferrari throw him back in his seat, as the needle quickly swung towards the hundred miles an hour mark. He let the car take control for a few miles before relaxing his foot from the throttle to cruise at a more sedate ninety. If he got a ticket at that speed, at least it would only be a fine and three points on his license, over a hundred could cost him a ban and any adverse publicity right now could be disastrous. Before he knew it, he was on the Edgeware Road heading for the City.

Once back at his flat, he called Maddy.

"How did it go?" she asked as soon as she picked up the phone.

"Well… at least I think so"

"Did you get the job or not?"

"It's not a job! It's a nomination. The problem is they have twelve candidates who they are then cutting down to a short list of three, who then have to go before the whole committee before they finally decide who they want as their candidate."

"You mean you've got to go back again?" she sounded incredulous.

"Yes, but I'm sure it will be okay. Oh and I've bought an apartment in Kenilworth." He tried to sound as matter of fact as possible.

"Why on earth have you done that for?"

"Because Giles told me that the constituents like their MPs to live in the area, so it's a commitment." He really didn't want to discuss the matter; as far as he was concerned, it made sense. If he ever got fed up with politics in the future, he could sell the property and make a profit. Even though property prices had fallen latterly he knew, in the long term, they would rise and he was in it for the long term.

She could tell by the tone of his voice that there was no point in pursuing the subject. In the short time that she had known him, she had learnt that once he had made up his mind on something, he acted immediately and, in truth, that was one of the qualities that had attracted her in the first place, that and the fact that he was a millionaire!

"See you later, darling, pick me up about seven, okay?"

"Fine," he replied, pleased that she had not questioned him anymore.

Chapter Twelve

Nearly two weeks later, on the Wednesday, he arrived home from the office earlier than usual as he was impatient to read his post. Sure enough, the letter he had been waiting for was amongst the usual collection of junk mail and bills lying on the mat. He checked the postmark, Kenilworth and walked into the kitchen clutching the bundle of letters. He put them on the table, and opened the fridge door and took out a bottle of champagne. *A mini celebration,* he thought. He set the glass and bottle down then reached for the letter, sliding his thumb into the flap of the envelope he roughly tore it open. He pulled out the letter and read its contents… and then he re-read it.

It must be a mistake! He read it for a third time as though by re-reading it then it would somehow change.

"Dear Martin,

A meeting was held on Monday to decide on the short list of prospective candidates for the constituency of Kenilworth and Southam.

It is with regret that I have to inform you that you were not successful in this case. May I take this opportunity to thank you for the interest you have shown in applying for the vacancy and wish you well for the future.

Yours sincerely,

David Smythe.

Chairman"

He felt numb. How could this have happened? He went over in his mind the interview with Smythe. He was sure that it had gone well and hadn't he winked conspiratorially at him at the end of it?

He decided to phone Giles and see if he knew anything. He rang his office. Fortunately, he was still at his desk.

"Giles, I've just received a letter from Kenilworth and you'll never believe…"

Giles cut in, "I know, they emailed me with their decision yesterday. I've been expecting your call."

"But why, I don't understand, I thought it would be a formality, what did I do wrong?"

"Nothing, fundamentally, they just felt you were a bit too flash for them. I think the Ferrari was the decider. The trouble with some of those boys from the sticks is that they are basically jealous of anyone who is overtly successful. It's the politics of envy I'm afraid."

"But I thought that was the cornerstone of Conservatism, to encourage upward mobility. Damn it, Giles, I made my money by bloody hard work, nobody left it to me." He was getting angry now.

"Calm down, old man, I'm sure we can find you something else, maybe not for the next election, but long term."

"I don't want to wait five bloody years." His temper was near to boiling.

"It will soon pass and we can get you into a safe seat as well."

Martin could detect the patronising tone in his voice. Giles was really not that interested, he could tell and that made him even angrier.

"Just fuck off, Giles, and stick your precious party up your arse." He slammed the receiver down not waiting for a reply. He was shaking with rage and stood for a moment gripping the back of one of the kitchen chairs. His knuckles were white when he finally calmed down. He poured himself a large whisky and sat in the kitchen staring into space.

He sat there for a few moments still unable to accept that he had been turned down. It was the first time in his life that things had not gone to plan. The realisation that he had also bought a property in Kenilworth suddenly dawned on him. What on earth had possessed him to buy the apartment before he had been chosen? Because he had expected to be chosen.

He phoned Maddy and gave her the news.

"Oh, darling, I'm so sorry. Never mind, you can forget about stupid politics and concentrate on making money. Would you like me to come round and console you?"

He knew exactly what her kind of consolation involved and right now, that was the last thing he wanted!

"I'm fine, think I'll have an early night if you don't mind. By the way, I told Giles to fuck off and stick his bloody Conservative party up his arse." He felt good just repeating the words.

"I'd better not tell Daddy, he won't be impressed." He could hear the laughter in her voice. Politics had never been of interest to Maddy.

He hung up and looked into his glass, it was empty. Pouring himself another large one, he went into the sitting room and switched on his iPod. The room was filled with 'The ride of the Valkeries' which he turned up even louder… *and fuck the neighbours*, he thought.

Chapter Thirteen

Martin had taken Maddy's advice and thrown himself back into his business. It was a difficult time in the City, the credit crunch was biting hard and the papers were depicting anyone involved in banking or finance as pariahs, but life went on and deals were still being done. He had scaled back his operations but still had that knack of being ahead of the game.

He and Maddy got married in the September, and honeymooned in Mauritius. He had deliberately chosen Mauritius as he knew it would be hot and had hoped that it would curb Maddy's carnal instincts. To a degree it had been successful, she was more than happy to lie in the sun displaying her range of designer swimwear... which never got wet. Nevertheless, he did not escape scot-free and her sexual appetite had to be satisfied. It wasn't that he found her undesirable, it was just his sex drive was at the opposite end of the scale to hers.

Once back in England, she had let her flat and moved into his, and it had not taken her long to change the décor and furnishings, so that it no longer bore any resemblance to the bachelor flat of old. The next thing on her list was a house in the country!

Martin was happy to let her make her plans. Getting married had strangely been good for his business as he was now invited to more and more dinner parties where he could grow his circle of clients. Many of the husbands gravitated towards Maddy, who always wore a low cut dress, often to the chagrin of the wives who were mostly older anyway. Martin was not at all jealous and, oddly, took it as a complement to him as if they were admiring his taste as you would a work of art.

All thoughts of entering politics had been pushed to the back of his mind that is until the Daily Telegraph broke the expenses scandal story. Martin was horrified as, day after day, another MP was shown to be manipulating the system by either claiming for 'duck houses', or flipping homes where they had received tax payers' money to pay for the mortgage on a second home, then selling it for a vast profit and not paying any capital gains tax. All this at a time when the country was on the verge of financial meltdown.

The more the system was exposed, the angrier Martin became. These were the very people that ordinary citizens had trusted with their votes to work for them not themselves and it wasn't just one party, they were all at it. Conservative, Labour, Liberal all had their rotten apples. There had to be a general election by June 2010, that would surely sort them out he thought, and that's when it hit him. He would stand as an Independent candidate in Kenilworth on an anti-sleaze ticket. That would show those pompous Tory bastards. If nothing else, he would split the Tory vote. Having made up his mind, he set about putting his plans into action. He would need an agent, someone local, who could give him background on the area and could keep him informed on what the other parties were up to once the election was announced and under way. He decided to put an advert in the local paper, The Coventry Evening Telegraph, and see what sort of response he got. What he definitely did not want was someone who had previously worked for another party. He realised that he would not be getting experience, but he wanted someone who felt as passionately as he did. He took a note pad from his desk and drafted a sample ad to put into the situations vacant page.

"Part-time position as a political agent for an Independent candidate for the next General Election. Must have no previous party loyalties. Must feel strongly about combating sleaze in politics. Experience not required, but enthusiasm a must. Preferably living in Kenilworth. Salary and hours by negotiation. Please apply in writing in the first instance to PO Box 14."

Satisfied with the draft, he rewrote it on his computer and emailed it to the newspaper, along with details of his credit card for the payment. He had booked it to run for seven days.

Let's see what that turns up, he thought.

The first advertisement was due to appear in that Friday's issue; he would now have to be patient and wait for any replies.

Maddy did not hide her disapproval. She had been quietly pleased when he was turned down by the Tories. The thought of being just an ordinary MP's wife did not excite her as much as being the wife of a millionaire, and all the parties and functions she attended. If there was one thing she loved more than anything else, it was being the centre of attention and being surrounded by men. Very early on in her marriage, she had discovered that Martin was nowhere near as sexual as she was and for a while, she had become moody. This led to a number of rows with Martin, which he always managed to diffuse with yet another expensive present. But there were only so many diamonds a girl could wear and in the end, they were no replacement for what she really wanted!

It had not been long before a 'replacement' came along in the shape of a young, Australian personal trainer.

She did not open the shop on a Monday and, until her marriage, had tended to use the time to keep her flat clean and generally take things easy. Since moving into Martin's flat, there was no need for her to perform mundane domestic chores, as a cleaner came in every morning for two hours to take care of everything on that front. With the constant round of parties and the increase in her alcohol consumption as a result, she had noticed that one or two of her dresses had been feeling tighter. Her looks were important to her, for business reasons as well as keeping the admiring glances coming. The solution was to join a gym and luckily, there was one within walking distance of the flat.

She had been a member only two weeks when Peter, who had been watching her on the running machine, came up and introduced himself. He was blond with a body builder's physic and strong aquiline features. He was just twenty-four.

She had jumped slightly when he spoke, her mind concentrating on the pedometer on the machine, sweat running down her face.

"Can I help you, madam?" his Australian drawl surprising her.

"Oh… I was just trying to lose a bit of weight," she mumbled, feeling embarrassed by her sweaty straggly appearance.

He had seen her coming into the gym and had noticed the expensive jewellery.

"If you want to lose weight, and may I say you look in excellent shape, then just running on a treadmill is not the answer, you need a proper programme of exercises. I'm a personal trainer and could easily devious the right programme to tune your body and make you look even more beautiful than you do already."

She was sold! If there was one thing that appealed to Maddy, it was flattery. The following Monday, she started having one-to-one sessions with Peter.

On the third week, Maddy asked him if they could break up their usual routine by going for a jog. The weather, although fairly cold, was dry and even the sun was trying to break through. Peter was happy to go along with the idea, so they put on tracksuits and set off from the gym.

Peter had suggested a circular route that took in side roads, keeping them away from the choking fumes of the buses and taxis. They were on the return leg of the journey when Maddy pulled up complaining of stitch and asking him to rest for a moment.

"My flat's just round the corner; can we stop off and get a glass of water?"

"No problem."

They continued their jog until they reached the flat.

"I'll wait here for you, shall I?" he said.

"No, come on up."

They went into the flat, the cleaner had finished her work for the day and it was empty. Peter followed her through into the kitchen where she poured two glasses of water.

"I'll be back in a minute, I just need to use the loo," she said and disappeared towards the bedroom. She had been gone a few minutes and he was beginning to wonder if everything was alright when she came back into the room… she was stark naked!

From then on, her weekly sessions with her personal trainer took on a whole new regime, the strenuous exercises being replaced by equally exhausting manoeuvers, but now Peter was doing most of the work!

Martin had noticed that, since she had taken to going to the gym, she had looked trimmer and had a glow about her; more importantly, she did not constantly bother him for sex, so it seemed to him that exercise was good for both of them.

A week after Martin had placed the advert, the replies began to trickle in. Most he discarded without really taking much interest. If they were from anyone who was retired, he consigned them to the litterbin. He was looking for someone young with vitality and a crusading mind, someone who wanted to change the status quo. One letter that caught his eye was from a man of twenty-five who had just completed a postgraduate course in politics at Warwick University. He lived in Kenilworth and had no full time employment at the moment. He seemed perfect. Wasting no further time, Martin picked up the phone and dialled the mobile number printed at the head of the letter.

"Hello, Tony Wright speaking."

"Tony, this is Martin De Glanville, you wrote saying you are interested in working for me as my agent."

"Oh yes, of course, thank you for contacting me."

"I'd like to pop up to Kenilworth and meet you to discuss the position in more detail. When would you be available?"

"Anytime you like, I'm not working at the moment, taking a couple of months off after completing my exams, so I'm available to suit you."

"Okay, can we say this Friday, about six at my flat at the top of the High Street opposite the Hotel?" He gave Tony his full address, and both the flat's phone number and also his mobile.

"I know those flats, they're the ones above the Almanac restaurant, aren't they?"

"That's right. I'll stop overnight, so if we need to meet again on Saturday, I won't have to drag up and down that bloody M1." He gave a chuckle, which Tony responded to similarly. "Good, I'll see you Friday then."

"Thanks, Mr De Glanville."

"It's Martin, if we are going to work together, we best get that clear up front."

"Sorry, thanks, Martin, see you Friday. Bye."

The line went dead. *Seems a nice enough chap,* Martin thought, *but a bit shy, let's hope that he loosens up when we meet.*

Martin looked at his watch, he was normally in the office by now, but fortunately, there was nothing pressing that his staff could not attend to. He called out to Maddy who was still dressing.

"Maddy, I'm off now. Oh, by the way, I'm going up to Kenilworth on Friday afternoon and stopping overnight. I'll be back Saturday afternoon. Don't worry I'll make sure I'm back in time to be ready for the Hamptons dinner party." He had anticipated that she would immediately panic that they might miss another social gathering.

She came out of the bedroom, still in her underwear.

"What are you going up there for?" she asked.

"To interview someone for the agent's post, remember?"

"Oh that bloody politics thing."

She turned and went back into the bedroom to finish dressing, her contempt for the whole thing plain to see on her face.

She heard the door close as Martin left. Well, if Martin could play his silly games, she would at least play her own games. She picked up her mobile and dialled Peter's number.

"Can I treat you to dinner on Friday evening?" Without waiting for a reply, she continued, "I'll pick you up at seven thirty."

Chapter Fourteen

Martin arrived at his flat just after five and checked the post stacked on the kitchen worktop, just the usual rubbish of circulars and begging letters from charities. When he bought the apartment, he found a lady who came in once a week to clean his flat and check everything was okay. She had been recommended by one of the other owners. He had not seen her since that first meeting and sent her money direct to her bank on the first of each month, in advance. The place was spotless, it had been money well spent and although he knew she had very little to do each week, at least it would not accumulate dust as even empty houses do. He had phoned her to let her know he would be staying overnight, and asked her to get him some milk and bread. At least, he would be able to make a drink and have some breakfast.

He made himself a cup of coffee and settled down to wait for Tony Wright to turn up. Precisely on the dot of six, the intercom buzzed.

"Hello, is that Martin? It's Tony Wright."

"Yes, come on up, just push the door, I've unlocked it."

A couple of minutes' later, there was a knock on his door. Tony Wright was slim, had sandy hair combed over to one side, which made him look even younger than he was. He wore glasses, which gave him a studious look. On the face of it, he was perfect for the role. Martin wanted someone non-descript so that at meetings and public appearances the audience would focus their attention on him, and no one else.

Tony followed him into the apartment and Martin pointed to one of the armchairs.

"Take a seat. Would you like coffee?"

"Thanks, milk and two sugars please."

Martin panicked for a moment; he had not asked Mrs Black to get sugar. But when he opened the cupboard, he found some packets in a dish and also some tea bags, neither of which he had thought to ask for. *What a treasure,* he thought.

Once the coffee was made, Martin sat opposite Tony in the other armchair and explained exactly what he was looking for. He took some time to reassure Tony that he did not expect him to have the knowledge of an experienced agent, on the contrary, he wanted someone new and fresh, but who believed, as he did, on breaking the mould of the old two party system with its inherent corruption.

Tony listened without interruption as Martin gave him a brief history of his abortive attempt at becoming a Tory candidate including his disappointment at not being chosen. He explained that he genuinely wanted to give something back to society and felt hurt by the attitude of the local Tory party. It had been the revelations in the Daily Telegraph that had fired him up, making him decide to stand as an anti-sleaze candidate. He outlined his views on Europe, Trident, the war in Afghanistan and a fairer tax system, but the fundamental thrust of his platform was to rid parliament of its leeches.

Martin finished speaking and drained the remains of his coffee, which by now had gone cold.

"Well, Tony, what do you think? Does it appeal to you or are you already committed to a party?"

Tony looked at him. He had sat listening for the last half hour without interrupting or asking questions. During his studies, he had made a point of attending all the major parties' conferences, being able to gain attendance as part of his course work. He had tried to keep an open mind, finding there were parts of each of the party's manifestos which he agreed with and parts he did not. In short, he was what is known as a floating voter and felt if he wanted to pursue a career in political journalism, then it was better to stay on the fence. Martin De Glanville was different. During his discourse outlining his views, he had not once criticised any of the other parties. There was nothing negative about him, a trait sadly lacking in many of the speeches he had witnessed at conferences. In fact, the only anger he had shown was towards individual MPs who had abused the trust placed in them by the electorate, but the most important factor that struck Tony was that this man had genuine charisma. He had wanted to interrupt him a couple of times, but had been almost mesmerised into listening to him.

"Well, Tony?" Martin prompted him. It had been a few seconds since he first asked the question and Martin had wondered if had just lost interest or worse, been bored.

"I would love to help you if you think I'm up to it. I have a little knowledge of what would be expected from my studies, most of it is common sense. We would need a small office and, once the election is called, some part-time staff to send out literature, etcetera. I know of a local printer who could do all the brochures, its run by two brothers. I was at Warwick school with the younger of the two. I can also sort out the computers for the office from another ex-school friend. I can…"

"Hey, slow down." Martin laughed. He had taken an instant liking to Tony and was genuinely pleased by his enthusiasm. "I take it you're in then. We need to discuss your remuneration and hours."

"Martin, I would definitely like to work with you and from what you have said so far, I will accept anything you offer. I believe you're a fair man and won't rip me off, plus it will be good experience for me."

Martin was touched by his remarks. It was a strange alliance in many ways as they were so different, but in a short time, a bond had been formed that Martin was sure would last a long time.

It was eight o'clock and Martin was feeling hungry.

"I'm going to get a bite to eat, would you like to join me?"

"That's very kind of you but I've arranged to see my girlfriend, sorry."

"No problem, but as you know the area, can you recommend anywhere?"

"We have an abundance of restaurants. What do you like, Indian, Chinese or Bistro?"

"Do you know of a Thai restaurant?"

"There is one in Coventry and one in Leamington, both owned by the same people and both very good. The one in Coventry is perhaps the easiest to find."

He wrote down some directions for Martin. All he had to do was take the A46 into Coventry, head for the city until he hit the ring road, then go all the way round the island back on himself and it was about fifty yards on the left.

Tony stood up and held out his hand which Martin shook vigorously. There was no need for a written contract of any sort, the agreement had been sealed in that handshake.

Martin walked to the door and watched Tony make his way to the stairs. He was pleased that things had gone so well. He must remember to get his secretary to write a reply to the other applicants. He was happy with his gut instinct, which had again proved to be his trusted ally.

He tidied away the coffee cups, putting them in the dishwasher and decided he would have a quick shower just to freshen up. He had not bought a change of clothing, other than clean underwear, as he only intended to stop for the one night. He would set off back to London first thing in the morning.

Within fifteen minutes, he was ready and took the lift to the basement where the car was parked. It was just twenty to nine when he entered the restaurant. He was pleased to see that it was busy but still with a couple of empty tables. He hated dining in restaurants that were empty and had no atmosphere. The Thai Dusit was not one of those.

He ordered his meal with a glass of Chablis, a bottle, although he could have drunk it, would be too much, and anyway, he had decided he would pop into a pub after his meal and try the local bitter.

The meal was delicious and he made a mental note to thank Tony for his recommendation, he would certainly come again. He thought if he could persuade Maddy to come with him on his next visit, this was just the place she would enjoy. He wondered what she was doing, probably curled up in bed watching the TV. He considered phoning her but thought better of it. She would not be pleased if he interrupted her evening's entertainment.

It was only ten o'clock and there was plenty of time for a couple of pints before he went back to the apartment. If he had one in Coventry and then drove back to Kenilworth, he could park the car in the basement, then call in at the Bistro in his block for a nightcap.

He called the waiter over and asked if there was a pub within walking distance, so he didn't have to navigate his way through uncharted territory. The waiter's English was not very good, but he managed to explain that a pub called Rainbows was just over the road, however, he had never been, so did not know if it was 'good' or not. Martin thanked him and said he would try it. He paid his bill and left a large tip. Martin, for all his wealth, was not noted as a generous tipper, he got very angry at restaurants that expected ten to fifteen percent whatever the service. He always tipped well if he had been looked after and refused to give a tip if the service was poor. His favourite watering holes had learnt this lesson very early and now he was always given the best service.

He left the restaurant and found his way to Rainbow's; he felt relaxed and strangely liberated, as he was unknown in this area and would not bump into any of his friends or associates. No one here knew he was rich; he could just be an ordinary man having a quiet drink.

He walked into the pub and was immediately struck by the décor, which was like no other pub he had ever been in. The walls were painted in pink and purple colours and the lighting was subdued. There were tables in alcoves where the lighting was almost non-existent. There were a number of people in the bar but it was not crowded. He could hardly make them out, but he was sure that they were all men. He walked up to the bar and ordered a pint. The barman, who wore a vest and was covered in tattoos, looked at him rather strangely, as he poured the drink. Martin stood there sipping his pint slowly whilst looking around for an empty table.

A young man of about nineteen sat on a stool at the end of the bar; he was drinking what looked like coke but no doubt was something stronger.

"You're new," he said, directing his comment at Martin.

Martin thought it a strange way of opening a conversation, as the lad moved down the bar towards him.

"Yes, I'm up from London, had some business in Kenilworth and was recommended to the Thai restaurant over the road. Have you ever been there?"

"No, but I'd like to go some time."

Martin had never had such an unusual conversation; it did not follow any normal pattern that he had known. He looked at the lad. He seemed fairly ordinary, a white T-shirt and denim jeans, and the obligatory trainers young men seem to wear all the time. What was different was his hair; it was a mass of curls and was carrot red. Martin also noticed, now that he was closer to him, the lad was broad shouldered with a body builder's physic.

"What's your name?" the young man asked.

Martin was slightly taken aback by this direct approach.

"Martin," he replied.

"I'm Joe, pleased to meet you." The lad held out his hand.

Martin shook his hand, the boy had a firm grip and Martin could feel the strength of his powerful body just in that handshake. Joe smiled at him… they were still holding hands.

Martin looked at the boy. There was something different about him, he felt strangely drawn to the lad. It was a feeling he had never really experienced before.

"Is this your first time? Joe asked.

"I beg your pardon," Martin spluttered. "First time for what?"

"First time in a gay bar."

Martin's jaw dropped open. He looked around and then the penny dropped, the pink and purple, the subdued lighting. It all fell into place. He did not move, still in a state of shock.

"You mean you didn't know?" Joe was trying to stop breaking into a laugh. "I'm sorry, are you okay?" He reached his hand out to Martin as a gesture of compassion. Martin did not resist the action.

Martin was confused; he felt an attraction to this young man that he could not explain to himself. He took a long drink of his beer trying to collect his thoughts together.

"Would you like to go somewhere else for a drink?"

Martin heard him ask the question, but was miles away.

"Would you like to leave, Martin?"

Still in a dream, Martin nodded his head and they left. Their drinks remained unfinished on the counter.

Outside, the cold air hit him, bringing him 'round in a second, like waving a towel over a flagging boxer.

"I have an apartment in Kenilworth, would you like to come over for a nightcap?" Martin heard himself asking the boy.

"I'd love to."

They walked across the road to where the Ferrari was parked.

"Fucking hell, is this yours?" Joe almost exploded.

"Yes, get in." Martin smiled at the lad's delight.

The engine roared into life and Joe sat there mesmerised by the dashboard. It was like the cockpit of an airplane. He had never been near a Ferrari before, let alone in one.

Martin did not speak on the drive back to Kenilworth, his mind in a whirl at the events of the evening. He kept asking himself what on earth had compelled him to invite this young man back to his apartment, but the more he raised the question, the more it seemed to be the natural thing to do.

He parked the car in its bay in the basement and switched off the engine. Joe followed him out of the car to the lift, alighting at the second floor. It was not until they were inside that Joe broke the silence.

"This must have cost a few bob," he said, looking around at the white leather chairs and the forty-six-inch TV in the corner.

Martin smiled at the young man.

"Would you like a drink? I'm afraid I don't have much of a variety to offer. I've got gin, whisky and some brandy, any good?"

"I'll have a whisky please."

Martin poured two large whiskies and handed one to Joe.

"Cheers." Joe chinked his glass against Martin's. "Here's to us and the future."

"Would you like some music?" Without waiting for an answer, Martin moved across the room and pressed the remote control, switching on the iPod. The steady beat of Bolero filled the room.

"I've not heard this one in the top twenty," Joe said with a chuckle.

"Oh sorry, don't you like it? I'm afraid I don't have any popular music."

"Don't worry. It's quite good."

The music was steadily building in the background as Joe reached his hand out to Martin. He stroked Martin's arm then his cheek, his touch unexpectedly gentle for a strong man. Martin did not resist, did not want to resist, a warm feeling passing over him as Joe came closer and kissed him. They held the kiss for some time, neither wanting to be the first to break away. Martin had never been kissed like that before. It was soft and tender, not like Maddy who always had to push her tongue down his throat as if she was eating him. He could feel the excitement in the boy's embrace and his heartbeat quickened, looking down, he noticed that other parts of his body were reacting as well!

Joe said nothing; he just looked at Martin and smiled as one by one he undid the buttons on the older man's shirt. Martin stood there as if frozen to the spot as Joe continued to undress him. He undid the buckle of Martin's trousers and they fell to the floor, still Joe said nothing, but kneeling in front of him, slid his underpants down and took his erect penis into his mouth.

Martin was in another world, a world of infinite pleasure, one that he hoped he would never have to leave.

Chapter Fifteen

At two o'clock in the morning, Martin woke to find Joe lying by his side, suddenly, the memory of last night came flooding back to him, but he had no feelings of regret. Joe had awakened something inside of him that he had not been aware existed.

He shook Joe until he woke.

"Sorry, Joe, but you will have to go. I can't risk us oversleeping and Mrs Black, my cleaner catching us."

Joe sat up and rubbed his eyes.

"Okay."

He swung his legs over the edge of the bed and stood up. He was naked and Martin looked admiringly at the young man's rippled muscles, realising how out of shape he was himself. *I must try Maddy's personal trainer*, he thought, *she swears by him.* A flash of guilt went through his mind as he thought of Maddy, but it did not last long.

Joe dressed quickly and collected his jacket from the living room.

"Can you call a taxi for me? Don't panic I'll wait for it outside the Almanac." He saw the look of concern quickly disappear from Martin's eyes.

Martin opened the draw next to the bed and reached inside for his wallet.

"Will a hundred pounds cover the fare?"

"Yes, thanks, that should be enough."

Martin walked into the living room and rang for a taxi.

"It'll be here in about five minutes," he said, turning as Joe followed him into the room. "Will I see you again?"

"If you want to." Joe tore a piece of paper off the notepad lying on the kitchen worktop and wrote his mobile phone number on it. "Just ring me when you're up next."

He turned and left without another word.

Martin had wanted to kiss him or at least hug him and felt a strange emptiness that he had just left like that.

Martin returned to his bed, but could not sleep, his mind recalling the events of the last few hours. Thinking back to when he had been a boy at Westminster, he remembered he had always admired his house captain and thought how handsome he was. He had watched him playing rugby and cricket for the school and had desperately wanted to be his friend, but he being older had moved in different circles. Thinking about him now, Martin realised that he must have had some sort of crush on the boy, which at the time he put down to hero worship and the fact that he was so much better than Martin at sport.

He had never bothered much with girls; even at university, he had been happy to go on drinking binges with his friends, but at the end of the night, when their thoughts turned from the delights of the bar to those of the boudoir, he had quietly slid away, unnoticed, back to his digs. He had put it down to a low sex drive and on the odd occasion, that the numbers dictated he had to pair up with a female, he went with the flow, but it was more often than not the girl had taken the initiative.

Maddy had been his first real girlfriend, having devoted most of the intervening years to making money. Often working round the clock, watching the markets around the world. Maddy had been different, she was beautiful and intelligent, qualities that in his experience were not natural bedfellows; more importantly, she had come along just at the right time when a suitable wife was part of the package he had needed to become a parliamentary candidate.

Maddy did arouse feelings in him, it was just that she was blatantly oversexed, which for most men would have been a blessing, but for Martin was a bind. Fortunately, since she had taken up her fitness regime, she had been less demanding. Obviously, the vigorous workouts were having a calming effect on her libido.

As he thought about Maddy, he was surprised at how little guilt he felt about the experience with Joe. Surely, it was possible to have feelings for two people at the same time. He still loved Maddy, it was just that Joe had opened up another world to him; after all, he knew of plenty of his colleagues who had mistresses as well as happy marriages. The only difference in his case was that Joe was a man!

Eventually, at about four o'clock, he dozed off to sleep, a silly smile playing on his lips as he thought of Joe.

It was nine o'clock when he eventually woke and dived into the shower to freshen up. He had intended to leave by now and although had nothing planned for the day, had wanted to be in London by mid-morning. Having showered and shaved, he quickly dressed and went into the kitchen to make himself a cup of coffee. It was now nine thirty and Mrs Black had told him that she usually came at ten. He desperately wanted to be away before she arrived, in case she noticed anything different about the place and started asking awkward questions.

He had nothing to pack as he kept spare toiletries in the apartment. As he closed the door behind him, he glanced at his watch, ten to ten, he breathed a sigh of relief and quickly walked to the lift. The Ferrari pulled out of the car park and round past the entrance to the building, he could just see a short dumpy lady carrying a shopping bag going through the doors. *That was close,* he thought.

The journey back to London was uneventful and the motorway was surprisingly quiet. He kept the car down to a sedate eighty miles per hour, resisting the urge to let it have full throttle, *too many bloody cameras these days,* he thought to himself.

Maddy was at the shop when he returned to the flat so he had the rest of the day to himself. For once, he did not feel like doing any work and instead walked round to the shops, bought himself a newspaper and a pastrami sandwich from the deli. Once back, he made a cup of coffee and relaxed on the sofa, the papers spread out, the sandwich on the coffee table, a strange feeling of contentment sweeping over him.

When Maddy returned at six that evening, she was surprised to find him asleep on the sofa, the empty cup and plate on the coffee table.

She shook him and he woke with a start.

"Hard work interviewing?" she asked.

"What… no… yes… I mean no," he mumbled.

"Did you get drunk last night or something? You look shattered. You haven't got a young woman hidden away up there, have you?" She laughed, knowing that would be the last thing on his mind. It often took all her natural skills to get him even remotely excited.

A look of terror momentarily flashed in his eyes when she said this but her laugh told him that she was teasing.

"I did have a couple of drinks but not until I got back to the apartment. I appointed Tony to the job and we went to a Thai restaurant in Coventry to celebrate. It was very good; I must take you there sometime."

He knew that would not happen as Maddy had let it be known that she was not interested in some Midlands backwater, and as far as she was concerned, he was mad even considering it.

"So this Tony Wright is the right man." She laughed at the pun and Martin smiled back at her.

"Yes, we hit it off straight away. He came back with me after the meal and had a few drinks then left, I tumbled into bed, but had a bit of a sleepless night. I guess I missed you, being alone in bed." He had kept close to the truth, just substituting Tony for Joe in his narrative.

This time, it was Maddy who felt a pang of conscience, she too had experienced a restless night, but that was because Peter had been on top of his game as well as on top of her!

The next couple of weeks seemed to drag by. Martin kept in regular touch with Tony, asking him to quietly spread the word around about Martin's intentions to stand at the next election, to sound out local people, especially businesses, on their thoughts regarding his views. He had also asked him to see if he could wangle an invitation to any functions especially civic ones. Martin had decided to try and become known in the area so when eventually the election was called, he would not suddenly appear as a stranger on their doorsteps. There was also the need for Martin to have a good reason to give Maddy for his proposed trips to Kenilworth and that he would have to stop overnight.

When, after only three weeks since his first trip to meet Tony, he explained to her that there was a dinner dance and Tony had got two tickets, he was pleased that she seemed relaxed about him going, but preferred not to accompany him, if that was okay. He feigned disappointment, but was secretly pleased, as this meant he would be able to see Joe again, that is if Joe wanted to see him. Maddy had immediately thought of other plans for that night.

Martin phoned Tony, and explained that Maddy had a heavy cold and would not be able to attend, but he would pay for the two tickets any way, after all, it was in aid of the local air ambulance appeal. He also said that he would send a cheque for two thousand pounds asking Tony to pass it on to the organising committee. His next call was to Joe. He let the phone ring but after a few seconds, it went to answer service. Martin did not leave a message. He was disappointed that the lad had not been there and wondered what he was doing. It was eleven thirty in the morning.

An hour later, his mobile went off.

"Martin? This is Joe, you rang me."

Martin felt relieved and excited at the same time.

"Hello, Joe, I rang you an hour ago, where were you?"

Joe did not answer the question directly.

"It's my lunch break now so I'm free to talk."

Martin felt stupid, of course, the lad had to earn a living, and anyway, why did he feel he should be at Martins beck and call.

"Joe, I'm coming up on Friday. I have to attend a function in Kenilworth, but I'll be free at about eleven, can you come over?"

"Yes, but I'll need you to pay for the taxi," the young man said in the same flat expressionless voice he always used.

Martin had hoped Joe would have been pleased and shown some excitement, but he was just matter-of-fact, exactly as had been on their first meeting.

"Do you want me to send you a cheque?"

"No, just reimburse me with the cash when I see you. Oh by the way, I've bought some new jeans and a 'T' shirt. Would you like to treat me to those as well?"

"Yes, of course, and if there is anything else you want, just get it and I'll pay you."

"See you Friday then, bye, Martin."

Without waiting for a reply, the phone went dead.

Maddy noticed Martin was in high spirits for the rest of the week and thought his flirtation with politics seemed to be filling him with a new enthusiasm, one she found difficult to understand, but at least provided her with extra time for her 'one-to-one sessions'.

On Friday afternoon, Martin left the office and drove straight to Kenilworth, arriving at six o'clock, which gave him time to shower and change before going to the function. Martin had asked Tony and his girlfriend to come along as his guests mainly, because he wanted Tony to point him in the right direction, introducing him to the 'movers and shakers' in the area, but also as a small thank you for setting up the office for him.

In his speech, after the meal, the chairman of the organising committee thanked Martin for his generous donation. *That was two thousand well spent,* thought Martin, *now everybody here knows who I am.* Once the plates were cleared and the tables stacked away the band burst into life, most of the men quickly making their way into the adjoining room where the bar was set up.

Tony introduced Martin to a number of local businessmen, most of who seemed to look on his ideas for cleaning up parliament favourably, though a lot expressed the opinion that he would have a job eating into the Conservative core vote, especially as they had such a strong lead over Labour in the opinion polls. They were in general polite, but not over enthusiastic. He took Tony on one side, and asked him to make a list of the people he had spoken to and mark them out of ten on their hoped for support.

At ten thirty, he excused himself, saying he had been up since five that morning and needed to get some sleep, though sleep was the last thing on his mind. He had left the car in the basement at the apartment and walked so he could have a drink. It was only a short distance and took just over fifteen minutes. He noticed his hand was shaking as he put the key in the lock and entered into the hallway. He needed a whisky to steady his nerves. The anticipation of seeing Joe again was making his heart race at an alarming pace.

At twenty past eleven, there was still no sign of Joe and Martin could feel the disappointment slowly washing away the excitement he had felt previously.

The intercom buzzer startled him. He jumped out of his seat and almost flew across the room to snatch up the receiver.

"Martin, it's Joe," the same monotone voice, but he did not care, Joe had come.

Martin pressed the door release button and within minutes, there was a tap on his door.

"I thought you'd changed your mind," he said flinging his arms round Joe.

The young man smiled at him but only gave him a cursory hug.

"I need a drink; do you want a top up?"

"Yes, why not." Martin held out his glass as the young man brushed past him towards the kitchen where the whisky was kept.

"It's late, shall we go straight to bed?"

Martin was slightly taken aback by Joe's off-hand attitude, but with his excitement having quickly returned, brushed it aside and followed the boy into the bedroom.

"Do you want a blow job or do you want to fuck me?" Joe said, as if he was asking if he wanted a cup of tea or a cup of coffee.

The words hit Martin like a blow to the stomach. This is not what he wanted at all. He wanted to caress Joe, to kiss him, to hold him and yes, eventually to make love to him.

Joe could see the look of disappointment in Martin's eye's and was quick-witted enough to recover the situation.

"Only joking, come here let me undress you."

A sense of relief filled Martin as the lad started to unzip his trousers. He felt his whole body shake. Joe continued undressing him until he was standing naked next to the bed.

"Well, I can see you're pleased to see me." Joe laughed as he quickly undressed himself and rolled onto the bed, patting the sheets to indicate to Martin to lie down next to him.

Joe, picking up from his mistake earlier, did not rush Martin, instead taking time to let his hands explore Martin's body and it was some time before he rolled onto his stomach.

Martin climaxed quickly and then lay there in a post coital embrace.

"Do you have any cigarettes? I could just use one right now," Joe said sitting up in the bed.

"There's some in a silver case on the table next to the TV." Martin still had his eyes closed, lost in a world of his own.

Martin did not smoke, having stopped when he was in his twenties, but unlike most reformed smokers, he did not mind other people smoking and always kept a few cigarettes for guests.

Joe returned to the bedroom with the lit cigarette hanging from the corner of his mouth and an ashtray in his hand.

"Nice case," he said.

The cigarette case had been an eighteenth birthday present from his father and was solid silver with his initials engraved on it.

"Um… was a present," Martin mumbled, still not back in the real world.

"Look, I've got to go… need to be up early tomorrow… you don't mind, do you?"

Joe could see by the look of disappointment on Martin's face that he did mind.

"Do you have to? It's only just after twelve and it's been three weeks since I saw you last," Martin's eyes had the look of a lost puppy.

"Sorry, I promise to stay longer next time," Joe's flat expressionless voice was cold.

The young man got dressed without saying another word and Martin watched him, his emotions in a turmoil, hurt and love fighting each other.

Joe was dressed now and ready, but he stood there as if waiting for something.

"What's the matter?" Martin asked.

"You said you'd pay for the taxi trips and the clothes."

"Oh God, sorry, yes of course."

Martin got out of bed and opened the draw in the bedside table. There was a bundle of notes held together by an elastic band.

"Is three hundred okay?"

Joe nodded.

"How do you want it, fifties or twenties?"

"Twenties please, I don't want people to think I've robbed a bank or something." Joe gave a hollow laugh, as if to soften the atmosphere that had appeared since his announcement he was going home.

Martin wrapped a dressing gown around himself, walked into the living room, and rang for the taxi.

"Five minutes," he called to Joe, who he assumed was still in the bedroom.

Joe had followed him out and was standing behind him. He put his arms around Martin, turned him around so that they were facing each other, and kissed him long and hard on the mouth. Martin felt the warmth course through his body as he held Joe in his embrace.

"You'd better go, the taxi will be waiting," he whispered hoarsely.

Joe turned and was gone. *But at least I've left him happy,* he thought to himself, as he walked to the lift, patting the three hundred pounds in his pocket.

Chapter Sixteen

Martin drove back to London thinking about the previous evening, wondering where the relationship was going. It was obvious that Joe did not feel the same as he did. He realised that he was falling in love with the lad but was confused, after all, there was still Maddy and he really did love her. These thoughts kept swirling around in his head until it ached. Finally, he decided to concentrate on something else, in the hope it would dull the thumping in his brain. Eventually, as he passed Luton, the pain subsided and he finished the journey feeling himself again.

Once back at the flat, he phoned Maddy at the shop.

"Fancy the Ivy tonight?" he asked.

"Yes please, you know I love that place, but will you get a table at such short notice?"

"Have I ever failed?"

She knew he hadn't. He always managed to get a table, much to the envy of their friends.

"What are we celebrating?"

"Nothing, I just want to take you out and have a special evening."

"Sounds good to me, see you later, bye, darling."

She put the phone down. *I might be in for a good night tonight,* she thought, *that'll be two on the trot.*

Over the next few months, running up to Christmas, Martin managed to get up to Kenilworth at least once a fortnight. Maddy could not understand why it was so important he had to be there as often as he did, but he explained to her that he was trying to establish a local presence, and anyway, Gordon Brown would have to call an election by June and then the visits would be even more frequent. Maddy did not protest too much, after all, it gave her the opportunity to see Peter, a pleasure that she looked forward to more and more.

His agent, Tony, had also thought it a little strange the visits followed the same pattern, arrive Friday afternoon, leave Saturday morning and was hard pressed at times to find a function or dinner party for him to attend. There had been no complaint from Martin on the odd occasion that there was no one for him to meet, but he still made the trip.

Martin's relationship with Joe also settled into a pattern, with the lad coming to the apartment at about eleven and leaving around two o'clock. It seemed he was always short of money and Martin found, with the taxi fares included, he was regularly handing over a few hundred pounds each visit. Martin did not mind, after all, he was wealthy enough and if it made Joe happy, then he was happy.

The week before Christmas, there was a dinner dance at Southam, which was the other small town, joined to Kenilworth in the revised constituency. Tony had obtained tickets and had stressed the importance of going, as up to then all his efforts had been concentrated on Kenilworth and he was hardly known in Southam.

It was a drive of about twenty minutes from his apartment and Martin had told Joe not to come to the flat until eleven thirty, in case, he could not get away earlier.

With the annual drink driving campaign in full swing, Martin resolved to stick to soft drinks all evening, a decision that found favour amongst the senior ladies, if not their husbands.

Tony had booked a hotel room for himself and his girlfriend, so they could have a drink with no worries and had tried hard to persuade Martin to do likewise. He had been surprised when Martin categorically refused, saying he wanted to be up early on the Saturday as he had a business meeting in London he had to attend.

The dancing was in full swing when Martin managed to sneak away and he was back in Kenilworth for a quarter past eleven, eagerly anticipating Joe's visit.

Joe rang his intercom just after eleven thirty and greeted Martin with his usual laconic 'Hi'. Martin had learnt that the young man was not as demonstrative as he was and just gave him a quick squeeze.

"Drink?" Martin asked.

Joe nodded and he sat down in the armchair whilst Martin poured them both a large whisky.

"I won't be able to see you for a few weeks, I'm taking Maddy to Courcheval, skiing."

It was the first time he had ever mentioned Maddy. Joe did not seem bothered and just nodded to show that he had heard him.

"I've bought you a Christmas present, hope you like it."

He passed the parcel to Joe who took it without a word and opened it. Martin had chosen the Omega Seamaster watch because it was large and he thought a smaller wristwatch would have looked silly, Joe having thick wrists and biceps. It was an expensive present and if he expected it would be received with a little more enthusiasm than Joe normally expressed, then he was disappointed.

"Thanks," he said in a matter of fact way, slipping the watch onto his wrist after discarding his own.

Martin sighed, if only the boy felt the way he did, but then, he was there and they would have the next few hours together.

Maddy was looking forward to the holiday. When they met, one of the things they had in common was a love of skiing and they would have gone away that first Christmas, had it not been for Maddy's father having a minor stroke. Martin had regularly spent Christmas at one skiing resort or another and always went with the same group of friends, so had not altered his arrangements. This year would be their first chance to go together, although still in the same group.

Maddy had managed to get in an extra workout with Peter, on the grounds she need to put in some extra training to strengthen her legs for the trip. If anything, the extra session turned her legs to jelly rather than strengthen them!

Martin too was looking forward to the break, not seeing Joe would be a wrench, but he felt he had been neglecting Maddy and, although she had not complained at his trips to the Midlands, she had not been her normal rapacious self either. He wondered if there was something on her mind or if she unwell.

On Christmas Eve, the group assembled at Heathrow for the flight to Geneva, where they would pick up their transfer to take them to the hotel in Courcheval. Maddy had met most of Martin's friends already and was soon chatting away to the wives. They were all seasoned skiers having their own boots and skis, so the check in was packed with cases and equipment as they lined up at the business class desk. Once everyone had checked in, they made their way to the executive lounge to start the holiday in earnest. The group consisted of four of Martin's long standing friends and their partners. They had met as young men starting their careers, and had remained friends over the years as wives and girlfriends swelled the numbers.

As they sat waiting in the lounge, Martin recalled their very first holiday together. They had met initially through work. John was in merchant banking, Andrew a stockbroker, Paul an accountant for one of the big five and Keith worked for Lloyds of London. They often met for drinks in the city and, on a whim, had all decided to go to Bangkok for a week of 'drinking and debauchery', as Keith had put it. The holiday had been a great success and to cement their friendship, after a particularly heavy drinking session on their last night, they all agreed to have a tattoo on their left wrist. After a long discussion on what form the drawing should take, John suggested, as they were like the three Musketeers, it should be a sword. Paul, as ever a stickler for accuracy, pointed out that the Musketeers were only three, the clue being in the title! It was Andrew who came up with the idea of a dagger, adding that it would be smaller and could be hidden by their watches. It was with a little trepidation that they went into the booth, Martin having drawn the short straw, being the first in.

Now sitting in the lounge, he recalled the pain, even though he had been partly anesthetised by all the alcohol he had consumed. Andrew had not been correct; their watches never did completely cover the design! As the years passed and they all became more successful in their careers, to a man, they all regretted what was after all a juvenile prank, but like many others who had made the same mistake, they had to live with the consequences. Martin had considered laser treatment to remove his tattoo, but Maddy had said she rather liked it and had talked him out of it.

By the time the call came to board, the group were, to say the least, in a very happy state.

It was late when the transfer cars finally pulled up outside their hotel and they just managed to get a meal before the kitchen closed for the night. A few bottles of wine with the meal finally tipped the scales and everyone decided to get an early night, so they would be up early for the morning's skiing.

To Martin's surprise, Maddy had dropped off to sleep as soon as her head touched the pillow. He had expected her to attack him once in their room, but even she had succumbed to the long tiring journey. He went to sleep thinking of Joe.

He woke on Christmas Day to find the curtains drawn and the sun streaming through the window. He felt across the bed for Maddy, but she was not there. He sat up and looked around the room trying to get his bearings, as he did so, Maddy came out of the bathroom, a towel wrapped around her head but otherwise naked.

"Morning, darling. Merry Christmas." She rummaged in her suitcase and withdrew a parcel, wrapped in holly and mistletoe decorated paper, and handed it to him.

He took the present and unwrapped it; an Olympus 500 camera.

"Thank you, darling, it's great. I can throw that old camera of mine away now, it's ancient anyway."

"I'm glad you like it. It's digital so you will be able to print your own pictures through the computer. There's also a stand that goes with it, which is back home and a remote so you can do a self-portrait. The beauty is that by printing your own pictures, we can take a few naughty ones!"

Martin could see the twinkle in her eye and knew she had not bought the camera solely for his pleasure.

He swung his legs over the side of the bed, got up, walked across the room to his own suitcase and pulled out a small package which he handed to Maddy. It was not wrapped in Christmas paper but something far more appealing, Asperys' own monogrammed paper. She gave a whoop of delight as her eyes fell on the package. Quickly ripping the paper away, she opened the box, revealing a beautiful bracelet of emeralds set in a gold band; each stone about a quarter of an inch square and each one surrounded by diamonds.

"It's absolutely wonderful, darling, how clever of you to buy emeralds, they are the one stone I don't have."

"Well, now you can say you have the full set, diamonds, sapphires, rubies and emeralds. I suppose we are going to have to move on to the lesser known stones next."

He laughed and held out his hand to her. She moved closer towards him and kissed him.

"Thank you, darling, it's absolutely beautiful."

The embrace was not lustful, but caring and Martin felt a warm glow as they stood, for what seemed like ages, holding each other.

When they finally released each other, she put the bracelet back in its box.

"This is too precious to risk wearing on the slopes. I'll save it until tonight when I can show it off and later I can thank you properly!"

For once, Martin was actually looking forward to Maddy's 'gymnastics'!

The holiday had started on a good note and continued in that vein, with some excellent skiing conditions and one riotous night after another. By the end of the week, Martin was exhausted and was looking forward to going back to England for a rest. The week had flown by and, as they waited in the lounge for their departure flight, it seemed like only hours since they had arrived. It was Andrew who suggested that next year they should make it two weeks not one, a suggestion that was unanimously endorsed by the group.

Chapter Seventeen

Joe sat in his room, fingering the watch Martin had given him as a Christmas present. He was thinking about Martin, not because he felt anything for him, he was just a punter, but wondering how he could up the ante. He had fallen lucky when he met Martin; normally, the men he met were regular gays who were just on the lookout for a one-night stand, often only wanting a blowjob. The most he got was twenty quid for oral and fifty for full sex, sometimes they argued about that, and he would end up with half the amount.

Martin was different, he was obviously loaded, you only had to look at the car he drove and the pad in Kenilworth to see that, he also had a place in London, though he had never talked about it. Most importantly of all, it was clear it had been his first homosexual experience when they had met and Martin had fallen in love with him.

The poor sap, Joe thought, *he actually thinks I'm in love with him and I'm gay as well.* Joe had been happy to let Martin's delusion continue; after all, he was picking up around two to three hundred pounds a fortnight for very little effort. It was much easier than working the bar and much more lucrative.

He looked at the watch and wondered how much he could get for it if he sold it, buying a cheap replica, so that Martin would never know. He decided after the Christmas holidays, he would talk to Jimmy about selling the watch, Jimmy bought and sold just about everything.

The best thing about Martin was he did not realise he was actually paying for sex! He believed he was just being generous. Joe laughed to himself that this obviously successful businessman actually accepted the cost of a taxi to Coventry was £100. What did he care if money was not that important to the man, it was another reason why he must find ways to increase the money flow without Martin getting suspicious.

Joe pondered the problem for some time, but could not think of anything that sounded reasonable, other than asking for money for more clothes, but then Martin would ask to see him wearing them. He could always say they were expensive designer labels, but get them as knock offs from Jimmy.

A thought suddenly came into his mind, it was his birthday on April1st and although a couple of months off, he could start preparing the groundwork to talk Martin into buying him a motor bike. It would make sense if he told Martin how much money he would save on taxi fares, though on second thoughts that may not be such a good idea as the taxi scam was worth £80 a trip. He was sure he could persuade Martin; after all, it was a special birthday.

He decided; he would sting Martin for £10,500 for the motor bike then sell it back to the dealer. He should clear at least £5000; that plus what he had saved over the last few months and what he could squeeze out of Martin in the next couple of months, should give him about £7500. It would be enough to get out of the sex scene and start afresh, though quite what he would do, he was not sure about. He had made a few tentative enquiries of Jimmy about maybe being his partner in the business, but they were quickly rebuffed, Jimmy did not do partnerships. Whatever, he would definitely make the break. He thought about Martin, he would be devastated, but so what, with his money, he would soon find another sucker. He laughed at his own joke, feeling no sympathy for the older man.

Joe felt exhilarated at the thought of putting this part of his life behind him. His mind went back, tracing the events that had brought him to his present situation.

He lived in a flat in a high-rise block near the centre of Coventry, which he shared with his mother. His father had left when he was only six. Joe had been asleep in his bed when he was woken by shouting, he remembered crying, wondering what was going on, and then his father coming into the room and kissing him, saying goodbye. He never saw his father again.

Next day, his mother had told him that his daddy had to go away on a job and would be gone a long time. He remembered how the weeks had become months and still his father had not returned, then his mother finally telling him his father had left them. He hated his father and vowed if he ever saw him, he would kill him.

It was not until his eleventh birthday and he was due to move up to the comprehensive senior school, that he discovered the truth. He had gone to his cousin's birthday party; she was also eleven and was the daughter of his father's sister. They had been discussing their move to new schools after the summer holidays. He overheard his aunt say what a pity that Joe's father could not be around to see his son making the transition.

Joe was full of rage and said 'that bastard if I ever see him, I'll kill him'. His aunt was stunned and had remonstrated with him, telling him he did not know what he was saying. It had taken some moments to calm him down, but eventually, she took him on one side, away from the other children and explained exactly what had happened.

His father had left because when he had come home earlier than usual from the pub, he had found his best friend in bed with Joe's mother. She had told him she didn't love him anymore and to go. Joe's father had been in a state of shock and had just moved out, living with his sister for a while before getting a job which took him to Canada. He had told his sister that when he had made good, he would come back and collect Joe so that they could start a new life together.

Joe had been confused; the story was the total opposite to the one his mother had told him. After the party, he had confronted his mother with his new-found knowledge and she admitted it was true. From that moment, his feelings towards his mother changed and he hated her as much as his father. Although he now knew that his father was the innocent party, he still could not forgive him for abandoning him.

Over the next few years, he receded into his own world, one without adults, who in his eyes only caused heartache. At school, he went through the motions, just doing enough to not cause any reactions from the teachers. He was bright but chose not to push himself, rather to be anonymous. One day, he promised he would show everybody; he would be someone.

His mother basically lived on social welfare, except on the few occasions when he had an 'uncle' staying; there was more money in the household budget, though none of it came Joe's way. As soon as he was fourteen, he got himself a job as a paperboy, which at least gave him a few pounds in his pocket, but still not enough to pay for his newly acquired smoking habit. It was the need to finance his growing dependency on cigarettes and the odd illicit drinking session with his friends, that opened up a new income stream.

If Joe was big for his age, then Danny was even bigger. At fourteen, they both looked more like sixteen or even seventeen. They had no trouble buying cigarettes, and could make a profit buying them and on selling to their contemporaries who could not get served themselves. However, this only garnered a few pounds, not enough for Joe. Danny always seemed to have more spare cash than Joe, but had been reluctant at first to tell him how he got it.

Joe had pestered him to let him in on the scam whatever it was, finally Danny told him. At first, Joe did not believe him and had laughed, saying he was making it up, but Danny was serious. He knew of men who would pay him to either masturbate them, or let them masturbate him, paying a tenner for the privilege! It was easy money; on a good week, he could make fifty quid.

Joe had been apprehensive at first, he was not gay, or at least, he was pretty sure he wasn't, and had enjoyed it when he and a couple of girls had gone into a shed and shown each other their 'privates'. He remembered the girls' eyes when he had become aroused, a look of apprehension mixed with excitement. The feeling becoming more intense as they fumbled with each other, none of them quite sure what they were doing, but knowing it engendered a warm feeling; but an old man, playing with your dick, that was another matter entirely.

Danny had said he just looked on it as job, just the same as delivering papers, except you didn't get soaking wet or frozen in mid-winter and the pay was far better!

Joe had wanted a computer, all his friends had one, but his mother had told him flatly there was no chance and there were no 'uncles' on the scene at the present time he could butter up too. It would take ages to save up with the money from his paper round and that would be if he gave up smoking as well. He decided to give the 'Danny' scheme a try; if he only did it enough times to pay for the computer then he could stop.

He remembered the first time as though it was yesterday. Danny had by now established some regular clients and he let Joe meet one of those, by taking his place.

The car pulled up at the kerbside, and the man lowered his window, he had been expecting to see Danny and was surprised when Joe bent down to greet him.

"Trevor?" Joe asked, it was not the man's real name, but one he had given to Danny.

"Where's Danny?" a look of worry creased his brow.

"He's got a cold, asked me to stand in for him," Joe realised the words sounded foolish, but could not think of anything better to say.

"Get in then." It was an order not a request.

Joe went to the passenger's door, opened it, and settled in the front seat. Trevor moved off and drove out of the city towards Berkswell. Once in the country, he found an entrance to a field which was partially hidden from the road and pulled up. Trevor switched off the engine and got out of the car, opened the rear door and got back in, waving to Joe to follow him. Once settled on the rear seats, he undid his flies. Joe's eyes focused on the erection that had burst from the man's trousers. *Christ,* he thought, *he's enormous!*

Half an hour later, Trevor dropped Joe back in Coventry, ten pounds richer. *That's what I call easy money,* he had said to himself; he had felt no desire, no excitement, it was just a job.

The money was easy and soon Joe had regular 'customers' of his own. One man had asked him to suck him off and Joe had refused, but when the man offered to double the money, his inhibitions disappeared, after all, he kept telling himself, it was just a job. Soon, he had saved enough money to buy a computer. He liked having plenty of money in his pocket and by now had ditched his paper round, he was making far more in this new venture. He had told his mother he was still doing the paper round and had got himself a Saturday job as well, when she had asked how he could afford to buy a computer. The money gave him a feeling of empowerment, and he made up his mind he would leave school as soon as he was fifteen and get a proper job.

By the time he had reached fifteen, he was six foot and looked over eighteen. He had not been questioned when he and

Danny had gone into a pub and ordered drinks, although they had always made sure that they never went into any of their local ones, just in case they were recognised. Both had left school that summer, but getting a job had not been that easy and they had signed on at the job centre. Joe's dream of earning 'proper money' disappeared in the aftermath of the credit crunch, but he still had his regular 'clients'.

It was Danny who suggested if he wanted to find some new punters, then the best place to start would be by visiting Rainbows, the pub which catered almost exclusively for gays.

Joe was not sure, he was not gay, but the lure of increasing his income overcame any reservations.

He had met Danny for a drink on the Friday and after a couple of pints with whisky chasers had decide to give it a try. Danny had said he would go with him, but at the last minute had cold feet and left him just outside the entrance to Rainbows.

Joe was wearing a white 'T' shirt and jeans. His muscles rippled under the tight shirt and, with his curly hair, looked like a young James Dean. He certainly looked older than his fifteen years, more like nineteen.

He entered the pub, and walked up to the bar and ordered a large whisky, the effect of the earlier drinks was beginning to wear off!

A number of men were sitting around the room, some in couples, others either on their own or in larger groups, they had all turned to look at him as he walked in; he was new kid on the block.

He sat there gripping the glass as though it was providing some kind of protection. A young man came over to him and tried to make polite conversation, but it was obvious he was just trying to chat him up and Joe was not there to make friends, he was there to make money! He had been in the pub for about an hour, and was on his third whisky and he could feel the effects slowly taking hold of his body. He decided that maybe this was not the best idea Danny had ever had. The only response he had received was from these bloody queers trying to get a date with him.

He slid off the bar stool and walked to the door. The cool evening air hit him as he went out onto the street and he swayed a little, the spirits having an effect on his legs. He suddenly felt a strong arm supporting him. He turned to see a middle-aged man, probably late forties, by his side.

"You okay, son?" the man asked.

"Yeah… fine, thanks."

"I've got my car just round the corner, would you like me to drop you somewhere?"

"Yeah, thanks."

Joe allowed himself to be led to the man's car, a dark blue Renault, about two years old. Joe looked a little closer at the man, he was not dressed in way out gear like a lot of the customers of Rainbows, but wore a blue shirt with fawn Chino's and brown shoes. He was shorter than Joe, about five nine and had the start of a paunch. His hair was dark with the first signs of grey showing in flecks to the sides and to his temple. His face was one of those that were easily forgotten, the only distinguishing feature being his bushy eyebrows, but he had a kindly smile and Joe did not feel threatened.

"Look, if you want to sleep it off, you can come back to my place."

Joe suddenly sobered up; he could here alarm bells ringing in his ears. The man saw the worried look in Joes face.

"Don't worry I'm not going to rape you." He laughed, but not in harsh way. "I was watching you in the pub, you're not gay, are you? I can tell."

Joe felt strangely reassured he was not being threatened; the man must be just friendly.

"You're a good looking lad and you went into Rainbows knowing it was a gay club, am I right?"

"Yes, so what?"

"That means you went in there for a reason and my guess is that you're on the look-out for a punter who'll pay you for your services, yes?"

"So what if you're right then?"

"I'm willing to pay, what do you charge?"

"Twenty for a blow job." Joe was now in full control of his faculties.

"And how much for full sex?"

Joe was taken aback, he had never considered full sex, but hell did it matter, after all it was just a job.

"Fifty quid," he heard himself saying.

"Okay, let's go back to my place."

They got into the car and the man drove off to his flat.

Joe never did get the man's real name and strangely never saw him again, but after this first initiation, he would make Rainbows his main pick up point, for nearly all his future liaisons. The regulars did not seem to mind and stopped trying to date him, leaving him to service the lonely ones amongst their midst who could not seem to be able to date naturally.

He still turned up at the job centre, but with little enthusiasm, after all, he did not need to work with his extra-curricular activities providing a regular income.

Now he had hit the jackpot and once he had his motorbike, it would be bye-bye, Martin.

Chapter Eighteen

Martin was looking forward to seeing Joe. The holiday had been fantastic and even his relationship with Maddy had been good, but he could not get Joe out of his mind. It was like being hooked on a drug, he needed his fix.

He phoned Joe's mobile and arranged to see him on Friday, then phoned Tony to say he would be coming to Kenilworth for a routine visit and was there anything happening he ought to know about. Tony had said that things were quiet, and there really was no need for him to come up as he had nothing new to tell him, nor were there any functions to attend. Martin said that it was fine, but he would call up anyway as he wanted people to get used to him being around, but Tony did not have to call in.

That evening, he casually mentioned to Maddy that Tony had been on the phone and he wanted to discuss some promotional work to get his name across in the area. He had suggested bringing a photographer to take pictures for an article, in the local magazine; he had wangled with the editor.

"I told him about your present, and said I would bring my new camera and tripod, and we could do our own pictures. If they turn out to be rubbish, then we can always get the professional in. What do you think?"

"Good idea," she said with little enthusiasm in her voice. She was not really interested and was disappointed, they had only been back five minutes, and he was off to the bloody Midlands again.

"I'm only going overnight Friday so if you want to go anywhere on Saturday, go ahead and arrange it, and I'll make sure I'm back with plenty of time to spare." He knew how she felt about his foray into politics and made sure that it did not inconvenience their social life.

"Fine, I'll sort something out," she said without looking up from the magazine she was reading.

Martin took his time driving up to Kenilworth. He had decided to go up via the M40 for a change, as he had nothing to do until Joe came, there was no need to race along. He had asked Joe to come earlier and said that he would buy an Indian takeaway so that they could have a meal together. This would be a first as Martin was usually out early evening and Joe had never previously arrived before eleven o'clock.

Joe, having decided over the holiday, that the arrangement would only last until after his birthday at the end of March, was going to make the most of these three months. Although the weather was cold, he intended to cycle over from Coventry, but still sting Martin for the taxi fare, that would bring him an extra £80 per visit.

Just after nine o'clock, the intercom buzzed and Martin unlocked the door for Joe. When the young man entered the apartment, the table was laid and the curry was already served; two cans of lager were half poured.

"Come on, let's eat before it gets cold and you can tell me what sort of Christmas you've had." Martin beckoned to the chair and Joe sat down.

They ate in silence, each seemingly lost in their own thoughts.

"That was good," Joe said as he pushed the plate away from him and opened his third can of lager.

Martin smiled, it was not often the lad showed any form of emotion and he was pleased his suggestion of a 'take away' had been so well received.

Joe did not want to talk about his own Christmas, after all, it had been nothing special, and he had spent most of the time with Danny and Jimmy at one of the city bars.

He did feign interest in Martins stories of the ski slopes and the fun he had enjoyed. *Maybe,* he thought to himself, *once I've made some money I'll go skiing with the fucking jet set.*

Martin cleared away the dishes while Joe sat watching him, having first helped himself to cigarettes from Martin's silver case.

"I've got something to show you," Martin said, as he finally wiped the kitchen surface clean and switched the dishwasher on.

"I can guess what that is," Joe said with a laugh.

He is in a good mood, Martin thought, *let's hope it lasts.*

"I didn't mean that. I had a present for Christmas." He walked across the room and opened the bag that contained the camera and tripod. "I thought we could have some fun and take a few pictures, if we don't like them, it's easy to erase them and we can print the ones we like on the computer."

"Whatever," Joe returned to his monosyllabic method of communication.

"Would you pour us both a large whiskey while I set up the camera in the bedroom?"

Joe got up from the chair, and poured two large glasses of scotch and followed Martin into the bedroom.

Martin had taken snaps before, but did not class himself as a photographer; the first few pictures were either out of focus or chopped off Joe's head. He took a series of pictures showing Joe in an ever-decreasing state of undress, until he was completely naked. He then got Joe to repeat the performance with Martin as the subject.

Their glasses were empty and Joe was dispatched to replenish them. He returned with the glasses almost full. The half-empty bottle wedged under his arm.

Martin had set up the tripod and fixed the camera to it, pointing it at the bed.

"Come on," he said laughing, the whisky beginning to take effect. "Let's try a few action shots."

"But how can you take a picture of us both?" Joe looked puzzled.

"Ah, it's got a timer on it so I can press the button, but there is a delay before it actually takes the picture."

He grinned giving Joe a knowing look, which implied he knew exactly what he was talking about.

Joe was also starting to feel the effects of the drink and his initial reticence had disappeared. *What the hell,* he thought, *if it keeps him happy what do I care.*

After a number of, what Martin had described as action shots, they fell into the bed both giggling like school girls.

Martin got up, and took the camera into the living room where his computer was and connected the camera to the machine. Joe could hear the whirring of the printer as the pictures fell into the tray.

After a couple of minutes, Martin returned with the pictures. The camera had been set up at an angle and, although the 'action shots', left nothing to the imagination, you could not actually see their faces, both of them having their heads pointing away from the camera.

"You'd better keep them somewhere safe, don't want your wife seeing them," Joe said.

It was the first time Joe had ever mentioned Martin's wife. Although the subject was not taboo, it was just neither of them ever raised it. Martin felt a small pang of guilt, but told himself it was not being unfaithful; it was not another woman so Maddy did not have a rival in the true sense of the word.

"I'll keep them in the drawer by the bed; it's lockable, so even Mrs Black can't open it."

The whisky bottle was, by now, three quarters empty, and both of them were tired and drunk. Within in minutes, they were fast asleep.

Martin woke with a start and turned on the light to look at his watch. It was four thirty. Joe was still fast asleep next to him. He shook the lad until he eventually woke.

"Joe, it's four thirty, you had better go before the neighbours start moving about."

Joe turned over, his head pounding from the effects of the whisky, and pulled the bed clothes up around him.

"Joe, come on, you've got to get up. Shall I call a taxi?"

Joe suddenly came alive, the last thing he wanted was a taxi, he had his bicycle downstairs; the thought of the extra £40 he would make overrode the ache in his brain.

He slowly rose from the bed and dressed.

"Don't worry about calling for a taxi, I've got my mobile, I'll walk over to the hotel and call one so it will look as though I've stayed there."

"Good idea. Here take this; it'll cover the taxi fare and those new trainers you were talking about."

Martin gave him a bundle of twenty-pound notes. Joe did not count them, but guessed there must be between two and three hundred pounds, he would check once outside.

"Right, see you; give me a ring when you're coming next." Joe grinned at the double entendre,

"Yes, bye."

Joe went to the door and without turning back, left, pulling the door shut behind him.

Martin sat for a few minutes, thinking to himself. It was always the same, little or no emotion, just a perfunctory goodbye and the boy was off; no warmth, no feeling, nothing. Martin wondered if there was any future in this relationship, that perhaps it would be wise to stop now, but however sensible the thought sounded, he could not shake off the desire to see Joe again and just hoped that the lad would change as things progressed.

Chapter Nineteen

Throughout January and February, all the papers were speculating on when Brown would call the election. It had to be before the end of June and most of the pundits were predicting early May, which meant announcing the date in April to give a month for canvassing.

Martin had decided to take the bull by the horns and hopefully catch his opponents on the wrong foot. He had phoned Tony to arrange a number of meetings in both Kenilworth and Southam, during the latter part of March and through April. Tony had queried if this was allowed, but Martin told him there was no law against inviting the public to hear a speaker address them. The meetings would be low key to start with getting more intense once the election had been formally announced.

"Look, I'll be with you on the 12th March, we can discuss it in more detail, and that gives you some time to find some locations for the meetings and book the halls. I've transferred £10000 to the account we set up and as you're a signatory, you can use it as you see fit. Be at my apartment at six o'clock and leave yourself free for at least three hours, okay?"

"You're the boss. I'll get cracking straight away."

Martin rung off, then immediately phoned Joe.

"This Friday about eleven okay? I've got a meeting first but should be finished by then."

"Sorry, I can't make it this week. I didn't know you would be up and my mates got us tickets for a rock concert, you're not angry are you?" Joe tried to sound concerned.

'Oh, no… of course not… I understand." Martin could not hide his disappointment.

"Can you make it the following Friday? I do want to see you, honestly," Joe tried to sound as sincere as possible. The last thing he wanted was to upset Martin just as his plan was about to mature.

"Yes, yes that will be fine, I'll probably be up every week now with the election looming," he replied, a little cheered by the lad's apparent enthusiasm.

"I'll look forward to it and I can tell you all about the concert."

Martin gave an audible groan; he was not the least interested in rock concerts.

Joe was just about to go out to meet Jimmy. He was still trying to persuade his friend to let him in on one of his scams, but so far without success. He looked down at the silent phone; it would be just a week before his birthday, so it would be a good time to put his little plan of action into being. Give the old fart a good night then, when he was sated ask him for a little birthday present. He must remember to take some brochures of bikes he'd been looking at. Martin was bound to go along with it, after all he liked expensive things and the Ducati he had decided on was only a drop in the ocean compared to the Ferrari.

Maddy arrived home from the boutique and flopped down in her favourite chair. Martin had already been home half an hour and was in the kitchen when she came in. He walked into the living room on hearing the front door slam shut.

"You look bushed, would a gin and tonic help?"

"Would it just! It's been chaotic today, but I suppose I mustn't grumble, we've sold more outfits in one day than we normally sell in a week." She took a sip of the drink Martin handed to her. "How's your day been?"

"Same as always really, everyone is on tenterhooks waiting for the announcement of the election before they make any real commitments, but life has to go on." Martin never really talked about his business in anything other than general terms. He preferred to keep his work life and home life in separate compartments.

"Oh, by the way, I've got to go to Paris the week after next for a couple of days. Thursday and Friday, the 18th and 19th I think it is. I'm meeting Monique; she's got some new lines she wants me to look at. Do you want to come with me?" She knew he wouldn't want to go, he'd already said he would be going up to Kenilworth, but thought it best to ask.

I just hope he doesn't change his mind and spoil my plans, she thought to herself, having already arranged for Peter to accompany her on her trip. It would have been difficult to change the arrangements if Martin had wanted to go.

"That's fine; I'm in Kenilworth anyway, and will be more often once the Prime Minister presses the button."

Maddy chose to ignore the last remark. She had made her feelings known on numerous occasions that he was wasting his time and money, but now that she had Peter in the background, she had to admit it had its compensations.

She sat drinking her gin, thinking exactly what she would be doing in Paris, a smile playing around her lips; Peter was so fit and never ran out of steam!

"You've cheered up since you came in. Do my gin and tonics have that effect on you? How about going out for something to eat? I've been told there's a new Japanese restaurant just opened. Shall I book a table?"

"Mmm… that would be lovely." But she was not referring to the restaurant, she was still planning what she would do to Peter.

Martin was pleased with the arrangements Tony had made for him. He had taken a short lease on some offices just off the High Street, and had fitted them out with a couple of computers and desks and already interviewed two ladies to work part time. Most importantly, he had booked six venues for meetings in the next two weeks and was waiting to hear on further dates. It was obvious that Martin would have to spend more time in the apartment or else drive back to London late at night. He decided he would see what Maddy thought before making the decision, maybe it would be wise to drive back and forwards, at least in the early days. As Election Day grew closer, whenever that was, he would need to be around day and night so he would hold back on telling Maddy until the very last minute.

Tony had been a real find and although rather shy in public, he excelled in pulling everything together. Whatever Martin thought of, it was almost guaranteed Tony had already put it in motion. Martin felt more and more confident as one after another, he put his messages across to the public at the meetings Tony had set up.

Tony had even got friendly with the political reporter for The Coventry Evening Telegraph and Martin was assured of a report, no matter how small, after each time he spoke. The fact his rivals were not holding meetings never occurred to Martin; the friendly reporter was only too glad of something to write about.

People were now coming up to him in the street and recognising him, though he found it a little disconcerting when one old lady asked him 'where his white suit was', obviously mixing him up with Martin Bell from years ago. What upset him the most was, Martin Bell was probably twenty-five years older than he was! At least, he was being recognised for being anti-sleaze and that was the crux of his campaign.

The more meetings he held, the more he believed he was connecting with the public. He had hit the right note, the general feeling of anger against those who governed us was apparent by the increasing number of people who attended. If the credit crisis was the fault of greedy bankers, then it was exacerbated by greedy politicians who, rather than look to control excess, were diving head first into the trough themselves.

Martin felt passionately about the whole expenses scandal, he was not against payment for MPs', in fact, he believed that their basic pay should be higher, as they were now earning less than some head teachers, but to fiddle expenses to make up for the low salary was downright criminal. It was when he expressed these feelings at his meetings he got the most applause. He had correctly understood the public's mood and, when taking questions from those present, had felt their almost universal resentment for all political parties, of whatever colour.

Chapter Twenty

Maddy had packed a small overnight bag for her trip to Paris and it stood in the hall whilst she looked in the mirror for the third time to check her lipstick was just right. Martin had offered to drive her to Heathrow, but she insisted on getting a taxi. He had pointed out that it was just as easy for him to drive up the M40 as the M1 and could easily drop her off, but she thanked him and repeated no, that was the end of the matter.

There was a call on the intercom to say that the taxi had arrived, and she kissed Martin goodbye and went quickly to the lift. Once settled in the back of the cab, she breathed a sigh of relief, if Martin had insisted on taking her to the airport, it would have caused a few problems, as the taxi was now heading for Peter's house to collect him.

Martin had taken the day off and had arranged to be at the new Kenilworth offices by lunchtime. He wanted to spend most of the day with Tony, going over the response they had received to a mail shot asking for support. He had no planned speaking engagements that evening so would have plenty of time to wind down before Joe arrived. He had asked him to come early and have something to eat, but Joe had declined saying he would not be finished work until seven thirty and then needed to go home and change, so it would be near nine before he came over. Martin was not too put out, he was pleased that Joe had a steady job, he always seemed to be between jobs and Martin had often given him a few extra pounds to tie him over.

The response to the mail shot had been excellent, with a hundred and fifty committed supporters who had pledged their vote to him at the election. Tony had suggested that Martin should reply to each person individually and had taken the initiative printing a thank you letter that only needed to have the person's name and Martin's signature added. As always, Martin was impressed with Tony, and happily spent the time personally addressing and signing all the letters. By five thirty, Tony had brought him up to date with appointments and meetings for the next few weeks, any functions he thought Martin should go to and shown him some drafts of election posters. All in all, Martin was satisfied that they were not only ready for the election, but would be first out of the blocks once the date had been officially announced. He thanked Tony for doing such a fine job. *Maybe when all this is over I could use him in the business,* he thought.

Martin walked back along the main street to the apartment. It was only six o'clock and Joe would not be there until nine, so there was time to shower, change and go to one of the local restaurants for a meal. The one thing he liked about Kenilworth was there was plenty of choice when it came to eating out.

Once changed, he glanced at his watch and as it was only a quarter to seven, decided to have a gin and tonic, and watch the news before leaving. There was still no announcement from Number Ten and he wondered just how long Brown would leave it before setting the date. The news was as boring as ever, nothing but doom and gloom. Although he did not enjoy eating alone, thought that anything was better than hearing yet another poor soldier had been killed in Afghanistan. It was the litany of wasted human life that had convinced him we should pull out and bring our troops home. *When, oh when will our Government realise we are no longer a super power,* he thought, as he drained the last dregs of his drink.

For a change, he had chosen a restaurant called Raffles which, according to the menu he'd read, in the window on his way back from the office, specialised in a mixture of Chinese, Malay and Indian cuisine. He enjoyed both Chinese and Indian, but had never tried Malay so was looking forward to a new experience.

It was early and there were no other diners when he went in. The waiter showed him to a table and left him for a few minutes to peruse the menu. Martin was not quite sure what to choose so called the waiter back and asked him to choose for him. The restaurant specialised in gin slings, made to the recipe of its famous namesake in Singapore, and as he was not driving, Martin had no hesitation in ordering one.

Although being empty with no atmosphere in the place, Martin enjoyed his meal and the two subsequent gin slings. In a way, he was content there were no other customers, as the last thing he wanted right now was for someone to recognise him and want to talk about his views on whatever was their burning concern of the moment.

He finished his meal, paid and was just leaving as the first customers of the evening came in. Fortunately, they were a couple who were either on their first date or an illicit one, as they only had eyes for each other and paid no attention to Martin.

He walked slowly back to the apartment and sat down to read the copy of the local paper Tony had given him. It was still only eight thirty. The next half hour seemed to drag by and by now, he had read the paper from front to back including most of the classified ads!

At last, the intercom buzzed and he pressed the button to unlock the street door. He had his door open ready before Joe had even got out of the lift.

"Hi, I've missed you," he said putting his arms around Joe once the lad was inside.

"Missed you too," Joe replied in his flat Midland vowels.

"Drink?"

"Yes, large scotch."

There was no please, or thank you, with Joe just the minimum amount of words necessary.

Joe took his drink and sat down on one of the easy chairs, reaching for the cigarette case as he did so.

"How was your concert?"

Joe had forgotten all about the imaginary concert he had made up on the spur of the moment.

"Alright, not your cup of tea, too loud for you I'll bet." He gave a crooked grin at the thought of Martin going to any concert, other than a classical one.

In truth, Martin was not bothered about the concert, but was just trying to show some interest. He reflected they really did not have a lot in common and the only thing that tied them was sex.

"I'm pleased you've got a steady job, what is it?"

The question hit Joe like a punch in the stomach. He had not expected to be questioned on a job which, like the concert, was a figment of his imagination. He needed to think on his feet. Playing for time, he asked Martin if he wanted another, and when he nodded to say yes, he walked to the kitchen area and filled both glasses.

"Oh, it's nothing special. I work in the loading area of a distribution company, they're a smaller version of TNT," he said when he returned.

He hoped that was vague enough to satisfy Martin's curiosity without getting himself too caught up in details he might forget in the future.

"I'm saving up to buy myself a motor bike."

Maybe this was a good opportunity to sound Martin out about his birthday present.

"How much is that going to cost you?"

"Well, it depends how much I can save. What I really want is a Ducati 848, but they cost ten and half grand, so I'll probably have to settle for a second hand one, which will only be a couple of grand. Look, I've got a brochure in my jacket if you're interested."

Martin nodded his head, and the lad went to the hall where his jacket was hanging and retrieved the literature from his inside pocket. At last, something they had in common; Martin loved speed and had thought about buying himself a motorbike, if for no other reason than the ease of getting around London.

Joe sat on the arm of Martin's chair as he turned over the pages showing pictures of the motorbike and details of its specification.

"Look, I might be able to help you with the purchase." Martin was holding Joe's hand and the boy responded by putting his arm around the older man's shoulders.

Now's the time to tell him about my birthday, Joe thought.

"That would be great if you could, especially as it's my birthday next week and it's a special one."

"Really, is it your eighteenth then?"

"No, I'll be sixteen."

For a few moments, there was silence. Martin could not believe what Joe had just said.

"Did you say sixteen? I thought you were about eighteen or nineteen. Are you telling me that you're only fifteen now?" Martin's voice rose as he tried to control the anger.

"Yeah, what's the problem?"

118

"What's the fucking problem? You're the fucking problem. You're fucking underage!" Martin was spluttering now, shouting; his face so red that it might burst. If this ever got out it could ruin me. "It's over, do you hear me, it's over," he bellowed.

"But what about my motorbike?" Joe could not understand what all the fuss was about, no one in the past had ever bothered about his age, they had only been too glad to get serviced.

"You can forget that. Look, I want you out of my life and for good. I never want to see you again. I'll give you five hundred pounds; call it a going away present, but I never want to see you again."

Martin was furious, struggling to hold himself together.

"But, Martin…"

"But Martin, nothing. I'm going to the 'hole in the wall' to draw out the cash for you and as soon as I get back, I want you to leave so have your last drink, I'll be back in ten minutes."

Martin slammed the door behind him as he left to find the cash machine.

Joe sat in the chair, stunned, this was not the way he'd planned it, Martin was his meal ticket, his exit strategy. He had to have another plan but what; five hundred quid was not enough, he needed at least ten times that amount. He had to think and fast, Martin would be back in a minute and then that would be it, all over, all that shagging for nothing!

Something was nagging in the back of his mind, something that Martin had said, no, not said, had shouted. If only he could remember… and then he did. Martin had said if it came out, it could ruin him; that was it. He would threaten to expose Martin and he would have to pay for his silence. Joe felt suddenly very pleased with himself, he would actually get the money without having to fuck the old fool, but he needed proof, what if he denied it. They would take Martin's word, not his. He looked out of the window and could see Martin walking back towards the apartment; he would be back in just a few minutes.

Then he remembered the photos and dashed into the bedroom. The draw was locked but it easily gave way to the blade on his sheath knife. *Thank god I kept that with me,* he thought as he pulled the draw open and took out one of the prints depicting 'the action shot'. He ran back into the room and lit

119

another cigarette to calm himself down. As he fingered the silver case, he thought 'why not' he won't miss it and slid the case into his trouser pocket.

Martin came back into the apartment, his face still showing the anger that had welled up inside him.

"Here's your money, now go and don't ever ring me or come to this apartment again." He pointed to the door, his whole body shaking with rage.

"Whatever," was all that Joe said as he scooped up the notes, grabbed his jacket from its hook and left.

Martin was shaking so badly, he spilt whisky on to the worktop as he tried to refill his glass.

Joe went down to the basement and retrieved his bike, still thinking how he would go about blackmailing Martin. He was sure he would pay up, once he knew he had evidence to prove they had been lovers and anyway, he was loaded, he wouldn't miss the money. He decided ten thousand would be a nice round figure which would set him up nicely, even Jimmy would have to show some interest if he said he could inject that amount into the business. As he peddled to the end of the main street and turned right alongside Abbey Fields Park, he relaxed thinking that maybe things had not turned out as badly as he first thought, at least he didn't have to go to bed with him this time, or ever again for that matter.

The road swung left down the hill towards the traffic lights then right onto the Coventry Road. He was freewheeling down the hill, congratulating himself on what had actually been a lucky turn of events, when the thought suddenly struck him that it was not a crime to have sex with another man, it was the age factor that was critical, being under sixteen years old was illegal. He slammed the brakes on as he got level with the entrance to the park.

He stopped and reached into his pocket for the photograph, he could just make out the figures in the light from the street lamp. Neither of their faces was visible, but he was sure with his blond curly hair, he could be recognised. Martin was more difficult, but you could just make out the tattoo underneath his gold watch and he was convinced that would be enough. The most important thing was the picture had automatically printed the date in the top right hand corner… 9/01/10.

He let out a whoop of joy. *Got the bastard, he can't deny that.* He looked around to see if anyone had heard him but there was nobody in sight. *I need to hide this picture somewhere safe,* he thought, *it's my passport to a new life.*

He felt in his pocket for the cigarette case he had helped himself to, took out a cigarette and lit it. Slowly, he inhaled the smoke trying to think where would be the safest place to hide the picture, not at home, that was definite; his mother was always going through his things. He finished the cigarette and was about to flick the stub into the gutter when a man walked by on the other side of the road with his dog. The man glared across, almost daring him to litter the pavement. Normally, he would have ignored the man, but the last thing he wanted right now was any confrontation, so turning towards the park, he walked to the rubbish bin, and having made sure the stub was extinguished, threw it in.

Although it was evening, it was a light night and looking into the park, he could just make out the play area and the café about five hundred yards away. Just past the play area, a pole reached towards the sky, it looked like a lamppost without the lamp. It struck Joe as being an odd place to put a pole that appeared to serve no purpose.

Then the idea came to him. It could serve a purpose after all; it could act as a marker. The more he thought about it, the more the idea made sense. If he buried the picture at the base of the pole, he would easily remember where it was hidden and no one on earth would ever find it. It was perfect.

He wheeled the bike along the path until he reached the spot, just past the play area and, leaning it against the hedge, looked around to make sure no one else was in the park or watching him from the road.

He had his penknife with him and for the second time that night was glad that he, out of habit, had brought it. He had, in the past, strapped it to his waistband whenever he was seeing a punter, just in case they turned nasty or did not want to pay. Fortunately, he had never had cause to use it, but tonight it had been a godsend.

The ground was soft after the recent rain, and after ten minutes of digging and scrapping, he had made a hole deep enough. The only problem now was how to protect the photo from any moisture, but that was soon solved as he patted his pockets and felt the cigarette case hard against his fingers. Emptying the contents, there were five cigarettes left, he folded up the picture and placed it into the case then dropped it into the hole. After another furtive look to see if anyone was nearby, he quickly back filled the earth and pressed it down with his heel, making sure that the sod of turf was covering the top.

He stepped back, pleased with himself, *That is as safe as the Bank of England.*

He walked back to the entrance, straddled his bike and set off back to Coventry. He would not ask Martin for any money straight away, but he would let him know he had the picture and then he would leave him to sweat a while before putting the squeeze on. Joe had not felt so happy for a long time.

Chapter Twenty-One

Martin had not slept well. The revelation by Joe that he was under the age of consent had weighed heavily on his mind. He kept asking himself why on earth he had got involved in the first place, but there was no logical answer. From their first meeting, he had been drawn to the boy and what he felt for him was something completely new. He had never thought of himself as homosexual, yes, he knew that his libido was not as great as that of his friends, and certainly not as great as Maddy's, but he still enjoyed making love to her. Whilst many of his male friends bragged about their numerous conquests, he had stayed silent, thinking they were not gentlemen to boast so loudly, but also because he had very little to boast about anyway.

The thing with Joe had been unreal as if in a fantasy, a sort of escape from his real life, but yes, he had to admit to himself he cared for the boy and it had not just been physical. Yet, on reflection, all their meetings had been short, and centred on the bedroom, although he had tried to engage Joe in conversation and other interests. Now that he looked back, it had always been Joe who wanted to go to bed. The more he reminded himself of their meetings, the starker the truth was that Joe had seduced him and he had been too weak to fight it. Joe was the villain of the piece, what a fool to let a young lad have such a hold over him. He should have been stronger and rejected the lad's advances.

Once Martin had established, in his own mind, that he was not at fault, he felt a little better and able to face the day. Fortunately, Tony had no appointments for him that evening so he decided he would go home early. He checked around the apartment, just to make sure that there were no traces of Joe ever having been there. He had washed the whisky glasses the night before and everything seemed to be in place. The only thing that was odd was that he could not find the cigarette case he kept on the coffee table and assumed Joe must have stolen it. He contented himself with the fact that it was a small price to pay for getting rid of the boy for good.

Picking up some papers and sliding them into his briefcase, he was about to leave when a key turned in the front door. His heart missed a beat, and for a moment he was paralysed, thinking maybe Joe had a key and was back again.

"Who's that?" he called out.

"It's only me, Mrs Black. I thought you'd be gone by now or I would have knocked. I hope I didn't frighten you."

The portly frame of his cleaning lady entered the room and he let out an audible sigh of relief.

"Oh, it's you. No, don't worry; I was just about to leave. See you next time no doubt. Bye." He swept past her and out of the apartment before she could even reply. He really could not face a half hour gossiping with Mrs Black.

As the Ferrari pulled out of the car park and headed towards the A48, he turned the stereo on full blast, The Ride of the Valkyries filled the car and he lost himself in the pulsating music. This was familiar territory; he could return to the real world and consign the last few months to the dump of history that never really happened.

He pulled up outside his London flat, eager to enter the safe confines of home. He desperately wanted to see Maddy, but of course, she would not be there, not being due back from her trip to Paris until the next day. Nevertheless, he had to talk to her; just to hear her speak would be enough.

Having parked the car, he took the lift to the flat and, as he walked in the front door, felt a warm feeling of reassurance. He was in his own domain, untouchable and strong again. He quickly looked through the post, nothing important, and went into the kitchen and switched the espresso machine on. He looked at his watch, twelve thirty; it would be one thirty in Paris.

On the off chance that she would not be in a meeting, he rang Maddy's mobile.

"Maddy? Can you speak or are you tied up?"

"I am rather tied up at the moment; can I ring you back in about an hour?"

"No problem, give me a call when you're free. Oh and by the way I love you."

"Love you too," her voice sounded a little surprised by his declaration of love; it was not that often he actually told her that.

Martin put the phone down and poured out his coffee, he took the cup into the living room and slumped into his armchair. *I'm really looking forward to her coming back,* he thought.

Maddy put her mobile down with two hands, she had to, they were tied together. She felt a little guilty when Martin had said he loved her, but it was only momentary. When the phone had rung, Peter had just tied her wrists together and was about to tie them to the headboard on the King size bed in their hotel. They were both naked and although they had spent most of the night making love, her appetite had not dulled. They had not left the bed since midnight the previous day, having had room service deliver breakfast to their room, consisting of Eggs Benedict and a bottle of Krug. Peter had suggested the bondage, not so much for its excitement, but more to get a little rest, although extremely fit, he was no match for Maddy's insatiable desires.

He finished by tying her ankles to the two bottom corner posts. She was now helpless and at his mercy, just the way she liked it!

He moved away and sat in the chair, his glass of Krug in his hand admiring the beautiful curves of her body.

"Peter, come on, don't tease me, make love to me," she looked at him in a plaintive way, almost childlike as though asking for an extra sweet.

He laughed. "You're going to have to wait, I need a rest, and this is the only way I can control you."

"You're so mean," she almost wailed. "I can't wait, I need you."

Peter just continued to smile.

"Please, Peter, please."

He could not resist, his self-control losing the battle with his desire. Slowly, he rose from the chair, his glass still half full of champagne, and walked to the bed. He sat beside her and trickled the champagne so that it slowly ran down over her breasts and he bent to lick it, as her nipples rose to the sensation of his tongue. Pouring more of the liquid onto her, it continued its passage down over her body followed by his tongue. She groaned as he carried on exploring her every curve until finally, the glass was empty. She wanted to wrap her arms around him and draw him into her, but the ties held firm. The agony and the ecstasy were almost too much to bear, and she gave a little scream as she climaxed.

Peter undid the knots and once loose, she jumped onto him, writhing against his body. If he hoped by satisfying her in the way he had she would be sated, he was sadly mistaken. Maddy had plans of her own and she would not be side-tracked.

It was nearly two hours later that she suddenly realised that she had promised to phone Martin after her 'meeting'. She rose from the bed, Peter was fast asleep, exhausted after all the activity of the last couple of hours, and walked to the bathroom. After a quick shower, she put on her make-up, dressed and checking that Peter was still sleeping, quietly slipped out of the bedroom and went downstairs to the hotel lounge.

She ordered a coffee and, having composed herself, phoned Martin.

"Sorry, darling, it took longer than I thought. You wouldn't believe how hard it was." She smiled to herself at the double entendre.

"Well, I just hope it's been worthwhile. I hope you've only spent money on the shop not buying more bags and shoes," he said it in half teasing manner. He had never been mean when it came to Maddy buying clothes for her own wardrobe.

"Yes, darling, it's been very rewarding, but I may have to come again." She struggled not to laugh out loud.

"Well, once this election is out of the way, I might join you and we can spend a long weekend, taking in the Opera house as well."

"That would be lovely. Anyway, I'll be home by lunchtime tomorrow, so can you book a table somewhere?"

"No problem; what about Simpsons on the Strand? It's always good for Sunday lunch."

"Yes, that sounds fine; why not ask Dick and Jenny if they would like to join us. Okay see you tomorrow. Bye, darling."

The phone went dead. Martin felt good. He would ring up Dick and Jenny straight away. The events of Friday evening now completely erased from his memory.

Chapter Twenty-Two

Martin had heard the news at his office and had left early to be at home to take in the full announcement on the News Twenty-Four programme. At last, the waiting was over, it was Thursday April 8th and Gordon Brown had called the general election for May 6th. The bastard had left it almost to the last minute and now there were only four weeks to canvass before polling day.

He switched the television on and watched Brown telling the world that he was asking the Queen to dissolve parliament. The race to Downing Street had started, and Martin had noticed how the opinion polls for the two main parties had been getting closer and closer. The Tories lead had been whittled down to just a few percent and the pundits were already talking about a hung parliament. He felt there was an even better chance of him doing well as an independent, especially with so many MPs standing down in the wake of the expenses scandal. His only slight worry was, as Kenilworth and Southam was a new constituency, no one could be really sure which way it would swing.

Having watched the same news repeated again and again, he finally dragged himself from the set and rang Tony.

"I take it you've heard?" There was a grunt at the other end of the line acknowledging that he had. "We need to get our nomination papers in quickly and start the canvassing. Have you got a proposer, seconder and the eight names we need for the nomination?"

"Martin, don't worry, it's all in hand and I've already been onto the printers to get posters printed. They have promised to have them here for Monday. I've also booked some advertising space in The Coventry Evening Telegraph and spoken to 'Mills' who have those bill boards you were asking about. I've managed to get some prominent spaces in all the villages, as well as half a dozen in Kenilworth and four in Southam. The only problem I have is the money has run out and I will need to pay for the printing on Monday."

"Tony, you're a star, what would I do without you. Don't worry about the money, I'll get my bank to transfer another twenty thousand straight away. When's my next speaking engagement?"

"Tomorrow, don't you remember? It's at the Women's Institute so put on your best smile."

"Don't you worry; I promise to be Prince Charming personified." They both laughed, but Tony knew that the women, especially the middle aged ones, found Martin very attractive and that counted for a lot in terms of votes.

Martin had arranged to take most of the month off from work, dividing his time, spending Mondays and Tuesdays in London, and the rest of the week in Kenilworth. Fortunately, with the impending election, business had slowed down and with a little help from his junior colleagues, he had managed to handle all current trading, keeping his customers relatively happy.

To his surprise, Maddy had been very supportive and had not complained when he had explained what his movements would be, in fact, she had even agreed to accompany him on the second weekend of the campaign. He wanted desperately to show her off to his future constituents and the opportunity had presented itself when the local paper had arranged for a 'Question Time' style debate with all of the candidates, to be held on Friday the 16th. Tony had said it would go down well if his wife attended the get together after the debate. The newspaper had hired a large hall and arranged for drinks for a select number of invited guests. Maddy had said she did not mind going to that particular event, but was really too busy to be with him all the time. For Martin, it was almost a complete turnaround from her often expressed disinterest of the whole 'circus' and he was more than pleased by her decision.

The Friday after the announcement, he had driven up to his apartment, arriving at about six o'clock, giving him enough time to shower, change and meet up with Tony before going to his first meeting as an official independent candidate.

As always, the apartment was immaculate. Mrs Black was certainly a treasure, there was never a thing out of place and he only wished his lady in London was as meticulous. He poured himself a gin and tonic, which he took into the bedroom so that he could drink it in between showering and dressing. He had just finished straightening his tie and making sure his aftershave was not too overpowering, when his mobile rang. He picked it up without even looking at the caller ID name.

The voice hit him like a kick to the stomach.

"Martin, its Joe."

Martin was shocked; he had never expected to hear from the lad again.

"I thought I told you never to call me again," he was shaking and he tried not to let his voice give away the anger he felt.

"I know, but I've got something I think you might want back and…"

"You can keep the fucking cigarette case, I guessed you'd stolen it," he interrupted almost shouting now, the bile rising in his throat.

"I'm not talking about the cigarette case; I'm talking about a photograph."

"What photograph? I don't know what you mean."

"I mean I have one of the pictures you took with your Christmas present. One of those action shots, as you used to say."

Martin felt the blood draining from him; surely, the boy was making it up. How could he have one, they were locked in one of his bedside drawers.

"It's not possible…"

"Just go and check."

Martin walked into the bedroom as if in a daze. Sitting on the bed, he reached into his pocket for his set of keys. Before trying the key in the lock, he instinctively pulled at the draw and to his horror, the draw slid open. His hands shaking, he reached inside and pulled out the pictures. With mounting fear, he counted them, there was one missing.

"Martin, Martin, are you still there?"

He could hear the boy shouting down the phone, but could not move his arms to put the phone to his ear; it was as if he was paralysed. Slowly, he regained his self-control and, taking a deep breath, spoke into the mobile.

"What do you want?" his voice was flat; he was totally at a loss.

"Now there's a good boy. What I want is very simple. I'll return the picture on condition, you pay me ten thousand pounds in cash. If you don't pay up, I'll go to the papers with the picture and tell them all about our little 'love affair'." He was sneering now; there was no compassion in his voice, more a sense of triumph.

"You want ten thousand pounds, are you mad? I can't get that sort of money in cash."

"Of course you can, and just thank your lucky stars I'm not greedy, you're a bloody millionaire. I'm letting you off pretty lightly so don't make me angry otherwise I might up the ante." The boy gave a hollow laugh; he was enjoying knowing that Martin would be squirming on the other end of the line. "You've got a week to come back to me and arrange payment. If I don't hear from you by this time next week, then you can forget all about being an MP, it'll be in all the papers the next day."

Before he could say anything, the line went dead and Martin sat, for a moment, on the edge of the bed trying to come to terms with the events of the last few minutes. How could he have been so stupid, why on earth had he kept those photos? He opened the draw and took out the remaining pictures taking them to the sink in the kitchen. One by one, he burnt them, flushing the ashes down the drain. If only he had done that the day after taking them then this nightmare would not be happening to him.

He noticed his glass was empty and although he needed to be leaving shortly for the meeting, poured himself another drink. He had to get control of himself, to focus his mind on his prepared speech, to block out all thoughts of Joe and his threat.

Maybe I should just pay what he wants and be done with it, he thought, but knew in his heart of hearts that once he paid, the boy would come back for more and more, going on bleeding him. He would have to find a way to get rid of the threat once and for all.

Having reached the conclusion that Joe would have to be dealt with in some way, he felt a lot calmer and finishing his drink, picked up his notes and slipped them into his briefcase.

It was not far to the hall where the meeting was being held so he decided to walk, hoping the fresh air would clear his head and give him more time to concentrate his thoughts on the speech he was about to give.

The meeting had gone very well and he felt what he had said had been well received. A number of the audience had stayed behind to ask him individual questions on local matters, which were obviously more important to them than Trident and Afghanistan. His only disappointment had been when a young couple, sitting near the front on the right hand side, got up and left before he had finished speaking. He had wondered if he had said something to offend them, but on reflection, could not recall saying anything too controversial.

Perhaps, he thought, *they were supporters of another party and they had heard all they needed to.* This had been the first time anyone had walked out on him, but he suspected it would not be the last and no doubt he would have to get used to it. The hecklers, Tony had warned, would make their presence known especially if his opponents perceived him to be a threat.

After the meeting, Martin asked Tony if he would like to have a pint with him before he went home, he felt the need to wind down after the upset that Joe's phone call had engendered. Tony had been surprised by the invitation, in the past, Martin had always been keen to get back to his apartment without any delay, but was happy to accompany his boss for a drink.

"How do you think things are going?" he asked Tony, once they had their drinks and found a couple of free seats.

"I think we're doing really well. I've had a lot of offers of support and volunteers to deliver your election literature."

Martin smiled, he was amazed at Tony's enthusiasm, he had been a real find, not like that little bastard Joe. The two men sat for a while discussing the diary for the next two weeks and before they realised the time, it was eleven o'clock. Martin rose, thanked Tony again for all his hard work, wished him goodnight and walked back to the apartment, his mind inevitably going back to Joe's phone call.

Once home, he slumped down in the armchair, he had to think rationally. Although his first thought had been to pay Joe the ten thousand, he had quickly dismissed the idea; blackmailers don't go away that easily. He had to find a way of making sure Joe never came back. The more he mulled over the problem, the more he thought the only way to stop him was to eliminate him. Martin was repelled the thought had even crossed his mind. There had to be another solution, though what that was he had

131

no idea. Finally, he went to bed, the problem unresolved. He would look at it again in the cold light of day and, when he was back in London, maybe he would come up with an answer.

Chapter Twenty-Three

Maddy had left a note for him when he returned home.
'I have asked Gill and Alan round for a meal tonight, hope that is okay with you? I will be home as early as possible and have arranged with The New Delhi to deliver the food for eight thirty. Love, Maddy.'

He smiled as he read the note. Gill and Alan were good company, and it was just what he needed to take his mind off of the problem of Joe. The more he thought of Maddy, the more he realised what a fool he had been to risk everything by seeing the lad, and he needed Maddy, she was his rock.

Maddy arrived back from the boutique just after six and found Martin in the dining room laying the table.

"Hi, how are things in election land?" She put her arms around him and reached up to kiss him.

"Good, but I'd rather be here with you." He bent his head and their lips met, Martin holding the kiss longer than normal.

"You old smoothie, you know you love all this playing at being an MP." She smiled at him.

"Oh be fair, I'm not playing at it, I'm serious. You'll be laughing on the other side of your face if I win."

"Yes, yes, I won't tease you anymore, but can we have a politics free night tonight? I don't want you and Alan falling out. He already thinks you're a let down by standing against the Conservative candidate."

"Okay, I promise. Now would you like a drink before you get changed?"

"Please, gin and tonic would be great, but not too heavy on the gin, it's usually a long night when those two come round and I don't want to get drunk too early."

He grinned at her, he knew exactly what she meant. Alan could drink wine like water and invariably they had to pour him into a taxi at the end of the night.

Martin made the drinks whilst Maddy had her shower and then, while she was making up her mind what to wear, he had showered and dressed. After another thirty minutes, she emerged from the bedroom, wearing a red, very low cut, dress with matching shoes that had heels so high, he wondered how she could balance on them, let alone walk. The dress was figure hugging and showed her curves off to perfection. He could see she was not wearing a bra, which was usually a signal that she would be expecting him to perform at the end of the evening. He was unusually excited by the prospect and made a mental note not to keep pace with Alan, or he would not be in any state to comply with the unspoken request.

Just after eight, the intercom buzzed and Martin answered, releasing the lock to the main entrance. Within a couple of minutes, Gill and Alan were in the flat, and Martin was pouring glasses of Dom Perignon.

Alan was an architect, a senior partner in a very successful practice, and was one of Martin's oldest friends, having met at university. He was part of the group who went skiing together and had been married to Gill for ten years. They had two children, boys, aged six and eight. The children were no problem as they had a live-in nanny who babysat for them. Martin had often wondered why they bothered to have children as it seemed the nanny spent more time with the boys than either Gill or Alan.

Alan was shorter than Martin and had the first signs of a middle-aged spread, a legacy of good living and hard drinking. His wife was stick thin, together, they reminded one of Laurel and Hardy, though no one actually said so in their presence. Gill did not work and seemed to spend most of her time either shopping or having coffee with her girlfriends. In spite of their different life styles, Maddy and Gill had hit it off from the first time they met. Martin had been pleased that the four of them got on so well together.

They were on their second glass of champagne when the food arrived. Maddy had warmed some dishes and quickly transferred the different courses on to them, then left them in the oven to keep warm whilst they ate their starters.

Within the hour, they had finished their meals, and Maddy and Gill cleared the dishes away and went into the kitchen to make coffee, leaving the two men alone.

Martin poured two large brandies. He did not even bother to ask Alan if he wanted one, he knew brandy was his favourite tipple.

"I'm glad we have a few moments alone, I wanted to ask for your advice on a little problem that I've got," Martin looked at Alan, his voice lowered in a conspiratorial way.

"I'm intrigued, what's the problem?"

"This is in the strictest confidence; you must promise not to tell a soul."

"Yes, yes, I promise, now go on what is it." Alan lent forward so that he could hear every word.

"I'm being blackmailed," Martin blurted out.

"What! Who? How?" Alan asked in disbelief.

"It's a long story, but an old one I'm afraid. You know I'm standing for Parliament?" He raised his hand to stop Alan interrupting. "Yes, I know you don't approve, but leave that aside for the moment. I bought a flat in Kenilworth, so that I could be near the constituents, thought it would look good," he added by way of explanation, "Well, I employed a local man as my agent, good man I can tell you, and he took on two part-time girls to help in the office. I'm afraid I got a bit too friendly with one of them, and we've been seeing a lot of each other and I do mean a lot." He sniggered at this to emphasise the nature of the relationship.

"You dirty old man, I never thought you had it in you. Until Maddy came along, you never seemed to bother with women." Alan was grinning, almost as if he was enjoying Martin's so-called problem. "So have you dumped her and is she blackmailing you?"

"No, it gets more complicated. One night we got a bit drunk and I took some photographs of the two of us in rather compromising positions, and I stupidly kept them. The problem arose when her brother, who is still at school, volunteered to help deliver my election leaflets and he came to the apartment to meet me. It turns out he is a bit of an unsavoury character and has been in trouble with the law; she's been trying to straighten him out. Anyway, he took a fancy to my silver cigarette case, which he pocketed but worse still, while I was in the bathroom, he must have gone into my bedroom to see if there was any money lying about. He found the pictures of his sister and me, and took one.

Now he is threatening to send it to the papers unless I pay him ten thousand pounds."

Martin took a large gulp of his brandy, he had kept as near to the truth as he could, whilst making it appear that he had just been one of the lads who had made a mistake.

"Is the girl involved in the blackmail?"

"I'm sure she isn't, she acts as though nothing has happened and I don't think she's that good an actress. I'm at my wits end. I can afford to pay him, that wouldn't be a problem, but I think he will just come back for more."

"You're right, once a blackmailer has his claws into you, they won't let go."

"I don't know what to do and he's given me till next Saturday to come up with the money."

Just then, they heard the sound of voices and the chink of cups as the girls headed towards the dining room.

"Look, give me a ring on Monday, I may have a solution," Alan just managed to finish speaking as Maddy entered the room.

Martin had been at the office since eight o'clock, but had waited until nine before phoning Alan.

He tapped his fingers impatiently on his desk while he waited for the phone to be answered. Eventually, Alan came on the line.

"Martin, how are you? By the way, thanks for a great evening on Saturday. Gill was quite pleased because I didn't get steaming." He laughed as he thought back to last Saturday. For once, he hadn't over indulged and had been rewarded with a romantic end to the night. "I take it you're ringing about the little problem you told me about."

"Yes. You said you might have a solution."

"Not a solution exactly, but I know of someone who could perhaps help you. His name is Stan Kenton, runs a private detective agency but really he's more of a problem solver. He is ex-army, SAS, I think, and can handle himself. He did a job for my brother who was having trouble getting paid for some building work. The customer was refusing to pay and had even threatened our Jim if he came calling. Well, Stan collected the money and sorted the problem, and Jim never heard another word. He charged him ten percent with a minimum fee of a thousand pounds. I've spoken to Jim and he gave me Stan's phone number, so if you want to ring him, you can say he was recommended by Jim."

"He sounds just the man. Thanks for that." Martin took the number down and rang off. He immediately dialled the number and was answered by a man with an East End accent.

"Stan Kenton speaking, how can I help you?"

"Good morning, my name is Martin De Glanville; I have been given your number by Jim Renwick, I understand you did some work for him."

"Yeah, I remember, collecting some money from some smart arse that had refused to cough up. It was an easy job really. Are you in need of something similar?"

"Not exactly, it's a bit more delicate, I'm being blackmailed, and I need someone who is discreet and can keep things confidential."

"Discretion is my middle name," he laughed. "Seriously, I give an undertaking in writing that any information you give me will not be disclosed to a third party, my reputation is at stake so don't worry on that score."

"Right, can we meet so that I can give you the details?"

"No problem, where do you want to meet, at your office or home?"

For a moment, Martin panicked, he didn't want the man at his flat and neither did he want him at the office. Too much explaining would be required.

"There's a pub, just around the corner from my office, the King William, in the city, can you be there in half an hour?"

"Okay, see you in half an hour."

"Just a minute, how will I know you?"

"I'll be wearing a red tie." He did not wait for Martin to say anything further and put the phone down.

Martin looked at his watch, twenty past nine. The pub was only a couple of minutes away so he would just have time to dictate a couple of letters before he left.

There were only a few people in the pub and Martin looked around to see if anyone was sporting a red tie. Having established there wasn't, he walked to the bar and ordered a ginger beer. It was too early in the day for anything stronger and he wanted his wits about him when talking to Kenton. He sat down at a table facing the door so he could see anyone who entered.

He went over in his mind the story he would tell Kenton. It was basically as he had outlined to Alan. He was pleased that the version he had made up when explaining to Alan about his 'problem' had sounded plausible, more importantly, he had not had to expose his guilty secret.

He had been there for about five minutes when Kenton entered. He immediately saw the tie and held his hand up to indicate to the man to join him. Kenton walked across and held out his hand.

"You must be Mr De Glanville. Stan Kenton," he said

"Please, call me Martin. Sit down; I'll get you a drink?"

"I don't drink, thank you, but a glass of lemonade would be fine."

Martin walked to the bar and returned with the lemonade. He studied the man as he drank half of the glass in one long draft. He was about five eleven, lean with a tanned face that looked as though he had spent a lot of time in a hot climate, Afghanistan maybe, when he was in the army. He had short-cropped hair, which was brown turning to grey and brown eyes set deep in his head. There was a small scar on his chin. He looked what he was, battle hardened.

"So, tell me about your problem."

Martin repeated the story he had told Alan, finishing with the fact he had only five days left in which to pay the boy.

"Let me get this right, firstly, are you prepared to pay the money to get back this photograph? Secondly, do you want me to make sure he never bothers you again?"

"Well, I don't really want to pay him anything, but if I have to and you can assure me he won't be coming back for more then, reluctantly, I'll pay."

"Look, from what you told me about the kid, he's just a chancer and I think I can scare him off with a few threats. If I can get your property back without you paying, then my fee will be two thousand pounds plus expenses, if you have to pay the money, then I'll only charge a thousand plus ex's. Is that okay?"

"I'm happy with that, but you will need to move fast."

"I'll email you the terms and if you can email me back with your acceptance I'll start straight away. Do you have the boy's address?"

Martin suddenly realised that he had never known where Joe lived; their only contact was via the phone.

"I don't have his address only his mobile number."

"That's okay, email it to me." He handed Martin a business card with his details on and Martin handed him one of his

"Right, thanks, Mr De Glanville, I look forward to hearing from you." He stood up and turning headed for the door.

Martin had been back at his desk for a little under an hour when the email came through from Kenton with his terms and a letter of confidentiality. He quickly read it and, satisfying himself that everything was okay, replied agreeing to the terms and giving Joe's mobile number. He felt a sense of relief as though a burden had been lifted from him. Kenton had impressed him that here was a man who would clinically and coldly deal with the matter, and he would never hear from Joe again.

Chapter Twenty-Four

Kenton was not an ostentatious man; he drove a pale blue four-year-old Renault Megan, the sort of car that went unnoticed, which was just the way he liked it. His business was very successful; his reputation for sorting out problems passing by word of mouth and, since leaving the army, he had earned himself a tidy sum. He could easily have afforded a smarter car but expensive cars attracted attention and he preferred to remain anonymous.

Having received the confirmation from Martin, he had wasted no time in setting about sorting out his 'bit of trouble'. Although he had a couple of other jobs on the go, there was nothing that demanded his attention immediately, so had decided the sooner he made contact with Joe the better.

Joe had been taken aback when Kenton phoned him and explained that Martin had asked him to act as the intermediary in paying for the return of the photograph. Joe was surprised Martin had told anyone else about their relationship, thinking that would have been the last thing he wanted to do.

"Did he tell you I want ten grand?" Joe asked.

"Yes, I will have it by Wednesday, but I will need to see proof you have the picture before I am prepared to hand it over. I can be in Coventry on Wednesday afternoon, can you meet me then?"

"Where are you phoning from?"

"London."

"Yeah, no problem. Are you coming by train or driving?"

"Driving, give me your post code; I have a satnav so I can come straight to you."

"I'll give you the code but I don't want to meet at my home. There's a pub just around the corner The Butts Retreat, opposite Coventry Rugby Club, I'll meet you there."

Kenton wrote the code down and made a mental note to check out exactly where the boy lived in case he needed to make a return call sometime in the future.

"Right, I'll see you at the pub on Wednesday at four. I'll ring your mobile when I get there, okay?"

"No problem."

The boy sounded pleased with himself, Kenton thought, *he may not feel so happy when I've finished with him.*

He reported back to Martin that he had made contact and had arranged to meet Joe that Wednesday. He did not ask for any money as he was confident the boy would hand over the photograph with a little 'persuasion'.

Kenton pulled into the car park of the pub and switched off the engine. Taking his mobile out of its hands-free harness in the car, he scrolled down until Joe's number came up and pressed send. The phone rang a few times before automatically going to answer phone. He was not happy. If that little bastard was messing him around, he would have to teach him a lesson. Kenton was meticulous and slackness or prevarication in others irritated him more than anything else. He sat in his car drumming his fingers on the wheel, wondering why the lad was not answering. He looked at his watch; it was five minutes to four. He waited until dead on four o'clock and tried the number again. This time the boy answered.

"I'm here," Kenton said tersely.

"Where?"

"In the car park, a blue Megan, it's the only bloody car there for Christ's sake," his irritation getting the better of him.

Kenton looked in his mirror and saw a young man approaching the car. He had expected a schoolboy, this lad looked about nineteen, tall and well built, maybe he wasn't Joe. The young man came up to the car and tapped the window. Kenton opened the door and got out. If anything happened, sitting in his car, he was at a disadvantage.

"I'm Joe," the lad said.

"Stan Kenton." Kenton did not offer his hand; this was not a social call. "Have you got the picture with you?"

"No, it's somewhere safe, but I can take you to it."

"Okay." Kenton turned to lock the car door.

"It's not around here, we need to drive to the place."

"Get in then," Kenton ordered.

Joe had a light haversack on his back, and before getting into the car, slipped his arms out of the straps and slung it on the back seat.

"What's in the bag?" Kenton was curious; he liked to know exactly what he was dealing with.

"It's only a trowel; the picture's buried in a secret place."

Kenton looked quizzical, how on earth could you bury a picture and not ruin it.

"Where are we heading for?" he asked the boy.

"Kenilworth," he replied.

He pulled out of the car park, and followed Joe's directions to the ring road then out of the city past the station and a large park on the left hand side and up to traffic lights. The signpost indicated Kenilworth was straight over the lights.

"How far is it?" Kenton asked.

Joe had not uttered a word other than give directions since he got in the car.

"Only a couple of miles, it's a straight road into the town until you hit some traffic lights then turn left, about a hundred yards down that road there's a park, Abbey Fields, go into the car park."

Neither said another word until Kenton had turned left at the lights in Kenilworth and had nearly driven past the entrance to the park, had not Joe shouted to him to pull up.

He steered the car in to a free space and switched off the engine.

"Now where do we go?"

"You'll see, but before I take you there, have you got the money?"

Kenton reached inside his jacket and pulled out a large manila envelope, it was about an inch thick.

"There's two hundred fifty pound notes in there all neatly wrapped, straight from the bank. So come on I'm interested to know how you buried a photo and expect it not to have rotted away."

"The answer to that is simple, I put it in a silver cigarette case. Didn't Martin tell you I had that?" The lad sneered feeling very superior at the man's apparent lack of any common sense.

Kenton had picked up the attitude of the boy and thought even more this lad needed a lesson in manners if nothing else. Joe got out of the car, opened the rear door and grabbed his haversack. He slammed the door shut and indicated that Kenton should follow him. All the time Kenton was struggling to keep his temper, the boy's arrogance was getting under his skin but he knew he had to stay calm and not let Joe rile him, this was a job and he was a professional.

He followed the boy along the path towards a play area where empty swings were swaying in the wind, any children having by now left for their tea. Apart from a couple of people exercising their dogs, the park was empty, even the cafeteria was closed. Joe walked past the play area and stopped next to the hedge that ran across the park. He had put his haversack down on the grass next to what looked like an old lamp standard, but without the lamp.

"It's buried at the base of this pole," he said to Kenton. "It's only a few inches deep, won't take long."

Joe had the trowel in his hand and had started to scrape away the turf surrounding the base of the pole. It came away easily as though it had only just been laid. He thought it odd as he remembered he taken a lot of trouble to stamp the turf down so that it would not look as though it had ever been disturbed in the first place. He continued digging, expecting to hear the sound of the metal trowel hitting the case, but nothing. He dug some more, widening the area so that the hole got larger and larger.

Kenton stood about a yard away watching the lad dig; he seemed to get more agitated the more he dug.

"What's the problem?" Kenton asked.

"I don't understand, it's not here." The lad looked at Kenton in disbelief, he had now dug a hole about two feet in diameter and at least a foot deep but had nothing to show for it.

"Look, son, are you pulling my pisser? I thought you said it was buried here, are you sure you remembered the right spot."

"Yes, yes, this is the spot. I don't understand, no one saw me bury it, I made sure of that." He was panicking now; without the picture, it was only his word against Martin's if he tried to expose him.

Kenton looked at the boy and realised that he was telling the truth, after all, there was no benefit in lying, the lad was not

143

expecting to get ten thousand pounds just for digging up a cigarette case.

"So it would seem that you have nothing to blackmail my client with," Kenton sneered as he spoke; he was enjoying the boy's discomfort.

"But what about the money? I promise I won't go to the press with my story if you pay me."

Kenton laughed. "You really are pathetic, go to the press, my client will deny it and without proof, no paper in the land would print it. It would be your word against Mr De Glanville's and we both know who will be believed, don't we?"

He reached in his pocket and withdrew the manila envelope.

"Here, take this for your trouble." He threw the package to the lad who caught it and tore it open like an animal would tear at its prey.

The look of horror mixed with shock when the boy pulled out what he thought would be fifty-pound notes, but turned out to be nothing but scrap paper, neatly cut to banknote sizes, brought a smile to Kenton's face.

"You fucking bastard." Joe's face was bright red with rage. "You can't do that, we had a deal."

"Yes, and you didn't keep your end of it, did you? Now listen, sonny, you got too big for your boots, you're playing out of your league, just go home and lick your wounds."

"Come on, then you can drop me back to the city?"

Kenton let out a laugh; he could not believe the gall of the boy.

"You also need a lesson in manners and I think a little while to cool off so I'm going to let you walk home."

Without another word, Kenton turned and walked back to the car. He was still chuckling to himself as he opened the door. In the distance, he could see Joe standing next to the excavation he had dug.

Kenton drove slowly back to Coventry, the events in the park had complicated what he thought would be a straightforward job. It seemed obvious that the boy had indeed buried the photo in the park and someone unknown had come across it. What bothered Kenton was if that person was a potential blackmailer or not, or if not knowing who the participants in the photograph were, would just throw it away and keep the case. He decided he

144

needed to try and discover who had taken the case, and that would mean going back to the park and asking a few questions, but that would have to wait for the next day.

As he drove back to Coventry retracing the route he had taken out, he found himself passing a park, now on his right hand side, and as the road curved round taking him towards the ring road, he noticed a couple of hotels on his right and pulled into the car park of the first one. It was a small hotel, the sort he preferred, that looked as though it catered mainly for commercial travellers, it was ideal.

He booked in for two nights, not sure whether that would be enough, but knowing he had to be in London on Saturday afternoon. It would have to do, if he didn't find anything out over the next two days, he could always come back.

He went to his room and thought back on his encounter with Joe. He smiled again at the thought of the boy and how he had still expected to be paid even though he had lost his 'evidence'. Typical little chancer, thinking he could make a fast buck. Kenton had been right when he guessed the boy was playing a lone hand and even if they had found the picture, there had been no chance of actually paying any money over. He would have just scared the kid to death and that would have been that. Kenton had handled a lot tougher characters than Joe and had always come out on top.

He lay back on the bed and dozed for about an hour, waking up to find that it was seven thirty. He took a shower and as he hadn't brought a full change of clothes with him, only a couple of spare shirts, he had to stay in the grey suit he had worn all day. In a way, it was useful, he fitted the image of a rep up in the area on business, in fact, just what he was.

Kenton ate in the hotel restaurant, and being teetotal retired to his bedroom to watch television before going to sleep. He wanted an early night as he had decided to spend the next day at the park and needed to be there as soon as it opened.

He was up at seven, finished breakfast and was in the car park for eight. He had been surprised by how busy the dining room had been, it seemed everyone had the same idea as him.

Although it was early, the roads were busy with early morning commuters making their way into the city. However, most of the traffic was going in the opposite direction to him, that is until he crossed the main A45 road when he suddenly got caught in traffic heading for Leamington and Warwick. It was not far to the park and he recognised buildings he had passed the previous day, so knew he was going in the right direction. He turned the corner at the traffic lights and this time remembered to slow down in time for the entrance to the park.

Fortunately, it was not raining, but the weather was not exactly warm and the thought crossed his mind that maybe the mums would not be out with their children if there was no sun. He locked the car, and strolled along the path towards the play area and past it to the post. The hole Joe had dug the day before was still there, looking like a miniature bomb crater amongst the unspoilt turf. He looked around, hoping to see some sign of life, but apart from a man throwing a stick for his dog, there was no one. He hoped the dog owner would make his way past him so that he could speak to him, he did not really want to go chasing people across the park to ask his questions, he wanted to appear more casual.

While he was pondering what to do next, a white van pulled up to the cafeteria and the driver got out, went to the back of the vehicle, and, opening the doors, started to unload some boxes. Kenton strolled across to him.

"Good morning, do you work here?" Kenton asked the man.

"Sorry, mate, I just deliver here, they usually open up about nine thirty to ten. I think they please themselves, nobody seems to check up on them." He looked at Kenton then suddenly realised he might have said the wrong thing. "You're not from the council, are you? I was only joking about the opening times."

Kenton grinned. "Don't worry, I'm not from the council. I'm just trying to find someone who might have found a valuable cigarette case a friend of mine, thinks he lost around here. There's a reward for it if I can find the person who found it," he added the last bit in the hope that even if the driver knew nothing, word would get around about the reward.

"Can't help you there, I'm sorry, but when they open up, one of the girls might have seen something."

Kenton looked around, one or two people had come along the path, but they had all being walking at a brisk pace, as though using the park as a route to work. He really wanted the strollers or the mums with pushchairs. The sort of people who would not mind being stopped and asked for their help.

Eventually, two girls in their early twenties arrived at the cafeteria, and unbolted the shutters to reveal a counter stacked with crisps and chocolate bars. Kenton watched as they took the boxes the delivery driver had left and opened them. Inside were freshly made sandwiches and cakes, which the girls transferred to the display cabinets below the counter. He made a move to talk to them, thinking he would get short shrift if he disturbed their preparations, instead, he sat on the bench opposite and watched fascinated as they went about what was obviously a well-rehearsed routine.

Kenton had learnt, from his days in the army, the need for patience. Not overreacting, but waiting for the right moment, had saved his life on more than one occasion. He was in no hurry; he had all day and tomorrow if needed.

The girls had finally unpacked everything and after a quick wipe down of the serving counter looked at each other as if waiting for a reward for their efforts. Kenton rose from his seat and walked up to the counter.

"Can I have a cup of tea please, strong no sugar?"

"Will you serve the gentleman, Sandra? I've just got to nip out the back."

The girl called Sandra nodded and held a cup under the water boiler that was sizzling away at the rear of the booth.

"Help yourself to milk," she said, as she pushed the mug of steaming tea towards Kenton.

He looked around, and then spied a basket, with cartons of milk piled in it, at the end of the counter.

"That will be two pounds fifty please."

He reached in his pocket pulled out some change and counted out the right amount. The tea was piping hot and there was no way he could drink it yet. He made no move to leave the counter, which prompted Sandra to ask if there was anything else he wanted. This was just the opportunity he was looking for and he seized it with both hands.

"Well, you might be able to help, do you work here every day?"

"Yes, me and Di, except for holidays, of course. Why do you ask?"

"A friend of mine has lost a very valuable cigarette case, well, its sentimental value more than just money, and he is convinced he lost it in this park, somewhere around here he thinks. The last time he remembers using it was when he stopped for a smoke over by that post. He'd been exercising his dog and stopped for a rest. I just wondered if you or your friend might have seen someone pick it up, or if it had been handed in to you."

Kenton realised his story was a bit long winded, but wanted it to sound as plausible as possible. It was a long shot that anyone would hand it in, he had little faith in the honesty of the human race.

As he spoke, the other girl, Di, returned and Sandra repeated Kenton's story to her. She shook her head when Sandra posed the question. Sandra turned to Kenton, an apologetic look on her face.

"Sorry, we can't help you, but if you leave your name and phone number, if we hear anything, I'll give you a ring."

Kenton took out one of his business cards and ringed his mobile number, and handed it to her with a curt 'thank you'.

He returned to the bench seat and finished his mug of tea. This was going to be like looking for a needle in a haystack.

As the morning slowly approached midday, one or two mothers with small children drifted in to the playing area. Kenton noticed, as they passed, they all seemed to give him the same half-curious, half-worried look and the thought struck him that he must look strange, a man in a suit sitting for ages just watching the mums and their kids. The last thing he wanted was someone reporting him as a suspected paedophile. He had spoken to a couple of the mums, repeating his story of his friend's loss, but none had known anything and had not really been interested in talking to him. He thought that maybe he was wasting his time. If someone had gone to the trouble of digging down to find the case, then they must have some idea of its value.

He decided to get something to eat and had almost reached the car park when his mobile rang. There was no caller ID so it was not anyone who he knew.

"Hello, Kenton speaking."

"Hello, this is Sandra… from the café in Abbey Fields… you spoke to me earlier about your friends lost cigarette case. Well, I was talking to Di about it and she reminded me of a chap that we often see who has one of those detector things they use to look for buried treasure."

"You mean a metal detector," Kenton interrupted her.

"Yes, that's right. Well, I'd forgotten all about him, we get so used to seeing him wandering around, he's almost like a piece of the scenery."

Kenton knew exactly what she meant, he had often asked people if anyone had called at their house and they would say no one until he mentioned the postman or the dustman and they always replied 'oh they don't count, do they'.

"Do you know how I can get in touch with this man?" Kenton was interested; this might be the breakthrough he needed.

"I don't know where he lives but I'll ask around for you if you like."

"Thank you, that would be great, if you could get his name and address. When do you think you will have the information?"

"I'll ask this evening and ring you."

Kenton got into his car feeling a lot happier; this was the most promising lead he had. It made sense that someone actually looking for buried treasure might unearth the hidden case. If he could get to speak to the man and offer him a small reward, then he could wrap the whole thing up and be back in London with the best part of two thousand pounds in his bank account.

He drove back to his hotel and put in a call to Martin. There was no answer and after a couple of rings, the message service clicked in. He left a short message asking Martin to ring as soon he could. He knew that Martin was actually in Kenilworth, but did not want him to make contact other than by phone, as he would be tied up with meetings for the election. There was nothing more that Kenton could do until he received a call from Sandra, so decided to walk the half mile into the city centre and have a look round.

He knew very little about Coventry except for the legend of Lady Godiva, the 1940 bombing by the Germans, which almost flattened the place and of course, the new Cathedral which had been built in the sixties. He was not a religious man, but nevertheless, headed for the two cathedrals which stood next to each other. The one just a shell following the air raids and the new one, designed by Sir Basil Spence, an example of modern architecture at its best.

149

After spending some time admiring the building and its famous painting by Sutherland, he walked into the adjoining visitor centre that gave a potted history of the wartime devastation. Being an ex-soldier, it was this that interested him the most and he marvelled at the fortitude of the British people who had suffered six years of war. At least, when he had been in a war he was able to fight back, but for years, people in places like Coventry had to suffer what was at the time a very one sided attack.

He had been so interested in his exploration of the city that he had not noticed how quickly the time was passing. It was now five thirty and he began to make his way back to his hotel so he could be in his room when Martin phoned.

Once back in his room, he switched on the TV and tuned the channel to news twenty-four. It was the same as always, another soldier killed in Afghanistan, the politicians each blaming the other side for the state of the economy and another stabbing of a teenager. He switched it off; it was too depressing to watch.

His mobile suddenly burst into life and thinking it was Martin he answered.

"Hi, thanks for ringing back."

"I've got that name for you." He was surprised to hear a woman's voice; it was Sandra from the park.

"Oh great, sorry, you caught me off guard, I thought you were someone else, I've been expecting a call." He wondered why on earth he was explaining all this to Sandra, all he had to do was take the call!

"That's okay, have you got a piece of paper?"

He reached for the pad and pencil that were lying on the table.

"Fire away."

Sandra read out the name and address, unfortunately, she did not have a postcode but explained it was only a short distance from the park and gave him the directions.

"His name is Shakespeare, the same as the playwright; you know Stratford and all that. Apparently, he is known as Will to his friends, but I don't know what his real name is. I hope that is of some help."

"Yes, that's very helpful, thank you. I'll pop over tomorrow with a little something for your trouble."

"Oh thanks very much, see you, bye."

He felt very pleased with the way things were falling into place. Fifty quid would be a fair amount to pay the girls and he could put it down to expenses.

Martin did not phone until a quarter to nine, by which time, he had finished dinner and was sitting, drinking coffee in the lounge bar.

"Sorry it's so late; I got your message but didn't have time to ring earlier. As soon as the meeting finished, we went straight out for a few drinks and I've only just got away."

Kenton understood, Martin had explained how important he took his candidature for the election; he also knew that Martin's wife was joining him on Friday, so would not want her knowing anything about their dealings.

"I just wanted to up-date you on what's happening." Kenton spent about five minutes filling in the details of yesterday's meeting with Joe and the discovery that the picture was no longer in Joe's possession.

"So, let me get this clear. There's no chance of Joe blackmailing me because he has no evidence, is that right?"

"Yes."

"But you now think someone else may have the picture, this Will Shakespeare fellow?"

"That's right and I'm going over to check up on him tomorrow, it's too late tonight, and offer him a reward for the return of the case. I don't think he will be bothered about the picture of you and this girl, even if he recognises you. Apparently, he is a teacher, so hardly the blackmailing type. I'll tell him the case is a family heirloom and offer five hundred pounds reward, is that okay with you?

"Yes, yes, whatever you think."

Martin sounded troubled. Kenton had thought he would be pleased by the news and was puzzled by his reaction. Martin had sanctioned the amount so at least he would not have to pay it out of his fee.

"I'll ring you tomorrow, hopefully, with the news that I've got your property back."

"Thanks, bye."

Martin turned the phone off. He was worried by this turn of events, if this teacher had seen the photo and recognised Martin then he might still be exposed. He just hoped that Kenton was as good as he had been told. The sooner he could destroy that picture the better.

Kenton was still thinking about the muted response he had received from Martin, he had expected he would be pleased that Joe was off his back, but he had not come across as showing much enthusiasm. Maybe there was more to this than Martin had told him. He pushed the thought to the back of his mind. He had a job to complete and two thousand pounds for a couple of days' work was good money, why complicate things.

Kenton did not rush down to breakfast; he had decided to let the restaurant clear, have a leisurely meal and read the newspaper. He planned to visit the park and give Sandra her 'reward', and then find the house where Will lived. He knew there would not be anyone there, but liked to check everything out before he actually made contact. He planned to call at the house early in case the teacher planned to go out later.

Having read the morning paper from cover to cover, Kenton went to reception and paid his bill, making sure he had a copy of the invoice to submit with his expenses when he sent in his account to Martin.

The day was sunny and he was in a good mood, with any luck, he would be back in London that evening, the cigarette case safely in his possession.

Sandra and Di were serving a group of elderly ladies when he arrived at the cafeteria, and he waited to one side until they had all been served. Sandra had seen him arrive and smiled to let him know she had seen him.

"Hello," she greeted him as he moved up to counter, the ladies having taken the tea and cakes to a nearby table.

"Good morning, as promised, a little thank you for all your help." He handed her a fifty-pound note.

"Thanks very much. I hope you get your friends case back." The two girls were both smiling; they had not expected as much as fifty pounds.

"Well, just keep your fingers crossed for me and hope this Will fellow did find it."

Having kept his promise, he walked back to his car, but on reaching it, changed his mind, and decided to walk to Will's house and leave the car in the park, Sandra had said it was only a couple of streets away and he had all day to spare.

Sandra had been spot on with her directions and within ten minutes, he had located the street. He was a little taken aback when he found that the number he had been given was in fact that of a flat, one of four in a small block. He had assumed he was looking for a house. He checked the names on the list outside the main entrance and confirmed Mr & Mrs Shakespeare lived at No 4. On the off chance someone might be home, he rang their bell and waited but after a couple more rings, with no response, he gave up and left.

Deciding to go back at about five o'clock, he checked his watch, it was not yet midday, he had about five hours to fill. On the way back to collect his car, he stopped off at a newsagent and brought a local paper. Once back in his car, he scanned the paper looking for the entertainment page. He found the cinema listings and the address of the nearest one, it was back in Coventry. He entered the postcode into the satnav and a map showing the location came on the screen. The cinema was just off the ring road at the same junction as the one he had used to meet Joe, but inside the ring road. He had remembered seeing an ice rink when he first came to meet Joe and guessed the cinema would be in that complex. A trip back to Coventry and a couple of hours in the cinema would use up the time nicely.

He pulled out of the car park and headed back to Coventry, retracing the journey he had made with Joe. The cinema was well sign posted and it had an adjacent car park. He parked the car and walked around the corner to the entrance. Inside, all the screens were listed with the different films that were showing. Kenton was not a regular cinema goer and was not really bothered what he saw; it was just a way of killing time, so opted for the picture that was due to start now. He would probably fall asleep anyway, but at least he would be in a comfortable seat.

The film was a romantic comedy and he realised, almost straight away, it had been a mistake choosing it, but he persevered and, apart from a section in the middle when he had dropped off, managed to endure the whole performance. He came out and looked at his watch, just after four, time for a cup of coffee and then back to Kenilworth to meet Mr Shakespeare.

Chapter Twenty-Five

He had been going over in his mind how to approach the teacher, and, after numerous ideas, decided the simplest way was to come out and ask if he had unearthed the case. The only thing that bothered him was that he would have to change the story about his friend walking his dog and losing the case, which would not account for the fact that it was buried. The best answer was to stick fairly closely to the truth, that it had been stolen by a young lad who worked for the owner and in his panic had buried it, planning to return, dig up the case and sell it. He knew that while the story sounded plausible, it was liable to be pulled apart by anyone who was at all astute, he just hoped the offer of a reward would stop the man asking too many awkward questions, especially if he had looked at the photo, and could put two and two together.

Try as he might, he could not think of anything better and decided to play things by ear when he met the man. If the worst came to the worst, he could always rough him up a bit, but that was to be a last resort. He wanted to tidy everything up nice and neatly without any unpleasantness.

He pulled up outside the flat, and turned off the engine, with any luck, he would be in and out in minutes. He always carried cash with him, which he kept hidden in the boot of his car, so unless the man wanted too much, he could clear the matter up in one visit.

He locked his car, and walked up to the main door and pressed the bell next to Shakespeare's name.

A voice came across the speaker.

"Yes, can I help you?" It was a woman's voice and Kenton guessed it would be Will's wife.

"Mrs Shakespeare? Is your husband there please?"

"I'm sorry, he's out, can I help?"

Kenton was annoyed, he had been sure this was the ideal time to catch Will before he went out for the evening.

"Are you expecting him back shortly?"

"No, I'm afraid he is out for the evening, he is visiting his father in Leicester."

Kenton swore under his breath, this was not going to plan and holding a conversation over an intercom was not helping.

"My name is Kenton, I run a private detective agency and I need some help with a case I'm on and I think your husband could help me. Can I come in, and show you some identification and explain how he might be able to help?" He tried to make his voice sound as reassuring as possible; the last thing he wanted was to frighten the woman.

"Okay, the main door is unlocked come down the passage it's the door on the right, number 4."

He walked through the main entrance, and down the passage and knocked on the door. The woman opened the door slightly to reveal that it was on a safety chain.

"May I see your identification?" she said through the small opening.

Kenton smiled at her and took out his ID with a picture, and his name and company address on it.

She compared the photo with the man facing her and, satisfied, slid the chain loose and opened the door fully.

"Sorry about that but you can't be too careful," she said almost apologetically.

"That's quite alright, I fully understand, in fact, I advise all my clients to do the same. It's amazing how many people never question strangers coming to their door." His words were reassuring and Julie relaxed, feeling that there was no danger from this polite man.

"How can we, I mean, my husband, help you?"

Kenton, having won the woman's trust, went with his initial plan of action.

"I understand your husband has a hobby, looking for buried treasure."

"Yes, but he's not found much so far." She gave a nervous giggle. "I'm always telling him that it's a waste of time."

"Well, I'm hoping that he may have struck gold, well not gold exactly but at least something of value. You see my client had a cigarette case stolen from his apartment in Kenilworth and he knows the thief, a young boy who worked part time for him. Well, I tracked down the lad to get my client's property back and he admitted the theft but said he had buried it in Abbey Fields."

She looked at him quizzically as if finding the whole tale a little far-fetched. He saw her look and quickly went on.

"I know it sounds bizarre but the boy said he panicked and hid the case until things went quiet, then he intended to go back, retrieve it and sell it. Well, I came on the scene, and persuaded the boy to get it and hand it back at which point my client would agree not to press charges. Unfortunately, when he went back to dig it up, it was gone; someone had beaten him to it. I'm hoping your husband has found the case, there is reward for its safe return as it is of sentimental value to my client." He finished speaking and waited for the woman to ask him how much the reward was, they always ask how much before anything else.

"I don't think my husband can help you, as far as I know, he has not found anything of value in Abbey fields and certainly not a silver cigarette case."

Kenton was surprised by her remark. She was lying, but why. He had not mentioned the fact that the case was silver, so why was she so specific about it being a 'silver cigarette case'

"That's a great pity, Mrs Shakespeare, because I do need to find that case and I intend to."

His voice was now cold, showing no sign of emotion; the friendliness had disappeared. "Here's my card, I'm staying in Coventry tonight and have to go back to London at lunchtime tomorrow. Please speak to your husband when he comes in and ask him to phone me, I think he will find it in his best interests if he can recall having found what I'm looking for. Don't get up, I'll let myself out."

Kenton left, banging the door shut as he went. Julie did not move for a few seconds, she was shaking; the threat in his voice had left her with a fear of what might happen if Will did not hand over the case and that bloody photo.

He got back in his car and sat for a few moments, trying to control the anger he felt. That silly bloody woman; she was lying, he was sure of that, but he did not understand why. He was as much frustrated as angry, every time he thought he had sorted things out and could get the case, go back to London and get paid, another twist to the story happened. There was something that he couldn't put his finger on. Why didn't she just hand over the bloody case and take the reward? The other strange thing was that she never even asked how much the reward was and that's the first thing they always ask. There was more to this cigarette case than Martin was letting on and if he was going to be able to sort it out, he needed to know what it was Martin was keeping from him.

Julie watched the man, sitting in his car, from behind her curtains. He had been sitting there for about five minutes and she had wondered if she ought to phone the police, but discarded the idea. They would probably think she was just being paranoid, after all, he hadn't actually threatened her, but the tone of his voice was intimidating.

Eventually, he drove off and she relaxed. When Will got home, she would get him to hand the photo over and that would be that. She still could not understand why she had not just given the man the picture in the first place; something had held her back, maybe because it was not hers to give, it was Will's.

Kenton had seen the twitch in the curtains and knew he was being watched. He deliberately sat in the car longer than he had first intended. Psychologically, he hoped that being there would add to the implied threat he had left with her. It was not always brute force that got results; he had learnt that at the detention centres in Iraq.

He turned the key in the ignition and headed back to Coventry. His first port of call was the hotel he had checked out of earlier that morning.

The girl at the reception remembered him and when he explained that he needed to stay another night to complete a business deal, there was no problem in finding a room. What he did not realise was that as most of the hotel guests were commercial travellers, they usually left Friday mornings and the hotel was virtually empty.

Picking the keys from the desk, he went to his room and made himself a cup of coffee. He needed to talk to Martin, not just to update him, but also ask a few pertinent questions. The phone rang without reply until Martin's message service cut in.

"Fuck!" he said just before the voice said 'please speak after the tone'.

"Martin, this is Stan Kenton, I really need to speak to you, can you ring me back? In case you don't come back to me tonight, I'll give you a brief update. I went to see that guy Shakespeare but he was out, spoke to his wife and I think she is hiding something, denied all knowledge of the cigarette case but I know she's lying. I told her there was a reward and left my card for her husband to phone me tomorrow morning. I'm staying in Coventry tonight and will go over to see him in the morning. If there's any chance of meeting you in Kenilworth tomorrow, I will hopefully be able to give you your property back. Give me a ring."

The last sentence was more of an order than a request, Kenton was feeling more and more he was being used, and did not like it.

Chapter Twenty-Six

Will arrived home at about nine thirty, too late to go to the pub for his regular Friday night with the lads. He was exhausted, and although not a big drinker, was desperately in need of a drink now. The call from his father had worried him as soon as he got it. His dad knew Friday was Will's night out and would never have tried to alter that under normal circumstances, and, anyway, they would be seeing each other the next day for Leicester's game.

His father would not explain over the phone, just said he had to talk to him. Will had been worried all day, and had rung to tell Julie he would go and see his father straight from school.

Will's dad had recently retired and was planning to go on his first cruise that summer, and Will had wondered if a problem had arisen over the holiday plans, but soon cast that thought aside. His father would not have bothered him over something like that, however important it might have seemed, no this was obviously more serious. It had been on Will's mind all day and he had struggled to concentrate on the needs of the children at school.

Try as he might, he could not get away from the thought that it must be something to do with his father's health, but that did not make sense, his father was as fit as a fiddle; he had not needed treatment of any sort, other than the odd cold, for over ten years and even then, it was for a cracked bone in his arm following an accident at work.

He had arrived at his parents' home within in half an hour of leaving school. His mother, as always, was in the kitchen. His father let him in and Will followed him into the living room.

"Dad, what's the problem?" Will had not meant to be so abrupt, but after worrying all day, it just burst out.

"Sit down. Just take your time, don't rush me."

Will could see the strain in his father's eyes and his chest tightened with the fear of what he would tell him.

"I've been told that I have bowel cancer and I need to have an operation as soon as possible. I…"

"What… when… how…?" Will interrupted his father.

"Listen and I'll tell you. I did a routine test; you know the sort that they send in the post for bowel cancer screening. Your mother kept badgering me to do it, though I have to say I wasn't keen. Anyway, I sent it off and after a couple of weeks had a letter back asking me to go to the hospital for further tests. I didn't say anything at the time because I thought it was just routine procedure. Well, this week I've been to see the consultant and he told me I need an operation as soon as possible."

"Have they told you what the prognosis is? Is it curable? Will this operation get rid of it?"

"You know as much as I do. I've contacted the hospital and they have told me that I am on the waiting list for the op and that it should be very soon. I just wanted to tell you what's happening and didn't want to be talking about this on the way to a football match. The Foxes are far more important!" He laughed at his attempt at a joke. Will did not find it amusing.

"Dad, for Christ's sake, be serious."

"Look, I'm sorry to drag you over here, but your mum wanted me to tell you straight away just in case I got a quick call to the hospital. She didn't want you to suddenly find I was in there."

"Bloody right too."

As he spoke, his mother came into the room with a tray holding three cups of tea.

"He's told you then?" she said as she put the tray on the table and passed the two men their cups.

"Yes, has the doctor said anything to you?"

His mother looked at him and shook her head, but her eyes said something else, she was holding something back, something she didn't want to say in front of her husband. Will knew that look and knew he would have to talk to her on her own.

After the initial shock of his father's news had subsided, they spent the next couple of hours chatting about their beloved Leicester and whether they would make it two promotions in consecutive years.

Will looked at his watch, it was after eight and Julie would be waiting for him to have dinner.

"Dad, I've got to go. See you tomorrow. It looks like you'll miss the last games of the season if this op comes though; but at least you'll have the summer to convalesce and be back fit for next season when, hopefully, we'll be playing the likes of United. I'll just pop in the kitchen and say goodbye to Mum."

He got up and walked through to the kitchen.

"What are you holding back?" he whispered so that his father could not hear.

"I've spoken to the consultant and he tells me that your father needs an operation urgently. If the operation is successful and they can remove the cancer, then he will be okay but if, when they open him up it's gone too far, then they give him only a few months. We won't know until he has the operation."

A tear rolled down her cheeks, and Will put his arms around her and squeezed. His father's optimism had allayed his initial worries, but now his mother had brought those fears back again.

"I've asked the consultant not to tell your father just how bad it is; you know how he hates hospitals. It will make him more depressed and I think he needs to feel confident that he will be fully cured."

Will nodded his agreement, if his father thought that he might not survive then he would go into the operation with a totally negative attitude, he was half pint empty man not a half pint full.

Will drove back home feeling washed out, the shock of what he had been told hitting him hard. His father was only sixty-five, far too young to die. The word die hit him like a kick in the head and he cried all the way back to Kenilworth.

He opened the door and Julie, hearing the key in the lock, called out from the kitchen.

"I'm in here. God I'm glad you're back, a man called and…" She stopped mid-sentence. Will had walked into the kitchen and she could see straight away by the redness around his eyes that he had been crying. "What's up? Is something wrong with your mum or dad? What is it, you look awful?"

Will slumped into a chair.

"Can you pour me a large whisky?"

She looked worried. Will rarely drank at home, other than a glass of wine with their meal, he was not a spirit drinker. She poured the drink and waited while he drank it, draining the measure in one go.

"It's Dad, he's got bowel cancer and needs an operation. He doesn't know how bad it is. Mum says the doctors say it's a fifty-fifty chance that they will be successful when they operate." The words came out in a rush as though he had to get something off his chest.

"Oh, Will, I'm so sorry. Are you okay? Do you want another drink?"

"I'll be alright, just need to get my head around things; it's a bit of shock. We've just got to be positive, if there's a fifty percent chance that he might die then there's a fifty percent chance he will survive."

She smiled at him; he had always had a positive attitude to life the exact opposite of his father. She poured him another drink even though he had shaken his head when she asked him if he wanted another. He took the glass but this time sipped it slowly.

"Sorry, love, you started to tell me something when I came in, about a man. What man?"

"I had a visit this afternoon, not long after getting back from work. He asked for you and I explained you would be out all evening. He then asked if he could speak to me, said he was a private investigator and he thought you might be able to help him with a case he was working on. Well, I checked his ID and then let him. At first, he was quite charming, and went out of his way to reassure me that he was genuine."

"So what did he want?"

"Be patient and I'll tell you. He wanted that bloody cigarette case! He said he was representing the owner; that a young lad had stolen the case, and he had tracked him down and promised that there would be no prosecution if the lad returned it. Apparently, the young man buried it in a panic and had intended to go back and dig it up, then sell it. When he went with him to retrieve the case, it had disappeared. He wondered if you had found it whilst out looking for buried treasure and that there was a reward for its return."

"What did you say?"

"I said no, you had found nothing."

"Why?"

"His story did not ring true; don't forget we've seen the photograph."

"Did you ask how much the reward was?"

"No, because that would have given the impression that you did have it. Anyway, I wanted to buy some time so I could talk to you and we could decide what to do for the best."

"Yes, good idea. Did he leave a card to get in touch with him?"

"Yes." She handed him Kenton's card. "I'm worried though, because when I told him that you had not got the case, he suddenly turned quite nasty, almost threatening. He did not actually issue a threat but his voice went cold when he said he would be back and 'it would be in your best interest if you remembered finding it'. It frightened me and when he left he was outside for about ten minutes sitting in his car. Do you think we should call the police?"

"I don't know. Perhaps we should just wait for his call tomorrow and be done with it. After all, it's none of our business and what two consenting adults do together is up to them. It's not my cup of tea, but each to their own."

For the first time that evening, they both smiled. *If that was a cup of tea, give me coffee every time,* he thought to himself.

She put her arms around him. As long as she did not have to speak to that man again, then Will was probably right, the sooner they got rid of the cigarette case the better. If there was a reward as well, then that was a bonus.

Chapter Twenty-Seven

Maddy looked around the apartment; it was smaller than she had imagined, but as she only intended to ever spend the one night there, she was sure she could suffer the inconvenience. She had driven up from London, having left the boutique at three to give her enough time to find the place, shower and change, before attending the 'Question Time' debate with Martin. He had given her a spare key as he was at the office with Tony and would not be back until about six.

Although only staying the one night, that was the promise she had made to Martin, she had still brought a case that most people would use for a week's holiday. She had not been able to make up her mind what to wear and had brought three separate outfits with her. There was plenty of time to spare before she needed to get ready, so made herself a gin and tonic, and sat down to put her feet up for five minutes.

She thought that it would be a shame that in just a couple of weeks, the election would be over and Martin would not need to visit Kenilworth again. She was convinced he had no chance of getting elected, which was a pity as his frequent jaunts up the motorway had provided ample opportunities for her extra curricula activities.

As she sipped her drink, she thought of the previous evening when Peter had taken her to a little Italian restaurant he knew near Cockfosters tube station. They had gone in his car as there was less chance of anyone recognising them, her car having personalised number plates. When they had finished their meal, she had put her coat on and while he settled the bill, she had excused herself to go to the ladies. Outside, they walked back to the car which had been parked in the station car park. Once inside the car, Maddy had undone her coat buttons, to reveal she was naked except for her stockings and shoes!

She remembered the look on his face and the panic in his eyes in case anyone was looking. She did not care and lowered the seat so that she was almost lying flat, the coat falling at her sides. She had covered herself whilst they negotiated their exit from the car park, but once on the main road, had let the coat slip open again. Poor Peter struggled to concentrate on driving and look at her at the same time. She had taken her dress and underwear off when she excused herself, and this was her little thank you for the meal. It had not taken Peter long to drive back to Maddy's flat. He had parked the car and they had walked to the lift, her coat streaming out behind her not caring who might be watching. They had got into the lift and he had been unable to hold back any longer, and had pressed her against the side of the lift and taken her. The lift soon reached her floor, too soon in fact and he had to quickly rearrange himself as they got out. Fortunately, no one was about and she had almost fallen into the flat she was laughing so much. What had started in the lift was finished in the hallway.

Maddy smiled to herself as she recalled the evening. It had not stopped there, they had made love three times that night and now she was exhausted. She just hoped that 'Question Time' would prove to be just as exhausting for Martin!

Martin had picked up the message from Kenton but had not been able to reply straight away as he had been busy with Tony. When he returned to the apartment, he had parked the car in the basement and tried to ring Kenton. There had been no answer so he left a message saying he would be tied up all evening and would contact him the next day, but would not be able to meet him as his wife was with him this weekend.

He took the lift up to the second floor and walked along the corridor to his front door. He had not heard from Maddy all day, and just hoped and prayed that she was there; having told Tony and his staff that she was coming; it would be humiliating if she let him down. The key turned in the lock, and as he opened the door, he could hear the hum of the shower pump and he let out a sigh of relief.

Maddy came out of the shower, the towel tied around her head like a turban being the only thing that she was wearing.

"It's a bloody good job I'm on my own," he said.

"Don't be silly, darling, if you'd had friends with you I would have secured their votes." She smiled at him, and walked across the hall and kissed him. "Would you like a drink?"

"Yes please, but not too strong, I'll need my wits about me if I'm going to make an impression."

She walked into the main room, and into the kitchen area where the glasses were kept and poured him a gin and tonic.

"Thanks," he said taking the glass off her.

He looked down at her body, admiring her beautiful curves, flat stomach and firm breasts. He must have been mad to neglect her for that little bastard Joe. He realised that, now more than ever, he needed her.

"Do you fancy a quickie?" he asked as he reached out and stroked her breast.

"Martin!" she said in mock horror. "This is not like you."

Her nipples had responded to his touch and were now firm, all previous thoughts of tiredness left her as she pressed her body next to his.

With her help, he quickly shed his clothes and carried her into the bedroom.

"Darling, you do realise we are christening your new bed, don't you?" She was on top of him now, the towel having been tossed aside, her hair still wet as it fell around his face.

A momentary pang of guilt went through him at her remark as he thought of previous encounters on this very same bed, but he quickly blotted them from his mind. He would have to learn to eradicate those thoughts permanently!

Their lovemaking was intense but short-lived. He had climaxed quickly and had left her wanting more, but despite her entreaties, he was unable to continue.

"Christ, look at the time, we'd better get ready," he said by way of an excuse.

Though Maddy was disappointed, she consoled herself with the thought that the previous night she had climaxed three times, so was not exactly unsatisfied.

By seven o'clock, they were in the back room of the hall that doubled as a dressing room when amateur plays were put on and a hospitality room for meetings. Tonight, it was filled with the five candidates who had declared so far, their agents and invited guests. The Coventry Evening Telegraph had provided a bar and canapés for them, and it was noticeable that the five candidates on the panel were all drinking mineral water.

The political editor of the paper was to chair the meeting and was now introducing himself to them whilst the audience was slowly filing in.

He came up to Martin and held out his hand.

"Jeff Bagshot, political editor of the Telegraph, I'm your chairman for the evening." It was the fifth time he had repeated the statement. "So you're the maverick of the group, my reporter has been to some of your meetings, thinks you are winning a few people around. Do you think you have a realistic chance?"

Martin looked at the man. He was short and overweight, and looked as if he had far too many liquid lunches, but Tony had briefed him not to be fooled by appearances. Jeff Bagshot had worked for one of the national newspapers and had been highly thought of, only returning to the Midlands because of his wife's ill health.

"If you want the truth, and after all, that is what I'm about, I really don't know. I accept I'm up against the might of the party machinery of the three main parties. I don't really count the Greens, but there is no doubt the average voter is pretty disillusioned with politicians in general and I am trying to tap into that dissatisfaction."

Jeff, nodded his head, his reporter had told him that this man was striking a chord with the electorate and he could see why. He shook Martin's hand and wished him well for this evening's debate.

Maddy had been talking to Tony and, as Jeff moved away, came up to Martin.

"Well, what did he say?"

"Nothing much, he's got to be impartial, can't really comment but wished me well and I got the impression he was being sincere."

It was now nearly seven thirty, the due time for the start of the proceedings. Jeff asked the five candidates to follow him into the main hall where a large table had been set on the stage with six chairs behind it; on the table in front of each chair was a name card, a glass and water jug.

The Green candidate, James Harrison, sat on the extreme right, then came Nick Milton, Labour then Jeff; to Jeff's left,

Jeremy Wright, Conservative, Nigel Rock, Lib Dem and finally, Martin.

Jeff introduced the panel and read out the first of the questions the audience had previously submitted.

The evening followed the pattern of the television show with some lively comments from the audience. Martin got the loudest applause of the night when he said it was an admission of their culpability by the main parties, that the last parliament had been corrupt by the fact that so many of the previous MPs had either been sacked or persuaded to stand down. The others had tried to belittle him by saying he would be irrelevant if elected but he had given a good account of himself, using Martin Bell as an example of people power. All in all, he felt rather pleased with himself. If he was to lose this contest, at least he would go down fighting. After the 'show' had finished, they went back stage for a drink before leaving. Maddy had been appalled by the hypocrisy of the candidates. On stage, they had been at each other's throats, name calling and blaming each other for all the ills of the world, and now here they were in the hospitality room, laughing and drinking with each other as if they were old friends. Martin had, to his credit, kept apart from the others; he felt like Maddy, that even though there were candidates that were new to the system, the other candidates really hadn't learnt from the mistakes of their predecessors.

Tony had congratulated him on his performance and told him that he had introduced Maddy to a number of locals, who had offered their support to his campaign. They had all been impressed with her, and expressed their hope that they would see more of her.

It was nearly midnight by the time they got back to the apartment.

"Thank you, darling, for your support, everyone fell in love with you, I knew they would." He put his arm round her and kissed her gently on the cheek. Maddy thought that it was times like this that she really loved him, if only he wasn't so conservative with a small 'c'. She smiled to herself at the thought.

"What are you smiling at?" he asked.

"Just thinking what a charmer you can be when you want to."

He smiled back at her.

"Come on, let's get to bed I'm shattered." He led the way into the bedroom, all thoughts of Kenton pushed to the back of his mind; he would sort him out in the morning.

Chapter Twenty-Eight

Kenton looked at the ceiling of his bedroom; the paper was peeling away at the corners and like the rest of the room, was in need of some decoration. He would be glad when he could get back to his house in London, he hated hotels, they were so impersonal.

He had not felt so dejected for a long time. He could not remember a case that he had worked on that was, on the face of it, as open and shut as this, and yet so bloody frustrating. He needed to take his mind of it and relax. He was hungry but could not face another bland meal at the hotel, what he really fancied was a curry.

He showered and put on one of the fresh shirts he had thrown into the car at the last minute when he left home. Discarding the tie he always wore when he was working, he immediately felt a little more relaxed. Picking up his mobile, he noticed there was a missed call from Martin, he must have phoned while he was showering. He punched the number for the message service, and heard Martin's voice saying not to ring tonight and that he would call him in the morning. *Bloody politicians, never there when you wanted them!*

He walked down the stairs to reception and waited whilst the young girl attended to a guest. Once finished, she looked up at Kenton.

"Can I help you, sir?"

"Yes, can you tell me where I can get an Indian meal?"

"Well, you've got plenty to choose from, do you know your way around the city?"

"Not really but I went to the cinema the other day so I know how to get to that car park, is there one nearby?"

"As a matter of fact, there is, the 'Turmeric Gold'. I've been and it's very good. It's in what they now call Medieval Spon

Street, the cinema is at one end, close to the ring road, so if you park in that car park, it's only a few yards to walk."

"Thank you very much." He turned and walked out of the hotel to his car. He knew he could have walked to where the cinema was, but feeling there was rain in the air and having no coat, opted for the car.

The cinema was literally a couple of minutes from the hotel and parking in their car park, he walked through the alleyway and soon found the restaurant. There were only a few couples eating and he was led to a table near the window. He perused the menu but still chose what he always had, chicken madras, with onion bargies to start, and a bottle of fizzy water.

The service was slow in spite of the few customers, but he was in no hurry, he had all the evening to waste. As he ate his meal, he could not help thinking about the case. There was a niggle in the back of his mind about the whole business, but try as he might, he could not put his finger on what was bothering him. He went over the whole thing since Martin had first approached him.

He could not see the sense in Martin wanting to get the picture back so desperately. If it had been published, it would most likely have wrecked his marriage, but would it really have wrecked his fledgling political career. Lots of MPs had extra marital affairs and it didn't always affect their future. He remembered Paddy Ashdown, who became known as 'Paddy Pants Down' and, in fact, had gained in popularity. So how secure was his marriage anyway, would it have survived an indiscretion, lots of wives forgave their errant husbands and stood by them.

He understood Martin's reluctance to pay a blackmailer, but after all, he was a millionaire and could easily have afforded ten thousand pounds, it was just a drop in the ocean. Then there was the worry that Martin had expressed about blackmailers always coming back for more, but Kenton had met the kid and he was no hardened criminal, just a chancer who thought he could push his luck. It didn't add up, why go to the expensive of hiring him, he could easily have handled it himself. Kenton was annoyed with himself that he hadn't thought it through more before accepting the assignment. He had broken his own rule by not waiting twenty-four hours before agreeing to take it on. He cursed under his breath.

He thought about the lad, Joe, why had he buried the picture. Why not just hide it at his home, it was only a picture of a couple making love, sure it was his sister, but was there any chance of her finding it when allegedly she never even knew Joe had it. To bury it made no sense. Kenton decided he would have another word with Joe tomorrow, before he went over to Kenilworth, if for no other reason than to satisfy his own curiosity.

Finally, he wondered why the teacher's wife had lied to him. He was sure she was lying, she had mentioned a silver cigarette case and he hadn't. Why was she holding something back? She hadn't even asked about the reward and they always did that. The teacher must have found the case, it made sense, no one else would have reason to dig into the ground, and the boy had been definite about where and how deep it was buried, and Kenton believed him. There must be something else in that case, something that Martin had kept from him, and he didn't like being kept in the dark. He would have a long chat with Martin once he'd recovered the case. Tomorrow would be very interesting one way or another.

He called the waiter to bring him his bill and pulled some cash out of his pocket. He was torn on whether to leave a tip or not as he had been kept waiting but in the end decided that the food was good enough to merit one. He put the notes on the tray and called the waiter back to collect it, telling him to keep the change. It was still only half past nine and he was not ready to go back to the hotel. He had felt better following the little chat he had had with himself. He walked out of the restaurant and along the road looking in the windows of the shops as he passed. The buildings were all medieval with oak beams being the prominent feature. At the end of the road, a plaque had been erected explaining how Spon Street had been preserved in its original state to show how ancient Coventry had looked.

It was at times like this he wished that he drank; being at a loose end, it was difficult to strike up a conversation in a pub if you only had a glass of water in front of you. Having retraced his steps back along the road, he came to the cinema complex that he had visited the day before and noticed the nightclubs in the area. Kenton thought that maybe a couple of hours dancing

172

would tire him out and get him off to sleep more easily. He checked on the door but they were not open until ten and anyway, he rightly assumed that there would be few people in there before the pubs closed. He had passed a pub on his way to the cinema, and walked back to it and went in. He could pass an hour or so before he took to the dance floor.

It was Friday and the pub was packed, mostly with young people in their twenties, although he did notice a group of men and women who looked more his age, late thirties. The barman had asked twice when he ordered a bottle of Perrier water, not quite believing that he had heard correctly. In all his time working in the pub, he could not recall anyone ordering water. Kenton took the glass and edged along the counter until he found a small space. He sipped his water and surveyed the scene; ordinary honest folk out on a Friday spending there hard earned money on a bit of entertainment or, as his cynical side kicked in, a few tossers spending their unemployment benefit. He didn't really care; he just wanted to get back to London where he was on familiar territory.

The chatter in the pub grew louder as the alcohol began to take effect. Kenton smiled to himself; he had never drunk even as a young man and could not understand why people had to drink before they could enjoy themselves. He preferred to be in full control of all his faculties. He stood at the end of the bar, people watching, fascinated by the sheer amount of drink that some of these young men consumed. He was surprised how quickly the time passed and soon the barman was calling last orders, the room slowly emptying.

Leaving the pub, he walked back along the pedestrian way towards the cinema and nightclub complex. A steady stream of young men and women were going in the same direction, and like water funnelling through a narrow gorge, congregated at the entrance to 'Jumping Jacks' the nightclub he had looked at earlier. Eventually, he found himself at the head of the queue and, having paid his entrance fee, was swept along with the flow of noisy clubbers into the main dance floor. The majority of people immediately crowded around the bar as if they were desperate for their first drink of the evening. He could wait, and instead walked around the room to familiarise himself with its lay out. It was something he always did when in strange surroundings; a legacy of his army training he could not shake off.

Once the initial rush had died down, he made his way to the bar and ordered a glass of orange juice, at least it looked more like the cocktails that some of the customers were drinking. The music was loud, very loud and it had been hard to make himself heard when he ordered his drink. As he looked around, he realised that maybe this had not been such a good idea. He felt a lot older than is thirty-nine years; the majority of those on the dance floor must have been in their early twenties.

He had wanted to tire himself out to get a good night's sleep, but it looked as though that plan would not materialise. He decided to have one more drink and then go; the noise beginning to give him a headache.

While he waited to be served, three women, who he had noticed earlier dancing together, came up to the bar to order drinks. Although he was the next person to be served, he stepped back and waved them forward in front of him.

The girl with long dark hair smiled at him and thanked him saying, "How nice to meet a gentleman for a change."

He smiled back and mumbled, "Not many of us left."

She grinned, whilst her two friends made some comment about her 'being in there', which Kenton did not quite catch. As he waited while the girls were being served, he looked more closely at the brunette. She looked a little older than her two friends, probably late twenties or early thirties, about five foot five, but in her high heels, as tall as he. She had big brown eyes and high cheekbones, and full firm breasts that were shown off by her low-cut dress. She turned and caught him looking at her, but did not show any disapproval, rather she smiled again. On the spur of the moment, he took her arm and asked if she would like to dance. For a moment, he thought he had read the signs incorrectly, but she followed him onto the dance floor without any hesitation.

The music was blaring out some record that he did not recognise, but it did not matter; the throbbing beat of the base pounding against his chest.

She could jive, unlike most young people, and moved easily to his lead. They had danced to three numbers without a break and, though he was fit, he needed a breather. He took back to the bar where her girlfriends were, but now they were three young men with them.

The girl looked worried when she saw the men standing there and quickly loosened her hold on Kenton's hand.

"What the fuck do you think you're up to?"

The speaker was a big man, with a haircut that was so short, at first glance he looked bald. He was about six foot two, weighing about sixteen stone, with muscles that rippled under his 'T' shirt. He glowered at the girl.

"I said what did you think you're up to?"

She said nothing, just looked away, but he grabbed at her arm and roughly pulled her towards him.

"I don't think that is any way to treat a lady," Kenton's voice was quiet but cold and although he could hardly be heard over the noise of the music, the man understood.

"You keep your fucking nose out of this or I'll bust it for you."

"I don't think so," Kenton spoke in the same cold even tone, his eyes fixed on the big man's eyes.

"Look, you piece of shit, just fuck off before I lose my temper," the big man was shouting now and was obviously a little worse for wear. His friends tried to calm him down for fear he would attract the attention of the bouncers, then they would all be thrown out.

"I think you had better try and control Dumbo before he gets hurt," Kenton said to the two other men who were now holding on to the big man's arms.

"I'll see you outside, then I'll rip your fucking head off," was his parting shot as Kenton turned away, walked to the far end of the bar and ordered another fruit juice. *So much for a quiet night dancing,* he mused.

The scene that had just been played out had brought Kenton's bad mood back again just as he thought he would be enjoying himself. He finished his drink and looked around to see where 'Dumbo' and his friends were, but he could not see them anywhere. *A pity,* he thought, *that girl was really attractive, what on earth was she doing with a thick lump like that.*

He decided he'd had enough entertainment for one evening and would make his way back to the hotel. It was one o'clock anyway, much later than he would normally retire. The dance floor was still heaving as struggled through the sweaty mob towards the exit. The cool night air hit him and he shivered slightly, wishing that he had brought a coat with him. It was not far to the car park so he would soon be in the warmth.

The street was strangely quite after the noise of the club, there was nobody about; no doubt the club would not be closing before three, so it was too early for most people to be leaving. He walked along the street looking for the gap in the buildings that led to the car park. He remembered it was between two shops and was dark, someone having broken the street lamp, leaving the lamp case hanging like a broken branch. He found the opening and started to walk the thirty or so yards that would open out onto the forecourt in front of the car park.

He had only walked a couple of yards when he heard a scraping sound behind him, turning he saw the outline of the big bulk of 'Dumbo'.

"Oi smart arse, fancy yourself as a bit of a ladies' man, do you? Well, you picked the wrong tart this time. I'm going to teach you a lesson about keeping your hands of other people's property." The big man was swaying as he walked towards Kenton.

"Look, sonny, I think you should go home and sleep it off, and by the way, you shouldn't really call your girlfriend a tart, she struck me as a very nice young lady, certainly too good for you," Kenton spoke in the same cold controlled voice he had used in the club. Although the man was big Kenton was not at all frightened, he had handled bigger and stronger men than this lump, and they hadn't been drunk.

"You're a mouthy little fucker; let's see how smart you talk with a fat lip."

As he spoke, the big man, who by now was only a foot away from Kenton, took a swing with his right hand, aiming at Kenton's head. The man was slow and the punch telegraphed, Kenton easily swayed back so that 'Dumbo' almost lost his balance and stumbled, the fist drifting harmlessly past. As he twisted round following the direction of his swinging arm, Kenton fired two rapid punches to the man's solar plexus. He coughed as his body doubled from the pain. He managed to just keep his balance by reaching out to the wall, but this left him more exposed and Kenton followed up with another blow to the body, and then a crunching hook under his chin, which nearly took his head off. The man fell crashing to the floor. Kenton looked down at him, but resisted the temptation to kick him, though he thoroughly deserved it.

Instead, he turned and began walking towards the car park. He had gone only a couple of paces when he was surprised to see 'Dumbo's' two friends from the nightclub. He was about to warn them to move out of the way when they suddenly rushed him taking him by surprise. He expected to have to ride punches from either side and was trying to decide who to sort out first, but instead they just grabbed his arms, pushing him backwards the way he'd come. The tactic momentarily threw him and he was rapidly re-evaluating the situation when he felt the blade rip into his back.

Kenton gasped, the pain was excruciating and he instinctively reached his hand to where the knife had entered. He could feel the hot sticky blood seeping through his shirt. He turned to face his assailant, but could not see him immediately in the dark. He just caught a flash of steel, but too late as 'Dumbo' lunged forward and the blade sunk deep into his stomach. Kenton fell to his knees, the blood pouring from the wounds to his body like a river in spate.

"That'll teach you, you fucking bastard," were the last words that Kenton heard.

Chapter Twenty-Nine

Detective Inspector Ferguson was not a happy man. He knew it was part of the job but could never get used to being woken up in the middle of the night, no matter what the reason was. His sergeant Sam Naylor had called him out at three thirty am to the murder scene, and now here they were back at Little Park Street police station, trying to piece together the reasons why a man from London should be murdered in Medieval Spon Street of all places.

It was seven thirty and his bad temper had not left him.

"Another coffee, boss?" Sam asked.

"I'll look like bloody coffee if I drink anymore, no thanks; just let's run through the details again, this case just doesn't add up."

Sam got out his notebook and read out the details of the dead man.

"Name, Stan Kenton, private investigator, office in London, lives in Marylebone Street London... I've got both addresses and phone numbers... Divorced, no children. Apparently, he is ex-army... Finished up in the SAS. Was highly thought of by his senior officers."

"Yes, yes I know all that." Ferguson had been through the details, he wanted to get to a reason for the murder.

"Sorry. His death was reported just after three by a guy who had just left Jumping Jacks nightclub; he was walking through the alley that leads to the car park, round the back of Ikea, nearly tripped over the body. He stayed with the man, not sure if he was still alive while his girlfriend called the ambulance and the police. The PC who went to the scene called into the desk sergeant who immediately called us."

"I didn't mean you to go over the bloody details that much, just cut to the chase." Ferguson had moved down to the Midlands from his native Glasgow thirty years ago, but had not lost his accent and when he was irritable, the accent grew stronger.

Sam had worked with Ferguson for ten years and probably knew the man better than even his wife did, so was used to his temper.

"The man, Kenton, had been stabbed twice; probably a short bladed weapon by the depth of the cuts, but it had penetrated his liver and spleen, and caused an extreme loss of blood. The doc will give us more details later this morning when he's finished his examination. He had not been robbed, there was five hundred pounds in his wallet, his credit cards were still in his pocket and so was his mobile phone. So I think we can rule out robbery as a motive."

"I never like to rule anything out at this stage, but I concede it's highly unlikely, go on."

"As you know, we found a receipt for a hotel he has been staying at, and they have confirmed he stayed Wednesday and Thursday, checked out Friday morning, but checked back in again on Friday afternoon for one night. He asked the girl on reception if she could recommend a curry house and she told him Turmeric Gold. I've checked with them and they confirm he had a meal there, leaving at about nine thirty."

"So what happened to him from nine thirty until he was stabbed at…" Ferguson looked at Sam for confirmation of the time.

"The doc thinks between one am and when he was found," Sam read from his notes.

"So we need to find out if he stayed in the area, which seems likely, or did he go away and come back, and if so, where did he go." Ferguson pulled at his chin, a habit he employed when he was thinking. "He had some car keys in his pocket, have we checked where the car is?"

"Yes, sir, I checked with the hotel who gave me the car registration and I got the foot patrol checking around car parks for it, I'm expecting some feedback any time now."

"Good. Now, what about the mobile? Have you traced any calls that he's made since he's been visiting our fair city?"

"Jack and Angela are on to that, shall I go and see how they're getting on?"

"Yes do that. We need to know why he was up here, if he was on an assignment and if so what it was. For all we know, this could be a contract killing, maybe he was getting a little too close to whatever it was he was looking into." He pulled his chin again. "Or am I letting my fantasies run away with me?" he said under his breath.

Sam left the office to go, and check how Jack and Angela were doing. It was at times like this that Ferguson missed smoking; it used to calm him and make him think more clearly. He had stopped when the smoking ban in all offices and public places became law, deciding that it was a golden opportunity to kick the habit and stop Madge from nagging him at the same time. Anyway, he was not going to be one of those sad bastards who even in the pouring rain huddled together on the pavement outside. He could now only resort to tugging at his chin, which is what he was doing when the Super tapped the door and walked into his office.

"How's the murder enquiry going? I've got to give something to the press, what do you think?"

"To be honest, we don't know what we're looking for, there seems to be no motive. I'm sure it wasn't robbery, but it would be a good idea to appeal for witnesses. I can get you a picture off his driving license. We need to find out his movements between nine thirty and three am."

"Okay I'll do that. Keep me informed if there are any developments." The Superintendent turned and left the office not seeming to hear Ferguson's "Yes, sir" as he left.

Ferguson slumped back into his chair; there were plenty of other cases on his desk without this one. *Why couldn't he have got himself killed in London, not on my patch.*

He was trying to put the different files he was currently dealing with in some kind of order, when Sam burst into the room. Ferguson gave him a look that said remember to knock in future, but pointed to a chair.

"Well, what's exciting you?" he asked his sergeant.

"Angela's got some numbers of outgoing and incoming phone calls. There are two that might be of interest. One belongs to a lad called Joe, no surname, and the other a chap called Martin De Glanville. De Glanville is the most interesting. It turns out he's a prospective parliamentary candidate for the forthcoming election and wait for it, he's standing for Kenilworth." Sam had a smile which said 'aren't I clever' all over his face.

Ferguson desperately wanted to say 'isn't Angela clever', but did not want to spoil his moment of glory.

"Well done. Have you contacted either of them?"

"Yes, the lad's coming in at one thirty and I've arranged for us to meet De Glanville at his campaign headquarters in Kenilworth in half an hour. So we'd better get a move on."

Ferguson got out of his chair and stretched, the tiredness from lack of sleep slowing his movements. He grabbed his jacket from the hook behind the door and followed Sam out.

"What do you think the connection with this De Glanville character is then, boss?"

"Your guess is as good as mine, but there's one way to find out," Ferguson replied as they strode across the tarmac to the car park.

Twenty minutes later, they were in the outer office waiting to meet the candidate.

De Glanville came out of a side door and greeted them. The two detectives introduced themselves, showed their warrant cards and followed him back through the doorway he had just come from.

The room was small with a table in the middle and four chairs, surrounded by cardboard boxes. Ferguson looked quizzically at the boxes.

"Sorry that it's so cramped, these," he pointed to the packages, "are all my election leaflets waiting for my loyal volunteers to distribute them. Anyway, how can I help you?"

Ferguson looked at Martin trying to weigh him up and deciding he wouldn't jump to any conclusions, rather wait and see how this little chat went.

"Do you know a man by the name of Stan Kenton?" Ferguson asked.

"Yes, as a matter of fact, I do, why?"

"He was found murdered in the early hours of this morning, in Coventry." Ferguson studied Martin closely as he waited for his reaction.

"Oh my god, murdered, but who, why?"

"We don't know the answers to those questions yet, but can you tell me what your relationship with him was?"

"Certainly. He's a sort of investigator, very discreet, recommended to me by a friend; he was doing a little job for me."

"May I ask what that job was?"

As Ferguson asked the questions, Sam wrote Martin's replies down in his notebook.

"Yes, well it was nothing really; you see I lost a cigarette case, silver though not very valuable, but worth a lot to me for sentimental reasons. I suspected one of my volunteers had pinched it and I wanted to get it back without too much fuss, so employed Kenton to make some enquiries for me."

"The person you suspected wouldn't be someone called Joe by any chance, would it?" Sam spoke for the first time. Ferguson thought he saw Martin's face redden slightly at the mention of Joe's name, but was not sure.

"Yes, yes it was."

"Did Kenton get your property back Mr De Glanville?" Ferguson was looking him straight in the eye, checking if the man was telling them the truth.

"No, unfortunately not, I understand we were too late, the lad had sold it."

"Did you notify the police of the original theft?" Ferguson knew the answer even before Martin spoke.

"No, I'm sorry, I suppose I should have, but it was not exactly the crown jewels and I did not want to get the lad into trouble, just get my property back."

The answer seemed plausible, but Ferguson had a nagging doubt in the back of his head that there was more to this than Martin was letting on.

"Well, thank you for your help, sir, here's my card. If you think of anything else that might help us with our enquiries, please give me or my sergeant a ring."

Ferguson stood up and Sam followed him, snapping shut his notebook as he rose. The two policemen walked back to their car and got in.

"Well, Sam, what did you think of him?"

"He seemed pretty straight to me, he's charming, but I suppose that goes with the territory, being a politician I mean."

"Yes I agree, he seemed genuine but I could have sworn he coloured up when you mentioned Joe's name. I just can't help feeling he's holding something back, but I certainly don't think he's our killer. Nevertheless, it wouldn't do any harm to discreetly check up on his movements last night."

Ferguson put the car into gear, and swung out onto the High Street and headed back to Coventry.

It was just before one thirty when Ferguson's phone rang.

"Hello, yes, bring him through, will you, and ask Sam Naylor to come in as well." He put the phone down and waited for the desk sergeant to bring Joe into his office.

The sergeant knocked the door and ushered the young man into the office, Sam following just behind them.

Ferguson pointed to a chair, indicating the lad should sit down.

"Joe, we have asked you in to help us with an investigation we are conducting. I believe you know a man called Kenton, a private investigator, is that correct?" Ferguson looked straight at the lad, noticing that he was a well-built young man who obviously looked after himself, and looked strong enough to take on the smaller Kenton.

"Yes, I've met him. Why do you ask?" It was the first time Ferguson had heard him speak and he was surprised the lad's voice was not as deep as he had expected it to be.

"How old are you, Joe?" The inspector asked.

"Just turned sixteen."

Ferguson's eyebrow rose slightly; he had thought the lad must be about nineteen from his build.

"I have to tell you that Mr Kenton was murdered last night and we are investigating the crime." He watched the boy's reaction as the words sank in; the boy looked genuinely shocked. "I have spoken to a Mr De Glanville who alleges you took a cigarette case belonging to him and M. Kenton came to see you to recover the same. It is my understanding you have already sold the said property, is that correct?"

Joe shuffled uneasily in his chair, but said nothing.

"Look, son, we're not interested in the theft and Mr De Glanville has said that he does not want to press charges, all we are interested in is trying to find who killed Mr Kenton."

The boy looked relieved and nodded. It was clear to him that Martin had not mentioned the blackmail for fear of being exposed and with the man Kenton dead, there was nobody who could know about their relationship.

"Yeah, I met the man you're talking about and he said there was a reward if I returned the case, but I told him I'd already sold it, only got a bloody tenner for it anyway," he added the last bit to make the story sound more believable.

"When was the last time you saw Mr Kenton?" Sam had said nothing up until now.

"Wednesday, he drove up from London, waste of a journey if you ask me."

Ferguson looked at Sam. That would tie up with the information from the hotel but still didn't answer the question why he stayed on Thursday and then decided to stay a further night on Friday.

"Can you tell me where you were on Friday between nine thirty and three am?" Ferguson didn't think the boy was involved, but wanted to make sure he could eliminate him from the investigation.

Joe hesitated for a moment before answering, he could not tell them the truth; that he had been entertaining clients on his old stamping ground at the Rainbow.

"I stayed in and watched an old video, couldn't afford to go out. My mum was there; she can vouch for me."

Ferguson pulled his chin, he didn't believe the lad for one minute, but he was still convinced he had nothing to do with the killing. If this young man had been involved, he would have taken the cash in Kenton's pocket, the credit cards and phone too. He had already admitted that he was a petty thief. Ferguson looked across at Sam, who nodded; they had both come to the same conclusion.

"Alright, that will be all for now, but we may need to speak to you again."

Joe stood up and Sam led him back to the reception desk.

When he came back, he sat down opposite Ferguson.

"What now then, boss? It seems to put those two in the clear."

"Yes, I tend to agree with you but there's more to it than either are letting on. I don't think it's got anything to do with the murder and we have enough on our plate without delving into their affairs. It just makes me wonder why anyone would employ a private detective to look for a cigarette case worth only a tenner and why did Kenton stay in the area after he had been told the case could not be recovered. Perhaps we'll never know, but it does make me wonder." He pulled at his chin and Sam smiled, he knew Ferguson hated a mystery that he couldn't solve.

Chapter Thirty

Martin was shaking as he watched the two policemen pull away. He had agreed to meet them at the campaign office as Maddy was still at the flat, and there would have been far too many questions raised by her if they had interviewed him there. He was convinced they had believed his story about the theft and, with Kenton dead, there was no one else, other than Joe of course, who knew about the photo. He suddenly stopped his train of thought; there was someone else, the man Shakespeare, Kenton was supposed to be seeing. Kenton had said he believed Shakespeare had dug up the cigarette case and still had it.

The news of Kenton's death had come as a surprise and had momentarily thrown him off balance. He was not sure what to do next. Kenton had not given him Shakespeare's address so he could not contact him, and he didn't want to get someone else involved snooping around for him, not while the police were investigating a murder. He decided it would be best to let things lie. At least, Kenton had got Joe off his back and if this new man on the scene was going to use the photo to blackmail him, surely, he would have been in touch by now.

Martin felt slightly easier having thought things through, he wanted to put the whole affair out his mind to concentrate on his election campaign, after all, it was less than two weeks until polling day.

Martin was still deep in thought when Tony tapped him on the shoulder making him jump.

"Sorry, I didn't mean to frighten you."

"No, no it's all right, I was just thinking about how things were going." He was finding the lies easily tripped off his tongue and it worried him that he might be falling into the trap of becoming like every other politician. If he was, then Tony, for one, hadn't noticed.

"I've had some feedback on last night, from the Telegraph; they rated your performance as the best of the night; said you came across as an honest man, not like the rest of them."

Martin winced a little at this remark and felt a touch of guilt at the compliment.

"That's kind of them but it's the man in the street that matters. We've got to get the message to them to stand any chance at all. Look, I'm just going to pop back to the apartment, Maddy's going back to London and I want to see her before she leaves. I'll be back to talk to you about tonight's meeting."

"Fine, I'll see you shortly then. I'll get your notes typed up ready so you can go over them and make any alterations you think are needed."

Martin laughed, he knew if Tony had prepared the notes, they would be perfect, he really was a find.

Maddy had stayed in bed for a lie in, when Martin had left earlier, but was now dressed and packed ready for the off. Martin had phoned to say he would only be a short time and be back straight away.

"Thanks for waiting. I just wanted to say thanks for being with me last night. Tony says the paper phoned up, thought we were the best of the evening…"

"Not we, darling, you were the best," she interrupted him.

"You know what I mean, we're a team. Anyway, Tony also told me everyone he spoke to thought you were enchanting. You made a big impression and that's important, the matrons of the parish like to see a happy couple."

He put his arms round and pulled her close.

"I do love you," he said, as he bent down and kissed her.

She held the embrace for a few seconds and then moved away.

"Are you coming back to London tonight?" she asked.

"No, sorry, I've got a meeting arranged, but I will be tomorrow, and staying in London on Monday and Tuesday, then back here for the rest of the week. The week after I shall have to be here all week right up to and including Thursday, polling day, and I'll be at the count most of the night. I think they are due to declare about two am, so I'll sleep here and return home Friday… win or lose." He laughed, in his heart of hearts, he did not really think he would win, but there was always at least one surprise every election, so it might just be him.

"Right then I'll be off, see you tomorrow, bye, darling." She pecked him on the cheek, picked up her bag and walked to the door.

Martin felt a sudden pang in his chest. He didn't want her to go. After all that had happened over these last few weeks, he realised just how important she was to him.

As she closed the door behind her, he promised himself that once the election was over, no matter what, he would pay more attention to her.

Chapter Thirty-One

Will was up early. Julie had said the man who had called the day, before asking about the cigarette case, had said he would be over to see him this morning and he wanted to be up ready for him.

They had talked about what to do late into the evening and finally Will had made up his mind; he would hand over the case to this Stan Kenton. As he had said to Julie, technically, it was lost property and should be returned to its rightful owner, the picture was irrelevant. There was no law to stop men having sex with other men and no law to say they couldn't take pictures of themselves. He had wondered if he ought to just hand the case into the police, but if he was going to take that course of action, he should have done so when he first found it.

Will, having recognised one of the men in the picture, could see why the man had employed a private detective to find the case; he would certainly not want the picture to get into the public domain. Not while he was fighting an election and especially as he was a married man.

Will was convinced the best thing would be to return it to its proper owner via this man Kenton and, who knows, there might be a reward for its recovery, which would always come in useful. Having reached his decision, the sooner the man arrived the better; he had more important things on his mind, with the worry of his father's illness.

The morning seemed to drag by; Will could not concentrate on anything, not wanting to get involved in any of the jobs Julie had asked him to clear up, just in case Kenton came while he was in the middle of doing something. As the hours past, he got more and more frustrated. He was meeting his father to go to the match and would have to leave by noon at the latest, and still no sign of Kenton. In the end he gave up, assuming the man would be sure to arrive just after he left, he called Julie to tell her he was off.

"Darling, I've got to go, otherwise Dad will wonder where I am, and start to worry and that's the last thing he needs right now."

Julie came in from the kitchen and nodded her head in agreement.

"What do you want me to do if he comes after you've gone?"

"Tell him you didn't know that I had it, I hadn't told you. Ask him if there is a reward for its return. Whether there is or isn't just let him take it. Then we can forget about the whole incident. You agree don't you?"

"Yes, but I don't like the man, he scares me."

"Well, he won't scare you if he gets what he wants, now will he?"

"I suppose you're right. Okay, of you go and give your dad my love."

Will gave her a quick kiss and dashed out to the car.

Will had not stayed long after the match was over; just long enough to get his father back to his house. His father had looked tired, though he kept insisting he was fine. Will was worried and was relieved when his mother told him the appointment for the operation had come through. They were taking him in next Friday and he would be in for at least a week. That meant he would still be in hospital on Election Day, Thursday 6th of May. His father was a died in the wool Labour man and Will could not resist a smile knowing his father would not be able to vote, especially as Labour, according to the polls, needed every vote they could get.

When Will opened the door, Julie came rushing out to meet him.

"Now that's what I call a welcome, have you missed me that much?" He laughed as he spoke, but suddenly the smile left his mouth, she looked worried. "What's the matter? Did that bastard threaten you or anything?" His voice was angry now his happy mood gone.

"No, no look at this." She was holding a copy of that day's Evening Telegraph. On the front page, there was a picture of a man and the headline read...

'Man Found Stabbed in Medieval Spon End'

The report went on to give the man's name as Stan Kenton and that the police were pursuing their enquires, appealing for any witnesses, or anyone who had seen the man in the area between nine thirty on Friday evening and three am on Saturday morning. Julie was shaking.

"That's the man who came here asking about the cigarette case look, I kept his card. It's the same man... Stan Kenton."

Will sat down, trying to take it all in. He read the report in detail but there was no mention of what he was doing in Coventry, or who he might have met.

"Do you think we should contact the police?" Julie broke into his thoughts.

"I don't honestly know. They say here that they are looking for witnesses who may have seen him in the Spon End area of Coventry. I can't see how his death has anything to do with us. I think we should just keep our council, at least for a couple of days anyway."

"But it's odd that he should be murdered in Coventry when he lives in London. You don't think the lad who stole the case in the first place murdered him do you?" she asked.

"What makes you say that?"

"I don't know, but what if the lad who stole the case is the one in the photograph? If he is, then maybe this Kenton fellow had threatened him and the boy killed him."

"Julie! You're letting your imagination run away with you. I think we should wait and see what happens before we get ourselves embroiled in this."

Will's head was spinning, just when he had decided to hand the case back and forget the whole incident had happened. He did not want to even think about the bloody cigarette case while he had his father's illness on his mind.

Chapter Thirty-Two

Ferguson was just taking his jacket off when Sam burst into his office.

It had been three days since the murder and they did not seem to be making any progress. Ferguson had resigned himself to the fact this would be one of those cases that lasted for months and months. The only person who had contacted them in response to their appeal had been a barman at the Shakespeare Inn, who thought he recognised the picture as a man who he had served on Friday. He had remembered him because he had ordered Perrier water and that had been a first, in all his time as a barman. The man had left at closing time. Ferguson had noted that at least it moved the time of death to between eleven and three, but other than that, they were no further forward.

Sam had not knocked before entering and Ferguson glowered at him.

"Boss, I think we might have a breakthrough." He could hardly hold back his excitement.

"What is it?" Ferguson's voice had a world-weary air to it. *This had better be good,* he thought. "Go on then, don't keep me in suspense."

"There's a girl outside who says she recognises Kenton. Say's he was in Jumping Jacks nightclub on Friday."

"Better bring her in then. Let's have a word with her."

Sam left the office and returned a couple of minutes' later, accompanied by an attractive young woman, looking rather nervous.

"Please sit down, miss…?"

"Dickson, Anne Dickson," she answered.

"Miss Dickson, thank you for coming in, can you tell me how you know Mr Kenton?" Ferguson had lowered his voice so that it took on a warm tone, which he hoped would make her feel more relaxed.

"I didn't know his name. I met him in Jumping Jacks on Friday. He seemed very polite; let me get served even though it was his turn. He asked me for a dance and we had three or four, but then my boyfriend came back and saw me dancing with your man." She hesitated at this point not sure whether to continue.

"Take your time, Miss Dickson; would you like a cup of tea?" Ferguson indicated to Sam to get the woman a drink.

"Thank you, yes please, no sugar."

Sam returned with the tea and she sipped it before continuing.

"Dan, my boyfriend, got angry and started swearing at Mr Kenton." She paused again to take a sip of her tea.

"Was there an argument?" Ferguson prompted her.

"Not really, Mr Kenton was very reserved, he spoke quietly, telling Dan to behave and not be so stupid."

"And what did Dan say?"

Her lip trembled as she looked into Fergusons eyes. "He threatened to bust his nose."

Ferguson looked across at Sam, who had been writing furiously during the conversation, and stroked his chin as he did so. "Interesting," he said.

"What did Kenton have to say to that?"

"He told Dan's friends to look after 'Dumbo' then walked away."

"I bet your boyfriend didn't like that." Ferguson gave a wry smile.

"No, he was furious."

"What happened next?"

"I don't know. He told me to 'fuck off' and walked off to the bar. I was upset, so decided to go home, my two girlfriends shared a taxi with me."

"Do you live with Dan?"

"Yes."

"When did he come home?"

"He didn't, I assume he stayed at one of his friends, he does that sometimes if he gets drunk."

Sam, as always, had sat there letting his boss do the talking, but was itching to say something and Ferguson realising it, nodded in his direction.

"Is Dan a violent man?"

"He's a body builder and fancies himself as a hard man. I hate it but when he's had drink in him, he does get into fights."

"Has he ever hit you?" Sam continued.

"Once, but it was my fault. I'd been talking to this man and Dan didn't like it. Took me outside and slapped me hard across the face, I had a bruise for ages."

"So it's fair to say he's a very jealous man, yes?"

Ferguson could see where Sam was heading and was happy to let him continue.

"Yes, I suppose you could say that."

"Was your boyfriend drunk when this argument happened?"

"Yes, he was, I'd hardly seen him all the time we were in the club, but I could tell he was well oiled."

"Did your boyfriend mention the incident when he returned next day?" Ferguson asked.

"No and neither did I. I didn't want to start another argument."

"Have you mentioned to Dan that you were coming here today?"

The girl looked down as though ashamed.

"No," she said shaking her head."

"Thank you, Miss Dickson, you have been most helpful. If you don't mind going with my sergeant, he will get you to sign the statement you've just given and take your address in case we need to contact you again. Could you also give Sergeant Naylor details of where Dan works and also the names of his two friends?" Ferguson stood up and smiled kindly at the young woman; she looked frightened and he could understand why, he made a mental note to ask uniform to keep an eye on her house for the next few days.

A short while later, Sam came back into Ferguson's office.

"Well, what do you think of that, sir?"

"I think we need to have a word with Dan and the sooner the better. Take Jack with you, he sounds as though he might be a handful."

"Any trouble?" Ferguson asked when Sam returned an hour later.

"No, sir, but he kept asking what did we want him for, came over all offended like," Sam put on his most sarcastic voice, which drew a smile from Ferguson.

194

"So he's the injured party, is he? Let's see what he has to say for himself. Have you told him anything?"

"No, sir, just said we need to ask some questions to do with an enquiry we are investigating."

"Good. Bring him in here."

Dan Carter was indeed a big man and Ferguson could see straight away why Anne Dickson was scared of him.

"Mr Carter, thank you for coming in to help our enquiries." Ferguson wanted to make the man feel at ease hoping he would not be too guarded in his answers when questioned.

"What's it all about? Your man here has told me nothing."

Ferguson ignored his question.

"Can you tell me, where you at Jumping Jacks nightclub last Friday?"

"Yeah, why?"

"Can you remember what time you left?"

"Not really, I was a bit pissed, about one, I'm not sure. Look, what is this all about?"

Again, Ferguson ignored his question.

"Did you leave on your own or can someone confirm when you left?"

"I left with a couple of mates of mine."

"Can you give me their names please?"

"Pete Davies and John Lowry. I don't understand, why are you asking all these questions? Am I being accused of something?" He was beginning to get annoyed and Ferguson did not want him to become defensive.

"Mr Carter, we are just trying to establish the times of people leaving the club. You are amongst a number of people we are speaking to, who like you have volunteered their help." He hoped he sounded sincere enough and watched the man relax a little in his chair. "How did you get home?"

"We walked under the subway and flagged down a taxi that was returning to the city."

Ferguson gave Sam a look and pulled at his chin. If Dan was telling the truth, that meant he did not pass the alleyway where Kenton's body was found so he would not have seen anything.

"I see, well, I don't think I need to detain you any longer. Thank you for coming in and helping. Oh, by the way, could you give my sergeant the phone numbers of your two friends so that we can cross them of our list of people at the club. It will save them coming in. Thank you for all your help."

Sam took Dan to his desk to take the numbers. Once they were out of the office, Ferguson rang the desk sergeant.

"Ted, can you pop in here, I've got a young man with Sam, I want you to escort him out but do it slowly, think of something to delay him. We need to make a couple of phone calls before he does; so whatever you do don't let him use his mobile."

Once Sam had handed Dan over to the desk sergeant, he rushed into Ferguson's office.

"One each?" he inquired as he handed a phone number to Ferguson.

The two men each rang one of the friends of Dan Carter.

When the calls were complete, Ferguson looked at Sam.

"You go first."

"Pete Davies confirms almost word for word what Carter told us, not sure about the time, thought it might have been later. He asked what it was all about, but like Carter, never mentioned the murder. What about yours?"

"Interesting, like your man confirms Carter's version but, interestingly, says they walked down Spon Street heading towards the Belgrade Theatre where they picked up a taxi. Like the other two, never mentioned the killing. It's odd, isn't it, that not one of them has read a paper or heard the local news. It might be me, but he sounded nervous as though he had something to hide. I think we should get them in to make a statement. We've got those calls recorded haven't we?"

"Of course. When do you want to see them?"

"The sooner the better; send Jack and Angela to pick them up… separately."

Sam left the office a little grin on his face. He had left Ferguson sitting at his desk pulling on his chin.

Angela and Jack were given the task of taking the statements from the two men once they were back at the station. They had been kept apart and neither was aware that the other was there.

Sam collected the statements and took them into Ferguson who quickly scanned them.

"Have you read them?" he asked Sam.

"Yes, I know what you're going to say. Lowry's changed his story, says they went under the subway to the other side of the ring road."

"Do you think they have been in touch with Carter?"

"I do, and I'm sure one, if not both, are not telling us the truth. Do you want to interview them?"

"Not yet, let them stew a bit, get Angela and Jack to check all the cab firms, and see if anyone can remember picking up three drunks, shouldn't be that difficult." Ferguson had a gut feeling that one, if not all, of these young men were somehow involved.

Chapter Thirty-Three

It was a week since the murder and Ferguson was being pestered by the 'Super' to come up with something. The press boys were getting restless that no progress seemed to have been made and he needed to issue another statement by Saturday at the latest. Ferguson hated being given deadlines, detective work wasn't like that, it took painstaking time to check on every little detail. He had not told his chief about Carter and his friends for fear he would order him to bring them in before he was ready.

Sam knocked the door breaking into his thoughts.

"Got the cabbie," he said.

"Good man. Where is he?"

"At the front desk, do you want him in here?"

"What do you think?"

Sam left before Ferguson could say anymore and phoned through to the desk to bring the cabbie through.

An Asian, about fifty years old, was ushered into Ferguson's office.

"Mr Asif, sir." The constable showed the man in and Ferguson pointed to a chair opposite his desk. The man sat down looking around nervously.

"Mr Asif, thank you for sparing your time to help us." Ferguson used his 'I'm your favourite uncle' voice to reassure the man and it had the desired effect as he immediately relaxed in the chair. "I understand you recall taking three young men in your taxi last Friday. Can you tell me where exactly you picked them up?"

"Yes, outside Belgrade Theatre."

"Can you tell me how they appeared; I mean did they look agitated at all? Were they drunk?"

"Very drunk and one, the biggest, looked as if he had been in a fight, he had a cut on his chin and splashes of blood on his 'T-shirt."

Ferguson looked at Sam and Sam nodded back; the remarks having been duly noted.

"Did you have any trouble with them? I mean did they pay you?"

"Oh yes. They pay... no trouble."

"Thank you, Mr Asif, you have been most helpful. We may need you to come to an identification parade and if so, my sergeant will contact you." Ferguson stood up to indicate that the interview was over.

Sam showed the cabbie out then returned to Ferguson's office.

"I think we've got the bastard, sir."

"Not too hasty, Sam, but the evidence does seem to be stacking up. Let's get John Lowry in, the one who changed his story; if we can break him down, then we might be getting somewhere.

Lowry sat opposite Ferguson waiting for him to speak. Ferguson just sat there looking at him, pulling at his chin, watching the man. He could see the fear in Lowry's eyes, he was visibly crumbling. At last, Ferguson spoke.

"You've not told me the truth, have you, John?"

"I don't know what you mean, I came here of my own free will and gave your girl a statement. It was all true."

"Strange that when I phoned you about catching a taxi, you said the three of you walked towards the Belgrade and picked up a taxi, but in your statement, you said you walked the opposite way under the subway and picked up a taxi on the other side of the ring road. Can you explain why you changed your mind?"

"I... I... I... was confused, sometimes we do go that way, just depends how we feel."

"Did you check your story with Mr Carter after I phoned you?"

"No, why should I?"

"That's what I would like to know. I think I should tell you at this stage that we are conducting a murder enquiry and I have reason to believe that you came into contact with the victim."

"I never spoke to him..."

"I didn't say that you spoke to the victim and neither did I say that it was a man," Ferguson interrupted him.

Lowry looked shocked and his face flushed; his hands started to tremble. Ferguson looked at him with contempt.

"I have some more bad news for you. The cabbie who took you home confirms that he picked you up outside the Belgrade." Ferguson was gambling that Lowry would not realise that the cabbie could not have identified them at this stage. "I don't think you are the person who did the killing, but you know who did and in the eyes of the law, you will all be guilty of the murder... that is unless you can help us identify the actual killer... then we can charge you with a lesser offence."

The words hit home like a thunderbolt, Lowry was now shaking violently, so much so, Sam got out his seat to calm the man down.

He suddenly burst into tears.

"It was Dan, he was pissed and mad with jealousy, we told him to forget it, but he just said he was going to teach the bloke a lesson. He was only a small guy and he would just bust his nose and give him a kicking. We followed the guy out and as he turned into the alley, Dan followed him. He sent us around the back to cut the bloke off if he tried to make a run for it. When we got to the other end of the alley and looked up, Dan was on the floor and the man started walking towards us. Pete grabbed me and said 'let's rush him'. We thought we'd catch him off-guard and I think he was surprised to see us. We grabbed an arm each and pushed him back towards where Dan had been doubled up on the floor. Suddenly, the man yelled out in pain and we automatically let go his arms, surprised ourselves. Dan had stabbed him in the back. The man turned 'round then fell to the ground. Dan had stabbed him again. We were in shock and I wanted to run, but Dan said just calm down and walk out down to the Belgrade as though nothing had happened and pick up a taxi. We went back to Pete's flat and all stayed the night there." The words had come out in a torrent, Sam having to scribble like mad to get them all down.

"The taxi driver said one of you had blood on their shirt, would that be Dan?" Ferguson did not feel sorry for this pathetic man in front of him, half an hour ago, he had been happy to let guilty man walk free, but he had given his word that he would only charge Lowry on a lesser offence and he would keep that promise.

"Yes, when we got to Pete's place, he took the shirt and burnt it."

Ferguson looked up at Sam.

"Sergeant, would you take this man to the desk and charge him? I think it would be wise if he stayed in the cells tonight... for his own protection."

Ferguson sat back in his chair; he would enjoy his meeting with the Superintendent in the morning. He was not going to call him now, better to wait until tomorrow, by then, he would have arrested the other two and charged them.

Ferguson was pleased that the case had been wrapped up and in record time too, but he still had that niggle in the back of his mind. Why had Kenton stayed in Coventry those extra days? He picked up the phone and dialled Martin De Glanville's number.

"Mr De Glanville? Inspector Ferguson here, just thought you'd like to know we have caught Kenton's killer."

"Really? Can you say who it was?"

"Turns out, it was just a case of being in the wrong place at the wrong time. A jealous boyfriend, who got drunk and went too far in his retribution."

"That's terrible, but thank you for letting me know."

The phone went dead. Had Ferguson imagined it or did De Glanville audibly give a sigh of relief when he told him how Kenton had died.

Chapter Thirty-Four

It was the first Saturday in a long, long time that Will had missed seeing his beloved Leicester play. He was in Leicester and not far from the Walker Stadium but not at the ground itself. He and his mother were sitting in the day room at Leicester Royal Infirmary waiting to see his father. The operation had taken place the previous evening but no visitors had been allowed. His mother had wanted to be there first thing in the morning, but Will had managed to persuade her to be patient and wait until lunchtime. Now she was getting frustrated as they had been there thirty minutes already.

Will got up and for the umpteenth time asked the nurse if they could see Mr Shakespeare yet, only to be told the same thing.

"The doctor is on his rounds and no visitors are allowed in until he has finished."

His mother was getting more and more agitated, thinking the delay was because something must have gone wrong, or there was bad news waiting for them. No matter what he said, Will could not satisfy her and he was getting worried that she might make herself ill.

Eventually, the nurse came up to him and said that the consultant had finished his round, but before they went in would like to see Mrs Shakespeare in his office.

Will's mother turned pale when he told her.

"It's bad news, I know it is. The cancer must be worse than we thought. Oh god, Will, what will I do?" She started to cry and Will put his arm around and gave a squeeze.

"Come on, Mum, you've got to be brave for Dad's sake. Would you like me to come with you to see the consultant?"

"Would you, luv? I don't think I could face it alone."

The nurse showed them into the consultant's room and he beckoned them to sit down.

"I'm Mr Shakespeare's son," Will said as they sat down in front of his rather imposing desk.

"Fine, good to meet you. Mrs Shakespeare, as you know your husband has had major surgery to remove a cancerous tumour."

She was gripping Will's hand as he spoke, trying to fight back the tears.

He continued, "I'm pleased to say that the operation has been totally successful and we've caught it in time. Your husband should make a full recovery, but obviously, will have to have complete rest for a week or so before he can leave hospital. I recommend..."

She did not hear the rest of what the consultant was saying. The relief at the news was overpowering and the dam broke tears streaming down her face, but they were tears of relief.

The doctor smiled at her, he had seen many tears shed in this room, but not many tears of joy.

"I'll ring for the nurse and she will take you in to see him. He's probably still a bit groggy so try not to wear him out."

Will's father didn't have to ask if they knew how the operation had gone; the look on his wife's face told him all he needed to know.

They spent half an hour with him before the nurse came in and said she thought he should have some rest. For once, his mother was happy to do as she was told and Will drove her back home, feeling as though a weight had been lifted of his shoulders. He had been dreading the result being negative and had spent the previous night hardly sleeping, worrying how his mother would cope.

He stopped at her house long enough to have a cup of tea and then drove home feeling so happy he never even bothered to switch on the radio to get the football results.

Julie was overjoyed at the news, especially as she had a soft spot for her father- in- law.

"Look, I didn't say anything because I didn't want to tempt fate, but I bought a bottle of bubbly to celebrate. I just knew it would be good news." She grinned at Will's look of surprise and he was supposed to be the optimistic one!

Later that evening, after dinner and with the last drop of red wine poured into their glasses, Julie pushed the Telegraph across the table to him.

"Killer's Charged with Night Club Murder."

Will read the story detailing how the police had found Kenton's killers following a tip off from a member of the public.

"So that's that then," he said.

"Not completely, what are you going to do about the cigarette case and the picture?"

"To be honest, I hadn't given it much thought, too busy worrying about Dad."

"Well, I think you should hand it back to its owner and then we can forget it and move on."

"Yes, I think you're probably right. I'll ring him on Monday and ask if I can pop round."

"You don't know where he lives."

"No but I know where his campaign office is, so I'll call in there and get his number. Now can we forget about that bloody photo and concentrate on something far more important?"

"And what might that be?" she said grinning from ear to ear.

"Making babies."

Chapter Thirty-Five

Martin had made breakfast in bed for Maddy. It was a special treat and unusual for a Monday, but as he was leaving to go to Kenilworth and would be gone all week, he wanted to make it a bit different. It was election week and he would be campaigning every day right up until the polls closed on Thursday night at ten o'clock.

Maddy was not really awake as he brought the tray in with her favourite Eggs Benedict and a glass of champagne.

"My, you have been busy," she yawned.

"Well, I won't see you until Friday so I thought you deserved something special for putting up with me being away so much. Anyway, it's back to normal from next week onwards."

She smiled and reached up and pecked him on the cheek.

"Thank you, darling, it's very thoughtful of you."

"Look, I'm sorry but I've got to go, Tony's arranged some sort of conference call for ten thirty so I must dash. See you Friday, bye."

Even at eight in the morning, the roads were already busy and he found himself caught up in one traffic jam after another, before finally reaching the M1. It had taken him the best part of forty-five minutes to get to the start of the motorway, so he would have to put his foot down if he was to make it in time.

He had just passed Milton Keynes as he glanced at his watch, it was nine thirty and he estimated that if he kept to about ninety he would make it on time, providing he didn't get pulled up by the police on the way. The car phone rang and he slowed slightly as he answered it.

"Martin, hi, it's Tony. Sorry to bother you while you're driving, but I've just had a phone call from a man called David Shakespeare, asking for your mobile number, says he wants to come and see you about some lost property. I asked if I could help him but insisted that he wanted to speak to you. Can I give him your number?"

Martin felt a chill run down his spine. He remembered the name that Kenton had given him, David Shakespeare.

"Can you ring him back and give him my number, but ask him if he can ring me at five. We should have some time to spare then, shouldn't we?"

"Yes, no problem, this evening's meeting starts at six thirty and is due to finish about nine. It's the only early one this week."

"Right, I'm racing up the motorway so will see you soon, bye."

Martin could feel the knot in his stomach. Did this man intend to blackmail him, was the nightmare starting all over again, wanting to see him this week of all weeks? Jesus, why, oh, why!

Try as he might, he could not get the man's name out of his mind. It was a Shakespearian tragedy all right.

All day, Martin found it hard to concentrate and Tony had to correct him a couple of times when he was talking to people. Tony wondered if he was ill and had asked if he could get him anything, but was brusquely told that there was nothing the matter.

For Martin, five o'clock could not come soon enough. He wanted to get this thing sorted out, even if it cost him money. He could not risk an exposé at this late stage.

The phone vibrated in his pocket and he stabbed at the receive button. He had left the office and was sitting in his flat having just made a cup of coffee when it went off.

"Hello, Martin De Glanville speaking"

"Mr De Glanville, my name is David Shakespeare I rang your office this morning."

"Yes, how can I help you, Mr Shakespeare?"

"I wondered if I could come round and see you. I believe I have something that belongs to you."

"When did you want to meet? I don't know if you are aware but I'm standing in this coming election and I'm rather tied up all this week."

"I'd like to see you as soon as possible if you can spare me a few minutes,"

"Well, I'm free right now, I have to be at a meeting at six thirty, do you have far to travel?"

"I live in Kenilworth, not far from you as a matter of fact; I could be with you in five minutes."

"In that case, do come 'round, I can spare half an hour if that's okay."

"Be right there, bye"

Martin sat looking at the phone wondering just what this man would want. He got up and poured himself a scotch. He had not intended to drink before the meeting, but right now felt he needed something to steady his nerves.

It seemed like only seconds before the buzzer sounded.

"It's unlocked, come on up, second floor," he said into the intercom.

Martin waited until he heard a tap on his front door.

"Mr Shakespeare? Please come in. Would you like a drink?"

"Thank you, I'll have a whisky if I may."

Martin pointed to a chair and Will sat down while his drink was being poured.

"Have we met before? I seem to recognise your face," Martin asked as he passed the glass to Will.

Will looked slightly embarrassed.

"As a matter of fact, my wife and I came to one of your meetings. I'm afraid we rather rudely left before it was over."

"Ah, yes I thought I recognised you. I thought at the time you were the opposition on a spying mission." Martin forced a laugh.

"On the contrary, we were most impressed with your presentation and your manifesto. I have to say I am in agreement with most of your views."

Martin relaxed a little; he had not expected to meet a supporter.

"What made you leave early then? Did I go off message?" Again, he gave a half-hearted laugh.

"No, it was just… we had a bit of a shock… I'll explain later if I may."

Martin looked puzzled, but did not pursue the matter.

"You said you had something that you thought belonged to me is that correct?"

"Yes, I need to tell you how it came into my possession though. I am a metal detector enthusiast, one of those anoraks who hope to find hidden gold, like the man who found the Staffordshire Hoard. Well, I have been searching in Abbey Fields, thought that with all its history something might just turn up. So far, I've found nothing that is except for this cigarette case. Which I believe is yours; it has your monogram engraved on the front." He took the case out of his pocket and handed it to Martin. Martin turned it over in is hands, checking that it was in fact his missing cigarette case, but he did not open it.

"Yes, that's mine alright, thank you for returning it. It was stolen from me by a young man who had been helping with my election campaign."

Will looked uncomfortable as he shifted in his chair.

"Look, I've got to tell you, when I found it, I opened the case and found this picture inside." He took out a folded piece of paper from his pocket and passed it to Martin.

The room fell silent as Martin unfolded the paper to reveal the photograph of himself with Joe.

"I recognised your watch and tattoo when we attended your meeting, that's why we left early. It was just the initial shock. I confess I was not sure what to do, whether to contact you or not and I just left it. I thought maybe the best thing to do was just dump it. Then my father suddenly became seriously ill and I forgot all about it. That is until a Mr Kenton came calling and threatened my wife."

"Kenton threatened your wife? I don't understand, I had asked him to recover the case on my behalf and to offer a reward to anyone who could help. He was not instructed to threaten anyone, please accept my sincere apologies."

"Well, perhaps threatened is a bit strong, but she was frightened. He was supposed to call back a week ago, but I understand he was murdered in Coventry."

"Yes, and I have been told his killer has been apprehended. An incident in a nightclub, he was just unlucky to be there."

An atmosphere had descended on the room neither man knowing quite what to say, how to take the conversation forward. It was Martin who spoke first.

"I think perhaps I had better explain." He was not sure why he was going to bare his soul to this man, but he felt a sort of confidence in him. He appeared to believe in the same things that Martin did and he was drawn to him. "I am married, but when I came to Kenilworth and bought this flat, to pursue my ambition to be the new MP, I met the young man in the picture and I am ashamed to say we started a relationship. I had no idea up to that point that I had any homosexual feelings, but I was taken in and really liked this boy. I foolishly took some pictures of our relationship. I did not realise at the time the boy did not feel the same, but was using me to obtain money. I realise now, how foolish I've been, but at the time I just thought I was helping him. It finished a few weeks ago when I found out what he was really like and I told him I never wanted to see him again. Then I got a call from him threatening to go to the papers with the picture unless I gave him ten thousand pounds. I panicked; I could afford to pay him, but was worried that he might keep coming back for more. I employed Kenton to contact the lad and pay him off if necessary, but to make sure he never came back. Well, Kenton found out that the case had been buried on Abbey Fields, but when they went together to recover it, it had gone. You know the rest." Martin gave a deep breath as though a large weight had been lifted from his shoulders.

"Look, your private life has nothing to do with me and I am not some homophobic nut, who wants all gays locked up, but I don't understand why you just didn't call his bluff, after all, there are lots of gays in public life and they still have good careers, and in some cases, even their wives stick by them."

Martin sighed, he had not intended to tell the whole story, but it was clear that this man was not totally satisfied with his explanation. He felt though, Will was sympathetic to his plight.

"It's a little more complicated. When I first met Joe, I thought he was about nineteen. When I finished the relationship, it was because he had asked me for money to buy a motorbike for his birthday... his sixteenth birthday!"

"Christ, so you're saying he was under age when the photo was taken?"

"Yes, I'm afraid so, only by a couple of months, but still under age and the date is on the picture. Of course, as soon as I knew, I kicked him out and told him I never wanted to see him again. So when he rang, with his blackmail threat, I was frightened. It would have ruined me."

Will sat back in his chair trying to take it all in, wondering why this man had confessed everything to him as though he was a priest.

"May I have another drink? This is a bit of a shock, why have you told me all this?"

"Because you know about the photo and I felt I owed you an explanation, and, well, I feel you have a certain empathy… I feel I can trust you… don't ask why, I just do."

Will drank his whisky in two large swallows. There was no doubt he did feel sorry for this man. He had admired the things he stood for and wanted him to succeed; he was a breath of fresh air on the political scene. It would be a complete waste of talent if, because of a mistake, he was lost from public life.

"Martin, as far as I'm concerned, this is a matter between you and your conscience, I have no right to pass judgment. I support completely your political ideas and wish you well in your ambitions. In that you have my full support. I can tell you I will never speak of this again to anyone." As he finished speaking, he reached across and snatched the picture from the table next to Martin and tore it into shreds.

Martin stared in disbelief. He could hardly speak, but managed to say "Thank you," in a hushed voice.

Will looked at his watch. It was just after six and he knew Martin had an appointment at six thirty.

"I'd better go you have to be somewhere, don't you?"

"Yes, yes thanks again. Can I have your address before you go? I'd like to drop you a line once the dust settles."

Will nodded, and wrote his name and address on the pad Martin passed to him.

"Goodbye, Martin. And best of luck on Thursday."

They shook hands and Martin watched Will walk to the lift. Only then did he let out a sigh of relief. At last, the nightmare was over.

Chapter Thirty-Six

It was the end of the road and by the close of the day; the votes would have been cast and the count under way. Martin, with Tony at his side, had spent the day touring around all the polling stations checking on the turnout. They had managed to get volunteers at all of the stations and they were able to provide some guide on the exit poll. It looked as though there would be a good turnout and Tony was feeling very confident. They had stopped in Southam for lunch and made their way back to Kenilworth in the afternoon to spend the rest of the day at campaign headquarters.

At about five, Martin slipped away to go back to his flat. On Tony's advice, he had decided to try and rest hoping, he might manage forty winks before he returned for what would be a long night.

He made himself a cup of hot chocolate and, slipping off his shoes, went to lie down on his bed. As he lay there, he thought back over the previous months since he made the decision to fight the Election. It had been a roller coaster of emotions and he wished he could put back the clock. If only he had not gone to that bloody 'Rainbow', then again, if he had never come to Kenilworth in the first place. If, if. Maybe if he had taken Maddy's advice and stuck to business then none of it would have happened. The thought of Maddy made him realise just how stupid he had been. He could have messed it all up through his madness. He resolved to take her on a long holiday once he was back in London. As thoughts of a holiday came into his mind, he drifted off to sleep.

The ringing of his phone woke him with a start.

"Martin, its Tony, where are you?"

"Sorry, Tony, I fell asleep, you've just woken me. I'll be with you in a few minutes."

He switched the phone off, quickly showered and dressed, and was back at the office within twenty minutes of the call.

The next two hours seemed to drag by until ten o'clock, the close of the polls, it was now a matter of waiting until the votes had all been collected and counted. They had been told that the declaration would be about two a.m. so there were four hours of nail biting to go.

At one o'clock, they made their way to the town hall for the closing stages of the count and the declaration. All his rivals were there already and politely shook his hand when he walked in. He watched fascinated as the counters busied themselves at the tables with small mountains of voting papers in front of them.

The clock slowly ticked around to two o'clock, but still no sign of a declaration. Eventually, the Recording Officer called them all onto the platform to make the announcement.

"I, Geoffrey Timmings, being the Recording Officer for the constituency of Kenilworth and Southam, declare the result of the general election of 2010. The votes cast are as follows.

De Glanville Martin	Anti-Sleaze	4873
Harrison James	Green	568
Milton Nicholas	Labour	6949
Moore John	UK Independence	1214
Rock Nigel	Liberal	13393
Ruskin Joe	Independent	362
Wright Jeremy	Conservative	25945

And I declare Jeremy Wright to be the duly elected member for Kenilworth and Southam."

Martin had a mixture of feelings, he had lost and by a long way, but he had only just been pipped to third place by the Labour candidate. Tony was vigorously shaking his hand and slapping his back. The other candidates came up to him and congratulated him. Jeremy Wright was giving his acceptance speech but he hardly heard him. He was lost in his own world, it was over, he felt totally spent. Still in a daze, he felt his hand being grabbed and looked up to see Jeremy facing him.

"I'd just like to say well done, you fought a good fight. I understand you originally applied to be the Tory candidate, well,

I hope we can get you to come back into the fold, I'd certainly rather have you on our side than opposing us. Keep in touch."

Martin was rather surprised by the compliment, who knows, he thought. In recent days, there had been a lot of talk in the papers about coalitions; maybe he might just have a rethink. It was clear, that if you wanted to win you needed one of the party machines behind you.

He was tired and just wanted to sleep, and get back home to Maddy, but he knew he had one more duty to perform.

He and Tony went back to the offices where his loyal supporters clapped him when they entered. He had laid on a few drinks for a celebration and they intended to enjoy the moment. He thanked them all for all their hard work and to their surprise handed them each an envelope with two hundred pounds in it as a bonus.

He took Tony on one side.

"Tony, you did a great job. I'd like you to have this as a reward for all you've done and, if you want to move to London, there's a job for you in my organisation."

Tony took the cheque for five hundred pounds that Martin had handed him.

"That's very good of you, thanks and thanks for the job offer, but I want to stay in this area, so I'll have to say no, but if you ever want an agent in the future give me a call."

The two men shook hands, then Martin said his good byes to them all.

The cold night cut through him as he walked back to the flat for the last time. He had decided to sell up since the result had been announced.

He flopped down onto his bed mentally exhausted and fell asleep thinking about Maddy.

He slept right through until midday. There was no rush; Maddy would be at work until six. He showered and dressed and made himself some toast. Once he had finished, he wrote a note to Mrs Black saying he was selling the flat and would not need her services any more. He thanked her for all her work and enclosed a cheque for two hundred and fifty pounds by way of compensation. There was just one thing left to do. He wrote a short letter to Will, thanking him for his understanding and adding at the bottom,

"Attached is the reward that I spoke of."

Reaching for his chequebook he wrote... D Shakespeare One thousand pounds.

That done, he phoned up The Ivy and booked a table for the evening. He packed the few clothes and toiletries he had at the flat. Checking each room to make sure he had all his personal effects, he closed the door for the last time. Once back in London, he would phone up the agents and put the flat up for sale, but there was no immediate hurry, that could be done any time.

He felt relaxed as he drove down the motorway. His political adventure was over and right now he had no intention of reviving it. All he wanted was to spend some time with Maddy.

The journey passed quickly and before he knew it he was in London. On the way back to the apartment, he called in the local florist and bought two dozen red roses. They were Maddy's favourite flowers, so he knew she would be pleased, especially with dinner at the Ivy to follow.

There was a spring in his step as he climbed the stairs, rather than take the lift, up to the apartment. He opened the door and walked straight into the kitchen to arrange the flowers in a vase. Having filled it with water, he took it into the living room and placed it on the coffee table. It was then that he noticed an envelope addressed to him, it was in Maddy's writing.

Strange, he thought as he slid his thumb into the flap and tore it open.

His jaw dropped open as he read the letter.

Dear Martin,

I'm so sorry but I've moved in with Peter. Please try and forgive me. I am very fond of you but I am in love with Peter. I will be in touch to sort things out. I promise I won't be difficult.
Maddy

Martin burst into tears, he could not believe it.
What had he done? Why, oh God, why?

He sat in the chair still holding the letter; his whole world had collapsed around him, just when he thought he had got it back.

"What a fucking mess," he shouted.

But there was no one to hear.

THE END